THE FORG(

Rachael H Dixon

TO
Dean

DReam is destiny

Rachael

X

www.slipperysouls.co.uk

Published by FeedARead.com Publishing – Arts Council funded

Cover art by Rachael H Dixon.

A CIP catalogue record for this title is available from the British Library.

For Clyde; for the laughs, memories and inspiration that will last a whole lifetime

Other Books by the Author

Slippery Souls (Book One in the Sunray Bay Series)

Acknowledgements

I'm always scared I'll miss somebody out of this part, consequently making me seem like a bit of an ungrateful git - which just wouldn't be the case at all. So if you think you should have been mentioned, but haven't been, feel free to let me know and, if I agree that you should have been, I'll apologise lots and then mention you twice in the next book.

Anyway, my heartfelt thanks goes out to the following...

Each and every one of my Sunray Bay fans; your support has been tremendous. I appreciate your emails and other communications more than you probably realise and I've been overjoyed at the level of enthusiasm you've shown in regards to this sequel. I hope you'll enjoy it just as much as you did *Slippery Souls* - if not more so.

Hannah Thompson, my copy-editor, who did another fantastic job of tidying my sentences and ensuring the story was safe from gaping whales and rifling chimps.

All of the entrants who took part in my character naming competition - and in particular Ginnifer Abell, who was the overall winner. I sincerely hope you enjoy your namesake, Gin! However I'll take this opportunity to point out to everybody else that vampire Gin is not meant to represent Ms Abell in appearance or personality, and if there are any similarities, other than name, then this was not intentional.

All of my family members and friends who've offered their encouragement and support over the past two years; I know writing books (especially vampire ones) can often be seen as folly, so it's nice that you all take what I do seriously and appreciate the hard work, time and effort that goes in.

Kathryn Roebuck for being an invaluable agent-of-sorts in the early days of *Slippery Souls*. I'm forever grateful for your dog-with-a-bone attitude to the local press - you got me places I probably wouldn't have got alone.

The members of Easington Writers (including former member Chris Robinson) for all your words of encouragement - and for lending me plenty of ears to chew.

My own subconscious for feeding me dreams every night - which without I'd probably still be stuck at chapter eight.

Derek, my husband, for putting up with another year's worth of head-bustery and for letting me continue with this craziness. I'm a very lucky girl!

Oh and, finally, apologies for the swearing in *Slippery Souls*, Nana. That said, you probably shouldn't read this one.

Prologue

With hands clawed, she applied unrelenting pressure to her fingertips; grinding them into the solid ground as though it would earth the pain. One of her nails creased halfway down and snapped off. It was so inconsequential she hardly even noticed, so she carried on scraping the rest of her nails against the cold floor. Her irregular gasping and panting was the result of another pain entirely; an excruciating jaw-clenching pain.

She was all alone in a darkened alcove (an insignificant alcove among thousands of others) in the stark grey mountain range that dominated the landscape. Lying on the jagged surface with her body tense and contorted, she wondered if she had the courage to kill herself - to end it all now.

The night was eerily still and her unrestrained cries carried far and wide. A chalky moon rode high but was, for the most part, hidden behind a thick blanket of suspended rain. The people below, in the surrounding villages, tossed and turned and shuddered in their sleep. Their dreams were to become disturbed and, after this long night, their harrowing lives were to become even more challenging - because something wicked was afoot.

The shark-skin clouds that suffocated the land were stealthily fermenting. Rolling and churning, growing and morphing as though agitated and gathering energy from each of her cries. At any moment they would surrender their weight to soak everything below in a cold wet fury. *Another* cold wet fury.

But, for now, it was the calm before the storm.

"Fergard, you lousy, miserable, feckless, cowardly piece of shit," she growled low between overwhelming contractions that squeezed her innards in a life-wringing grip. Long strands of white hair clung in sweat-splayed bands across her forehead and cheeks. "I'll kill you. I promise."

Her face was creased into a scowl, she was furious. None of this should be happening to her, none of it was what she wanted. Her hopes and ambitions had been taken away; she'd been raped of her freedom.

Each time she wailed the sound was now fuelled entirely by rage rather than the horrendous spasms that overtook her body. She threw her head back and focussed on channelling her energy into the clouds above - she imagined they were her release, a product of her wrath. And goodness knew how she wanted everyone else to suffer for her own misgivings.

In recent weeks the rain had ruined fields and crops below, the sodden ground not having enough time to recover during infrequent dry spells. The clouds were too quick to replenish, ready to pummel the earth once again - and, because of this, she'd taken great satisfaction in seeing the farmers and their families suffering.

An uncontrollable urge overcame her; her body telling her to push. Bearing down with all of her might, pushing and squeezing, she felt something rip. Skin tearing where skin shouldn't tear - but she was too numb to feel any more than a burning sensation. She held her breath, her face throbbing with exertion - and then, surprisingly, an enormous amount of physical relief washed over her. Upon sensing that the thing in her body had been ejected, she looked down for confirmation...

A small glistening mound lay wriggling on the craggy surface between her legs; its skin translucent despite the lack of light. Sighing inwardly, she relished the quiet moment before it took its first lungful of air and then squealed its own ear-ringing angst into the night.

Wincing, she curled her lip and silently cursed the thing. Its face was small and undeniably beautiful, its limbs and digits all perfectly formed. But still she hated it - hated it with every bit of her being. She was almost tempted to nudge it off the side of the mountain with her foot. But she didn't because she knew that it would be foolish in the long term, she'd be punished without doubt. She and the infant were now bound together. An uncompromising union sealed by the obligatory maternity law set out by the almighty one, Casiphia.

Instead she picked it up, cringing at the contact of its bare flesh against her own. The sides of her mouth curled down as she held it aloft. Its black tear-soaked eyes locked onto hers and she saw there a level of neediness that made her feel faint. She whimpered piteously, a sound that was drowned out by the baby's own cries.

And then, as though the baby's nerve-shattering screams had aggravated the clouds, a fat raindrop fell onto her upturned brow. She continued to look up to the sky, hoping the rain had at last come to wash her sweat-drenched body clean. A few more raindrops spattered down onto her bare flesh, sparse and soothing. Then, after not even a minute had passed, torrents of ice cold water splashed down from the sky, hammering the drenched land of the valley down below. Her body was instantly invigorated but her heart was filled with an indescribable amount of dread for what was to be.

Rain continued to gush into the alcove for the next hour. She cradled the infant in her right arm, both of their bodies glistening and slippery. After daubing a grubby white cloth into the diluted blood and goo of the afterbirth, she held the makeshift teat to the baby's mouth and watched as it suckled enthusiastically. Rainwater and blood washed over its pudgy chin in pink rivulets. The sight may have been cute had she have given a maternal shit, but she didn't. So it wasn't.

Unexpectedly, the hairs on her body stood upright - a signal that she was no longer alone with the baby. Just as she'd felt the natural urge to push the child from her body, her instincts were now making her aware of the presence of another - another she couldn't yet see. As she stiffened and looked up to the sky, a large figure stepped onto the ledge of the alcove from the blackness of the night making her jump. White-blue lightning flashed as though to further dramatise the surprise arrival.

The visitor's broad face was pale and his eyes were set deep in recesses (recesses that appeared blacker than any of the alcoves in the whole of the mountain range), and his chin was capped with wiry hair.

"*Fergard,*" she hissed, her eyes alight with pure hatred. Thunder clapped and the mountain shook as though quaking in its very foundations.

"Ah, my son," the unwelcome visitor said, ignoring her whilst tipping his head to the baby. "I could *feel* it. I knew you'd arrived."

"You felt *nothing,*" she spat furiously.

He chuckled in a way that made her want to rip his beard off and shove it down his throat.

"Oh look at you." He smirked, finally meeting her gaze. "Motherhood has certainly taken its toll on you, hasn't it? You look like shit, my dear."

Before she could retaliate he stepped closer and bent to take the infant from her arms. As he lifted it into his own embrace, her face was momentarily hopeful.

"Have you come to take it away?" she asked, eagerness making her voice slightly higher than usual. "Will you have it?"

This triggered more amusement from him, only this time he roared with a bellowing belly laugh.

"Don't be preposterous, woman. Nursing is no job for a man, that's your tough luck.

She gritted her teeth together tightly.

"So why have you come? Won't you even share the burden?"

"Absolutely not." He stopped laughing and looked gravely serious. "His upbringing is to be your encumbrance alone. I come only to greet my son, Fergard Told the Seventh, into the world."

"How very disappointed you must be then."

He looked questioningly at her with his unyielding dark eyes, confusion creasing his brow.

"Don't be ridiculous. Why would I be disappointed? He's perfect."

"Physically, I agree - yes he is perfect. But his name is *not* Fergard. And nor shall he carry your surname, you presumptuous, arrogant shit." Her eyes glinted with spite and she relished the look of shock on his face.

Laying the baby down onto a deep ledge, Fergard's eyes burned fiery and he stepped up close to her. Raising one of his large hands he slapped her heavily across the face and, as her head jerked backwards from the force, he boomed, "Of course he's called Fergard, you audacious bitch. He's *my* son."

She stayed facing away from him for a moment whilst she drew strength, and then she reared back her own arm and landed her fist into his face. Satisfied with the cracking sound that the cartilage of his nose made, she smiled smugly. His face was instantly covered in red and his nose was broader and flatter.

"Since you refuse to play any part in rearing him, I think you'll find he's *my* son," she growled. "Therefore it'll be *my* decision what his bastard name will be."

Fergard spat some of the blood from his lips into her face.

"I should kill you right here and now," he rasped, his voice thick and phlegmy.

"Again, how very disappointing for you," she goaded, running the tip of her tongue over her lips, licking his blood from her mouth tantalisingly. Circling him slowly, she crowed, "You wouldn't dare."

"Don't tempt me, *whore*."

His last word incited a new rage in her and she took on the demeanour of a wild animal; stalking, calculating and readying herself to pounce. He watched her cautiously, his own stance hostile - yet there was an element of uncertainty that quivered on his face and a nervous tic pulsated strongly in the fleshy bit below his right eye.

"You have no power over me," she continued. "Yet I have you right in my clutches."

"You have no such thing," he spat; although the anxiousness had now crept into his voice.

11

"Oh but how you contradict yourself," she cackled, shaking her head with her own amusement. "Do you forget that if you kill me then *you* get to raise the...the..." she pointed at the baby. "*That*. So I'd say you wouldn't dare. Am I right?"

She savoured the look on his face as the full meaning of her words dawned on him. Those ferocious eyes that overwhelmed her in the past were now pathetic and desperate.

"I think, therefore, you'll agree that this puts me in a much stronger position?"

By now she was standing at the very back of the alcove, balancing on the balls of her feet in an attempt to match his height - to show that she wouldn't be intimidated by him. He'd dominated her once, but never again.

Exasperated he opened his mouth to speak but instead, as though he'd thought better of it, he crouched down slightly, ready to leap into the air. She was already one step ahead of him; expecting him to take flight because the cowardice in his eyes surely denoted that he would try to escape. And so, once again, she punched him on the nose.

As he howled at the new level of pain inflicted upon him, she sliced her hand through the air. In one long ripping motion her fingernails carved his abdomen wide open, like a blade through canvas. Before he had time to react to this new horror, she'd already plunged her hand deep inside. Fingers gripped and clawed, tugged and scratched up through his innards and then she ripped out his beating heart in one fluid movement. The squelching noise it made upon exiting his body made his eyes bulge even wider, as though the pain was nothing in comparison to hearing and seeing the still-pumping organ in its entire mass of dark, glistening meatiness. He stood and watched, mouth agape, as she dropped the throbbing mass to the floor and stamped on it with her bare foot.

With this last action, all life force was finally driven from him and Fergard Told VI's body crumpled and fell forwards. To prevent herself from being squashed by his burly frame, she leaped into the air and drop-kicked him squarely on the chin. The impact of the blow smashed the vertebrae of his neck and sent his body toppling backwards with such force it careered over the edge of the mountainside into the darkness.

She stood for a moment basking in her glory, then turned and picked up the baby.

"Your father was a prick of the highest order, little one," she said, looking into his eyes. "And I've no doubt you'll be just like him one day."

Leaning back against the stony wall she looked thoughtful as the baby suckled warm blood from her fingers; blood from his own father's heart. She smiled. This gave her an immense feeling of satisfaction.

"I suppose you'll need a name," she said eventually. "Because, unfortunately, we're going to be together for a very, very long time you and I."

The baby smiled and gurgled, a cluster of pink spit bubbles emerging from his lips.

Looking up to the moon, which was now peeking from behind a mass of clouds, she announced, "From now on I'll call my burden *Reeve*."

Chapter 1

Alex was scowling, his skin tone a mid-shade of grey and his mouth and eyes black.

"I can't believe you left me," he was saying to her, his lips unmoving.

"Oh, like you're really bothered. At least you'll have more milk for your coffee now."

Her reply seemed to fuel his rage and he reached for the mug that stood on the kitchen counter next to him. His arm arced as he threw the mug and its contents across the room. It shattered against the black splash-back tiles behind the sink and, as hot coffee flecked up onto the white of the adjoining wall, the whole house literally came crashing down all around them. A huge crack, which split the room from floor to ceiling, caused the bricks and mortar to crumble as though the house was made of nothing more substantial than chalk.

Rufus's tail was between his legs and his ears were folded back. He hid behind her legs, cowering and unspeaking.

"Are you happy now?" Alex screamed. This time his mouth did open, but it didn't move in sync with the words. "You've ruined everything!"

He stormed towards her, his clenched hands reaching out. She reeled backwards when she saw his nose begin to extend, the tip turning black like a piece of coal. Coarse hair, like the bristles of a heavy-duty paintbrush, developed at a rapid speed all over his exposed skin and she watched in horror as his teeth popped out one by one. He looked at her for a brief moment, piteous as his hands reached up to catch white fragments as he spat them from his mouth. The tip of his tongue flicked around, exploring the squidgy crevices.

14

Libby dry-heaved at the sight and then watched as large pointed teeth accommodated the bloody gaps. They rose up quick from his pouring gums, and at the same time his mouth and nose stretched further outwards to form a lean snout. Whilst this was happening, his whole body began to distort and rearrange itself. Elbow joints popped forwards and knee caps snapped backwards, he roared in pain and fell to the floor on all fours.

With his back arched he stood amidst items of his own clothing, now torn and discarded on the floor all around him, and he snapped his jaw up and down with vigour as though testing out his new elongated facial arrangement. All the while she edged backwards trying to gain more distance, but in a stomach-jolting lurch he was bearing down on her; his breath hot and smothering. Her legs buckled beneath his solid weight and he easily pinned her to the cold tiles of the kitchen floor.

Looking up wide-eyed, Libby couldn't see a scrap of her ex-boyfriend left at all. He'd been replaced by some sort of enlarged Alsatian-type dog, which judging by its bared teeth and lack of playful tail-wagging wanted to seriously maim, if not eat, her.

Reaching up to its throat she buried her fingers into its thick fur and battled to keep its snapping teeth away from her face, desperate to remain in one piece because being eaten alive had never featured high on her list of things to do - in fact it was right at the bottom alongside burning to death, drowning and eating cold tapioca pudding.

Alsatian-Alex's fetid dog breath was heady - but at least the obnoxiousness of it kept her from passing out. She didn't try to fool herself she was match enough for a gargantuan dog creature, the fact it hadn't already torn her limb from limb made her think that it was merely toying with her.

Closing her eyes she willed the power to brace her arms out straight so that she could gain a greater distance from its snarly drooling mouth. It was so close, each time it exhaled strands of her hair blew about and there was a sweaty moistness that clung to her cheeks. Low marrow-chilling

15

growls rumbled in its throat, vibrating through her hands, and its big black eyes bore into hers with an intensity that matched its stale breath. After much effort she managed to push the hairy dog-beast backwards. Locking her arms out straight, she panted, "You know, you shouldn't play with your food, arsehole. Did no one ever teach you that?" She felt its weight press down a little harder, crushing her chest and squeezing the air from her lungs, but she carried on regardless, "You also have to earn your food or at least beg for it, and you did neither. So get off me you stupid hound or I'll be forced to teach you some new tricks - and believe me, I'm like a psychotic Victoria Stilwell when I get started."

It snarled and snapped its teeth close to her bare skin in direct response to the threat. She was pleased it appeared to understand what she was saying because if she was going to be eaten alive then she certainly wasn't going down without a fight - and her best defence had always been her smart mouth. If she couldn't kick its arse in a physical fight then she'd damn well insult the hell out of it until she no longer had the ability to talk.

Closing her eyes once again as though doing so would help her summon more strength, she raised her leg in preparation for a well-aimed knee to the gonads, but much to her confusion the struggle came to an abrupt ending. The ribcage-crushing force of the ginormous hairy-wolf-dog was no longer bearing down on her. In fact it had gone completely flaccid in her hands and its skin was now smooth and furless.

When she opened her eyes she was stunned to see that it was her mother's neck she gripped in a choke-hold. There was an alarming look of fear and desperation residing in Merilyn Hood's broken-blood-vesseled eyes, one she had never seen before. Upon releasing her grasp she cowered backwards, scrabbling away across the floor as though her mother was even more terrifying than the wolf-man. All the while their eyes never left each other's.

Merilyn looked ragged. Blackish upturned crescents rimmed her lower eyelids and a gaunt, sallow face highlighted cheekbones that were too prominent. Her skin had a yellow-ish hue and there were lines on her top lip that Libby had never noticed before. Libby wondered whether her mother had been giving her liver and lungs an all-out hammering since Tuesday just gone. She looked like hell.

"Libby? Is it you?" Merilyn's voice sounded muffled, as though she was talking and Libby was under water. "Is it really you? Can you hear me?"

Libby continued to stare, but for the life of her she just couldn't find any words at all.

"*Libby?* Libby!" Merilyn's words became louder and more pleading. "I need to talk with you…"

And then Libby awoke with a gasp.

Another bad dream.

Alex, her ex, wasn't really a dog-ish looking werewolf. Her mother didn't really look like a broken, decrepit version of herself. And Rufus…well, Rufus wasn't anything anymore.

During the two days she'd been in Sunray Bay, Libby had had similar nightmares each time she'd attempted to sleep; her unconsciousness filled with struggle and unease. Catching her breath and feeling somewhat disorientated in the darkness, she patted her hand out to the left. Upon feeling nothing but empty space she sprang up into a sitting position and looked around blindly.

"*Grim?*"

Chapter 2

Thursday, 3:58pm: The Girls' Chamber, Sun Castle, The Grey Dust Bowl

"How long's it been now?" Mord asked, her voice husky and her usually-vibrant blue eyes lacklustre in the dim light. She shuffled a deck of cards in her graceful white hands, working them up and down with little effort. And even though she didn't look up as she spoke, everyone around the table knew she was addressing Gin.

Gin shifted her weight on the hard wooden bench from her aching left buttock to her right. Feeling instantly gratified, yet wishing for the umpteenth time they had some scatter cushions lying about the place, she cleared her throat and answered, "Three days."

Nobody said anything for a while. They all knew very well how long it had been, but it was as though talking about it might accelerate things.

"So what's the hold up?" Mord said eventually.

Shrugging her shoulders, Gin breathed in deeply while looking around the table at the faces of the four other women she was playing cards with. Three of them, including Mord, looked back with a certain air of expectancy but the other had her head low, pretending to study the joker card that lay face up on her palm. In truth Gin didn't have a clue what the answer to Mord's question was, but she hoped things might drag out for at least another week or two. She wasn't psyched up enough to partake in the next instalment of the Queen's big mission just yet. Even though she felt physically re-energised since Monday's shenanigans in Sunray Bay, she still found herself dumbfounded and a little apprehensive about all the changes Rembrae's plans foretold. She'd never let her companions know how disconcerted she was feeling about it all because she saw herself as the brave protector of the group, she felt personally responsible for the safety and wellbeing of her four roommates - there was no room for fear or doubt.

Trying to wear a confident, blasé look she drew a breath ready to respond but was cut short by a loud rapping on the door. Everyone around the table jumped at the sound; each woman with a look of threatened unease and suspicion etched onto her face. Gin was quick to jump to her feet; signalling with her hands for the other four to remain seated.

Moving to the door, stealthy and cat-like, she listened for any clue as to who might be calling. They certainly weren't expecting anyone. Nobody *ever* came knocking at their door. Her muscles tensed and her pupils dilated; she braced herself for whoever was on the other side. Narrowing her eyes, she asked bluntly, "Who's there?"

There was no answer.

In fact, all that could be heard was the distant whine of wind filtering through the network of old stony chambers they inhabited. Gin looked to the others, who were watching in anticipation, their bodies rigid and ready for immediate action should it be necessary. She shrugged her shoulders and, after a moment of hesitation, reached for the door handle.

"*Wait*," hissed Mord. "What if it's one of *them*?"

Gin looked momentarily perplexed.

"One of *who*?"

"*You know*," Mord urged, her barely-there eyebrows arching upwards as though the answer was blatantly obvious.

Gin looked even more stupefied and raised one of her own eyebrows questioningly.

Crossing her arms, Mord huffed; resisting the need to say out loud what she really meant for fear of sounding foolish.

Van, who was sitting to Mord's left, asked, "You mean one of the *men*?"

Mord rolled her eyes but nodded her head all the same. "Yes! It's just a matter of time before they become aggressive. And what if they stop listening to Rembrae?"

"They wouldn't dare go against the Queen," Gin snapped. "But if it is one of them," she added, thumbing towards the door, "I'll kick him between the legs so hard that his dangly bits will become an internal feature." With that she kicked the air to demonstrate the conviction of her words, grinning all the while.

"What if it's more than just one though?" Mord challenged, her arms still placed over her chest in a manner of defiance.

"Well, in that case, they can form an orderly queue. I'll deal with them one by one."

"For pity's sake calm down, Mord, they know better than to hound us," Brinda, the youngest of them, whose long tapering limbs also made her the lankiest, said. "At least, they should do if they know what's good for them."

They all laughed at that, including Mord, but then another knock on the door hushed them into silence once again. This time Gin didn't pause for thought, she grabbed the handle and thrust the door open to face whoever it was interrupting their twilight game of cards.

A filthy, repulsive creature of male specification stood before her in the fusty shadows of the passageway outside. Despite the god-awful way he looked, he had a non-threatening manner about him. In fact he was so gormless she found she could do nothing but roll her eyes and groan with impatience. No words at all formed on his opened salivating lips and he stood completely motionless whilst holding a piece of paper in an outstretched mouldy-looking hand.

"Good grief," Gin muttered, to herself. "Thackery's been busy again, I see!"

Thackery was one of their male peers and he was both studious and mischievous by nature. He bored easily during the seemingly-endless nights in The Grey Dust Bowl and spent his time experimenting and working out how things worked. Only two weeks ago he'd been reprimanded by Rembrae for having blown up a small section of the old buttery. Gin wasn't sure how the hell he'd managed it, but the boom had been so colossal she'd thought the whole castle was falling down. He'd sustained substantial burns to his face and even his white hair was now singed black at the front. Rembrae had told him to let it be a reminder of his thoughtless foolishness and if he ever did anything like it again she'd personally burn the rest of his hair off. And so, since the unfortunate buttery incident, Thackery's latest favourite pastime had seen him teaching new tricks to Sun Castle's servants.

The servants had been serving Sun Castle for some years. Their only duties, prior to Thackery's input, was to draw water from the well and to deter unwanted visitors from the perimeters of the castle during daylight hours. Now it would seem they could perform personal deliveries too.

Wonders will never cease to amaze me, Gin thought. *Whatever next?* Laundry duty or housekeeping services? Goodness knew the place could do with a good tidy. Or maybe Thackery would give them lessons in alternative therapies. Neck and shoulder massage, reflexology and reiki - she wouldn't rule anything out.

Snatching the bit of paper from the servant's feeble grip, she unfolded it carefully and read the contents, her lips moving as she did so. When she'd finished she crumpled it in her hand, closed her eyes and sighed. "Oh buggering hell."

"What is it?" Mord's eyes were wide with alarm.

"I have to go," she answered, rubbing her forehead in agitation.

"*Tonight?*" Mord had been the one to broach the subject only moments before. In doing so she now felt as though she'd somehow managed to jinx the situation. The ball was rolling again - which was clearly to Gin's dismay. The others around the table drew in sharp breaths of shock.

The messenger at the door remained silent, not reacting in the slightest to what was going on inside the room. He stood and continued to gawp at Gin in the same stupid way, though there was no real depth to his gaze, his eyes as lifeless as glass buttons. His slack-jawed gape could have been

21

misinterpreted as awe of her wraithlike beauty - but she knew that wasn't the case because his type didn't ponder such things. In fact, his type didn't ponder anything at all.

Filthy clothes hung on him like rags and his skin, what little of it was exposed, was an odd purple-blue colour like fading bruises; the mottled skin of a dead body. His hair was greasy from the roots to the very ends, plastered down to his scalp. But worst of all, the rancid smell of his putrid body, akin to festering meat, wafted in through the open doorway making Gin feel nauseous and even more displeased about his presence.

He stood frozen as though captured in suspended animation. His hand still extended even though she'd taken the message from him. He gave the impression that he was hanging about like some sort of nuisance concierge waiting for a tip.

Making a sound of distaste Gin swung the door shut then turned back to face the room. The light was low in the cosy open-plan living space; black iron wall sconces held thick yellow-cream candles which were all alight. Shadows throbbed and danced but she could see remarkably well despite the creeping darkness. Her companions sat around a large rectangular oak dining table on sturdy bench seats. And the white of bed linen glowed invitingly from bunks that were located around the circumference of the room.

Lilea, Gin's closest companion, threw the joker card facedown onto the table and huffed, "Are you sure I can't come with you this time?"

Lilea was around five feet tall, a curvy little package with a face that could be deemed sweet, an aura that could be deemed innocent and smooth waist-length white hair that shone almost lilac in the light which gave her an ethereal quality. Gin, on the other hand, was five foot ten. She was willowy and long-limbed, and there was a faint harshness to her otherwise pretty face that had come from a long lifetime of fighting and training. To add further to her less-than-angelic demeanour, her own white hair was ratty and knotted - arranged on top of her head in a carefree manner that spoke volumes of her nature. In just over three-thousand years, dreadlocks denoted that she'd long since stopped caring about hairbrushes and ornate hair-slides. She doubted the time would ever come when Lilea and the other girls stopped brushing their hair and adorning themselves with jewelled clips. They were all stereotypical girls - they loved the art of preening - but she on the other hand was a bit of a tomboy, always had been. And so she wore her hair in the same style as the menfolk. Long and bunched together in thick strands that looked similar to grotesquely large rats' tails. It was, in fact, a trademark of Blōd Vampyre masculinity - and perhaps the reason she'd opted to wear the style herself. Gin was rebellious and headstrong.

According to some unwritten Blōd Vampyre law, the longer your hair the wiser you were deemed. That, of course, wasn't always strictly true. Even a couple of millennia weren't enough to make some people pass as clever, however long their hair grew. Stupidity was genetic, or so she believed, and there was no getting around that. But she was smart and her hair was very long - so she conformed to that Blōd Vampyre belief perfectly. She was no weakling either, she'd stand up front with the menfolk during any battle that might come their way - she thought herself a brave warrior and certainly equal to any man. The other four Blōd Vampyre girls, although no push-overs themselves, felt comforted with her around - now that she was being sent away on another of Rembrae's errands they shifted in their seats and looked hesitant.

Gin walked back over to the table. Straddling the bench seat so she faced Lilea, she said, "No that would not be wise."

Lilea began to answer but Gin's index finger pressed against her lips, stopping her from uttering another word.

"Don't," Gin whispered. "I'll be back before sunrise. We can sit outside and watch the beginning together, if you like? Who knows, it might be our last time."

"*Our last time?*" Lilea's face turned even whiter than it already was.

"I meant our last time *here,* silly," Gin said, shaking her head in despair, her eyes alight with humour. "At Sun Castle."

"Oh, okay. But really, I don't see why I can't…"

Gin gave her friend a warning glare. Lilea's eyes narrowed and she breathed out in exasperation, knowing it was pointless arguing.

The other three Blōd Vampyre girls, Brinda, Van and Mord, sat quiet. They all kept their eyes downcast, unsure what to say. The moment was awkward. They all knew that in the long term Rembrae's plan should ensure a better life for them all, but in the short term they had to stand by and watch as Gin underwent dangerous errands - from which nobody could ever be certain she'd return safely.

Gin looked around the table at each of the other women, their mouths all twisted with apprehension. She rolled her eyes and clapped her hand down hard onto the surface of the table, stinging her palm and making them all sit up straight.

"For heaven's sake, cheer up you lot. Anybody would think I wasn't capable of doing this thing."

At first they looked nothing but startled, but eventually her words seemed to strike a chord and they all nodded and smiled sheepishly. When Gin stood up and opened her arms wide, they all jostled to their feet and gathered round for a group hug.

Breathing deep, Gin closed her eyes and relished the mass of silky hair, soft skin and chiffon fabric that was enveloping her. It was her calming moment of comfort before she headed back out into Sunray Bay. She made an appreciative purring noise as someone rubbed the muscle of her left shoulder and she smiled when Lilea stretched up and pecked her on the cheek.

"I'll be back in a few hours, carry on without me," she said, untangling herself from the group embrace. Then pointing to the cards on the table, she was quick to add, "I suck at this game anyway - the Queen of Hearts always escapes me." Turning to Lilea, she whispered, "Wait up for me, yeah?"

Lilea smiled thinly but nodded. Gin flashed her a mischievous wink before turning and making to leave. As she pulled open the door she was surprised to see that the messenger was still standing exactly where she'd left him. Same stupid look on his face, same stupid hand outstretched - the only thing different was that the thread of drool hanging from his open mouth was significantly longer and was now almost reaching his chest.

"For crying out loud," she sighed, jabbing her finger out past him and pointing in the direction of the black corridor. "Kindly bugger off, will you?"

When he showed no sign of obeying her command she grabbed him by the shoulders, spun him round and pushed him forwards - landing him a kick up the arse for good measure.

Rolling her eyes to show her impatience, she turned back to her four roommates and said, "Catch you all later," and tried her best to give them a sincere smile.

Chapter 3

***Thursday, 3:42pm: The Battlement, Sun Castle, The Grey
Dust Bowl***

With his back to the faded sunset, Reeve perched himself in
one of the battlement's crenels. It was the fourth one along
from the north tower and for as far back as he could
remember it had always been his favourite spot within the
castle's confines. He knew all of the mottled markings in the
stonework and was particularly fond of the carved drawing
on the merlon to his right. The lines were almost crude, yet
the subject matter lent the image a simplistic, elegant quality.
The deeply engraved white lines depicted a naked lady
whose hair was long and voluminous, whose hips were
exaggeratedly rounded, whose waist was miniscule and
whose breasts were amazingly gravity defying.

Her name was Hope. At least that's what he'd come to
call her over the years. In truth he had no idea who'd
engraved her image into the limestone. He supposed a
soldier from back in the days when the castle had been
glorious most probable. Whoever the anonymous artist, he
was very appreciative of the time and effort taken. Hope was
perhaps the main reason this particular crenel had come to be
his favourite place. The battlement itself was peaceful and,
of course, it was also privy to a fabulous viewpoint - Hope
just made it even better.

By now the sky was losing most of its red hues, the sun
almost out of mind, and a pleasant breeze buffeted his
exposed skin. It warmed his body but was not quite frisky
enough to move his mass of thick, heavily-knotted hair.
Heated by the sun's rays earlier, he liked to think it was now
sharing the warmth with him. Like hundreds of sun-kissed
kisses covering his face and hands, allowing him to feel what
he could never see. He closed his eyes, enjoying the tender

sensation - imagining that he was somewhere else; that he was someone else.

After a while of quiet contemplation, he looked out across the expanse of The Grey Dust Bowl towards the town of Sunray Bay. It was an orange slit on the horizon. Buildings were still burning and smoke belched out in a fuzzy haze, blocking out the band of sea that was usually visible.

He wasn't at all surprised that Rembrae wanted to get things moving along. He'd been watching the events of Sunray Bay unfold from the distance of Sun Castle with great interest. The day after he and Gin had stolen the paperwork from the archives was the day, so it was said, that some reprobate Peace & Order Maintenance Officer had been the catalyst for a revolution. Talk about timing. It wasn't at all bad for him and Gin though - theoretically, it gave them an easier way in. The town's guards were lowered, meaning their second stint of thievery should be a piece of cake to exact - they would be able to sneak around virtually unnoticed.

That wasn't to say he was any happier about the fact he'd been chosen to fulfil the mission - and especially not alongside Gin. In fact, he really disliked that he had to go along with her. He wasn't keen on spending time with any of his fellow Blōd Vampyres, but it was even truer of the girls - he seriously wasn't keen on them. He saw the way they looked at him and the way they quietly judged him. *Nasty and vindictive pretty things,* he thought. *All of them.* He'd swear that sometimes he could feel the actual weight of their contempt. It was Gin, the ringleader, whose level of watchful scrutiny held most clout though. Out of all the other Blōd Vampyres she was the one he was most wary of. She was the one closest to Rembrae.

Just before leaving his sleeping chamber, not long after the sun had dipped safely below the horizon, he'd been notified that Rembrae requested his presence in The Great Hall in an hour's time. That had been the extent of the written message given to him by one of Thackery's trainee servants but that was all he'd needed to know, he knew exactly why she wanted him.

It was time.

Time to claim the invaluable weighing scales from the courthouse of Sunray Bay.

Once he'd dismissed the servant with a polite, "Thank you kindly," he'd decided to spend some time up on the battlement before going to The Great Hall. He needed a chance to gather his thoughts, to mope a little, to build strength for what lay ahead - and, of course, he meant to see Hope. He knew he'd be saying a final goodbye to her soon enough. The faceless carving was his one and only friend.

Not being at all sociable, he always did prefer his own company. He was a general misfit amongst his fifteen male counterparts, even Thackery who was a bit of an outcast himself, because they were always bickering and fighting and talking about sex. He would join in with training exercises, where necessary, to practice transition control and fighting techniques, but aside from those occasions he would distance himself as much as possible. He had no interest in being involved in their petty backbiting or juvenile boasting about how many times they'd been laid - or how many more times they'd get laid once they left Sunray Bay. They often accused him of being frigid because he never joined in their lewd conversations, but it simply wasn't true. He liked women as much as the next man. What he longed for was true love; something he doubted they could even begin to understand right now - none of them was as mature as he was. Love was a rumoured emotion that he wanted so desperately to believe in, it was something he latched onto with every bit of faith that he possessed in the vain hope that there must be someone, *anyone*, out there in the universe that could learn to care about him. And it was this longing that made him something of a Blōd Vampyre rarity, setting him aside from the rest of his peers, for the moment. They sought nothing more than carnal indulgence and no emotional ties, but he swore that when he shared his most intimate parts with another he wanted it to be mindfully meaningful too.

28

He wanted everything about it to be consensual and binding, thus leading to a partnership with its good times and bad. He wanted to be in it for the long-haul.

That's not to say he was a virgin though, he wasn't a complete wet blanket. He'd been around for thousands of years and had indulged plenty in that respect. It was just that every time he'd done the deed it had always felt as though something was missing. He put it down to lack of spiritual connection; lack of mutual feelings of a deeper desire. So, for those reasons, he had absolutely nothing in common with the other Blōd Vampyre men.

And god forbid he even try to consort with the Blōd Vampyre girls - they were nothing but a bunch of fierce harpies who hated men as much as the rising sun. But that was pretty much the order of things around Sun Castle, there was a clear male/female divide - and he was a tortured soul amongst them all.

Gazing across to the long route into Sunray Bay, Reeve imagined it looked like an expansive stretch straight into the Devil's own backyard. The Grey Dust Bowl, a barren landscape of ashes, led to the no-hope town which, at that moment in time, was filled with fire and even more animosity than usual. Realising he'd be travelling that path later that very evening, he sighed long and hard.

Everything about it looked drab, charred and depressing. *Yes*, he thought, *depressing is a good choice of word to sum it all up*. It was a particular word he often pondered; wondering if he might be depressed himself. He wasn't sure how depression was identified though, so he had no way of knowing. He presumed there must be a test to take that would tell if you were depressed, or a medical device that would measure how depressing you were to *others*. What he did know for definite was that most times he felt pretty damn low, some nights he didn't even want to wake up, and goodness help him - if he was so depressed with himself and so depressing to others then how would he ever find someone to *love* him?

This thought depressed him further.

"Oh woe is me," he muttered, holding his head in his hands, his words lost to the breeze.

Apart from his hair, face and hands, which were all glowing in the dusky post-sun gloom, he remained pretty much invisible at night - the way he preferred to be. Whereas the other Blōd Vampyres wore light fabrics in whites and antique creams, he adorned a long-sleeved black top and a pair of black trousers (both garments ludicrously tight-fitting); he became one with the night. A slinky shadow, save for his mane. He thought himself a silent observer of the world; a hushed spectator of the night sky; a quiet ponderer of deep thoughts - mostly thoughts surrounding the meaning of life, where he spent his time worrying that he'd missed the point altogether.

Embossed black cowboy boots that were intricate in their design, and which he'd stolen from a fancy boutique in town, gave him that extra edge of sophistication - or so he liked to think. All of the other Blōd Vampyres walked around bare-footed which, to him, made them all despicable cretins with no class whatsoever. He found the idea of walking around shoeless quite frankly disturbing. If a Blōd Vampyre must live with the same feet for thousands of years, then preservation *should* be paramount. No excuses. But, as it was, some of his peers had feet akin to those of a rhinoceros, heel skin as tough as the leather that his boots were made of (and those bad boys were so tough they'd taken him three whole years to break in). So yeah, the two-and-a-half-inch-heeled cowboy boots were his pride and joy. They kept the soles of his feet smooth and, as if that wasn't enough, the metal segs in the heels made a very satisfying *clip-clop* noise on hard surfaces.

With his legs draped over the edge of the crenel he tapped his feet together and looked downwards, past the boots. On the ground, below the battlement, in the dried up trench that had served as a moat at one point, he could see servants wandering about without any real aim - their lethargic meandering giving the impression of highly-medicated sleep-walkers. As he watched them his curiosity stirred and

30

he wondered what provoked them to act in the despondent way that they did. They usually gathered in the courtyard after dark, but every so often some of them would wander off like stray sheep. He tried to imagine what they must think or feel. What it was that made them roam.

Were they looking for escape?

Searching for food?

Hoping to die?

In all likelihood, he supposed, they were probably looking or hoping for nothing at all. Poor wretches. He felt a slight tug of empathy towards them, primarily because he felt just as pathetic as they were most days.

Turning his body sideways so that he was wedged between the two merlons at either side, he twiddled a pencil in his right hand and fingered a notebook in his left. It was a perfect night for scribbling down thoughts and verses; a perfect night for releasing some of his emotions onto the page. Poetry filled with sorrow and angst was his usual coping mechanism for dealing with the life fate had dealt him.

He couldn't wait for Rembrae's newfound plans to be enacted. He and all of the other Blōd Vampyres had been hanging around for what seemed like forever in The Grey Dust Bowl. In his mind they were a bit like hermit crabs, having taken an opportunist claim to the shell of Sun Castle many years ago. It had been a building of great presence and grandeur, but one that didn't quite fit their lifestyle. It had never felt like home - at least, not to him. Soon they were going to leave the dreadfully depressing place, and he for one couldn't wait to be free from Sun Castle.

Oh the irony of it, *Sun* Castle indeed.

He'd spent goodness knew how many lousy years residing there, yet he'd only ever caught mere after-glows of the real sun. Such a tantalising reminder of what he was missing, what his life could never really entail. He hated being a vampire at times.

He swore that once he managed to escape Sun Castle, The Grey Dust Bowl and Sunray Bay - he'd never set eyes on another Blōd Vampyre again. He'd find himself a woman to fall in love and settle down with. Perhaps he wouldn't even mind all that much if she was a modern-day vampire, he'd just about decided he could live with that. And it was the thought of this imagined woman that kept him going night after night. She was all he ever hoped for and dreamed about.

It'd be super if she had a body like Hope, though he reasoned that that wouldn't be a necessity - or even a likelihood. She *would* have coloured hair though - beautifully coloured hair with nothing white about it in the slightest. Absolutely not. Even though Hope had white hair, he was sick to death of white. It was all he'd ever known - a heartless colour devoid of love. After all, it was the colour of the Blōd Vampyre.

In the same vain, ideally his lover's eyes would be brown or green. He didn't envisage that they'd be any shade of blue, like that of his own eyes or those of his peers, but that aspect wasn't as essential as hair colour. He could waver on the eyes if need be, but there was absolutely no budging on the hair. In fact, he felt so strongly about it he didn't think he could stomach yellow hair either. No, she'd need to have hair that shone luxurious earthy brown, more alluring even than chocolate. Or hair that was so black it radiated blue in brilliant light. Or hair that blazed fire-red like the remnants of every sunset to which he'd ever borne witness. Yes, that was it. Red hair would be perfect.

Rembrae often chastised him for being a foolish romantic, an accusation he didn't deny because it was true. Yet the irony of it was, although she mocked him she didn't appreciate the truth of her own words. Only a true gentleman would be deemed romantic (foolish or not), but still she saw him as she did all other Blōd Vampyre men - a brutish, potential threat to the female kindred. It was reasonable to say that Rembrae hated men with a burning passion. *Especially* him. This saddened him beyond words, but he could do nothing other than keep himself to himself, write poetry and dream about his future wife - of what she would look like and of the life they would have together.

After thirty-odd minutes of mulling things over, he finally clapped his notebook shut and rubbed his right index finger over the familiar blank face next to him.

"Wish me luck, Hope."

Chapter 4

Thursday, 9:02am: North Point, Sunray Bay
"I'm over here."

His gruff response caused her to sigh heavily with relief.

"Oh I thought..." Libby shook her head dismissively, not exactly sure what it was she'd thought. She relaxed further when a low beam of light illuminated the outline of Grim up ahead in the tunnel. He was in a sitting position, his back propped against the ragged wall of the cave and his knees drawn up with his elbows resting on them. He was shining his torch down to the ground near his feet, to let her see where he was. She felt a little embarrassed about her outburst and murmured, "It doesn't matter."

"You okay?" he asked.

"Yeah, fine. Did I keep you awake?"

She could just about make out that he shook his head, but she wasn't sure whether his response was genuine or not. The previous morning, in Gloria's spare room, she'd woken up all alone despite the fact she'd fallen asleep cradled in his solid arms. She'd come to in a panic, the remnants of a bad dream lingering and a deep hurt at the remembrance that Rufus was no longer there twisting her guts. She'd needed the sanctity of Grim's embrace to make it all feel a little more bearable, but he hadn't been there. He'd snuck downstairs at some point, leaving her to plough through troubled sleep alone. And now awaking again this morning to find him not within arm's reach was very discomfiting. She wasn't sure whether her bad dreams were disturbing him or he was battling his own nightmares. She knew hardly a thing about the horrors his mind harboured, but she promised herself she'd be patient and that in time he would surely open up.

Since they'd slept together on Tuesday night she thought she'd perhaps made a massive breakthrough into the mystery that was the man hiding behind the alter-ego Grim, but as it was he was still detached and emotionally unreachable. She didn't think he was being intentionally difficult and she didn't feel as though he'd taken advantage of her either - he wasn't like that. At least she hoped not. Besides, it could hardly be deemed being taken advantage of when it was *she* who couldn't wait to get her hands on him again. And regardless of his despondency he was company nonetheless - for which she was eternally grateful. She didn't think she could have gone it alone in Sunray Bay. Not now Rufus was gone.

Grim certainly conformed to the old adage *a man of few words*, but that wasn't to say he was emotionally cold. He'd held her close once or twice (when it had suited him), wrapping her in his sturdy arms. She'd loved the feeling of being able to nuzzle her face into his chest because everything felt safe there, serenely safe, if a tad cold. But now it was beginning to seem as though every time she closed her eyes he gave her the slip. At this rate she was going to develop a phobia of sleeping. Not only was her sleep haunted by troublesome dreams but she also tended to lose Grim somewhere along the line.

If she was honest with herself, she was completely and utterly in lust with him - and what was worse was that those feelings had intensified ever since he'd allowed her to get intimate with him the night before last. Her feelings were stirring and shifting, and she gulped with dread in case they were turning into something else.

Not love; that wasn't possible.

Not yet.

But whatever it was she could feel it was growing. And sooner or later she knew she *would* be offering her heart on a plate - whether he wanted it or not.

The thought terrified her. He was so complicated.

To her dismay he'd also gone back to wearing sunglasses all the time; a permanent feature that kept part of his ruggedly good-looking face hidden. She'd seen his eyes (and face in its entirety) on Tuesday night, but not again since. And even then, as they'd shared the single bed in Gloria's spare room, he hadn't given her the opportunity to *really* look. She'd sensed how uncomfortable he was without his cover-up; he'd practically cringed when she'd removed the sunglasses. But to have seen his eyes at all made her feel strangely honoured, because she'd experienced the Grim not many others had. Although, subsequently, she hated the fact he felt the compulsion to wear the wrap-around shades even when the two of them were alone together. She could never tell what he was thinking or feeling - which she realised in dismay was *exactly* why he wore them.

They were his barrier for keeping people out, yet she also appreciated that they were a way of guarding his own shame by keeping it hidden from the casual observer. Whatever had caused his eyes to turn white and whatever events surrounded the death of his wife and daughter, that's where all of the answers lay. But it was hard for her to broach the subject uninvited. Not this soon anyway.

Some might say he was damaged goods. Even Gloria had said as much. Libby knew and accepted that fact, and although pretending to herself that she wasn't trying to fix him, deep down she was hopeful that she could. She'd had an insight to his potential and believed him to be a good man beneath the brooding façade that he put forth for the rest of the world to see. After all, he'd put his own plans on hold for her and he'd saved her life in the tunnels of Sunray Bay's ghost train. Even in the aftermath of the metaphorical shit Finnbane Krain had blown up in her face, and especially after what had happened to Rufus, he'd stuck around to offer words of comfort. Then, of course, there was the fact he was sexier than she could even describe.

There hadn't been much opportunity for them to talk properly as yet. After the whole Finnbane Krain incident two days ago things had seriously kicked off in Sunray Bay. There'd been an uprising between werewolves and vampires. Nobody apart from the vampires themselves wanted vampires to be in power any longer - and as a result there were all-out riots going on in the streets. Sunray Bay was now even less of a safe place to be.

Buildings and houses had been vandalised, looted and burnt out. Prospect Point Fair had gone up in flames. She'd watched in awe as the ferris wheel had been rolled to the end of the boardwalk by a mob of masked hooligans of unknown species, who'd then pushed it off into the sea. The whole town was in disarray - a complete bloody mess.

At first Libby and Grim had anticipated staying to battle their own little war of survival. They'd made a trip to Booze 'N' Stuff to catch up with their possible monster-slaying allies, The Ordinaries, but Thad Daniels' convenience store had been trashed beyond repair and there was no sign of him or any of the others. The stark realisation had then come to them that there was very little point in hanging around. Of course, Libby still had a death-wish out on Kitty for her having killed Rufus - but putting her own life in danger to carry it out seemed absurd. Besides she felt rather numb about it all now. The initial vengeful anger caused by having lost her dog in such a brutal and wasteful way had now given way to a morose feeling of regret and sadness. She realised that killing Kitty would never bring Rufus back. He was gone and all she had left now was Grim. That is, if she could even make such a claim.

Meanwhile, Gloria and the rest of the Knickerbocker Pack had headed underground; taking to the sewers after their café-come-exotic dance lounge was seized by a feuding pack of werewolves. Frighteningly, not only were werewolves fighting against vampires but they'd turned on each other too. Taking the opportunity to lay claim to territory; a chance to thrive and bag more space and dominance. With nowhere else to go and being the underdogs of Sunray Bay, the Knickerbocker Pack had scarpered - with no time to worry about where they would go or what they would do once they got there. Libby felt bad for them - she'd liked Gloria and Stan.

Not long after their departure, Libby and Grim had decided to take to the underground themselves. Grim had suggested they head for The Grey Dust Bowl, which is what he'd originally planned to do himself. He had small hopes of there being something else, something better, beyond the vast planes of the great grey desert - so Libby had agreed it was worth a shot. It didn't escape her attention that he could have made it to the borders of The Grey Dust Bowl at ground level on his own, but he'd insisted they take to the underground so it would be safer for her. It had been reported that the barren stretches of land between the back of Sunray Bay's industrial estate and the borders of the ominous grey desert had been seized by a pack of particularly psychotic werewolves, headed up by alpha male Big Mad Bonzer. Big Mad Bonzer was said to be as wide as he was tall - which was very - and he was, as his name might suggest, as mad as a bag of badgers. His pack of seven dogs and five bitches was completely feral. They were indiscriminate killers therefore it did not sit easy with Grim to lead Libby directly into their territory. Although it all sounded pretty terrifying, her heart swelled at the sentiment - it was proof enough that he really did give a shit.

Unlike the Knickerbocker Pack, Grim had said that he didn't much fancy trawling through the shit pipes of Sunray Bay. He knew of a place at North Point - an opening in the craggy cliff-face just up from the north pier. It was a large cave system that was said to be home to countless nefarious creatures, namely cave trolls. Nobody tended to venture inside the North Point cave system because the trolls were said to be great ugly creatures that could bite a man's head off with one chomp. Grim said that was highly unlikely and that he didn't believe in them. Sunray Bay was plagued with vampires, werewolves and zombies, but according to him, trolls were taking it too far. Libby trusted his judgement and placated herself with the fact that even if he was wrong in his assumptions, then he was capably big and strong enough to protect her against such underground terrors. And besides, he had a point - she hadn't fancied traveling to The Grey

Dust Bowl in the confined spaces of the sewers either. It was North Point cave system over sewers and floating turds any day.

They'd entered North Point some hours ago. It was dark, dank and claustrophobic. Libby had lost all sense of time and direction. The only thing she *was* sure about was that Grim was still there with her - and that made her feel insanely relieved.

"So, we survived our first night," she said, pushing herself up off the ground. It was the first thing that came out of her mouth, yet she had no idea how long she'd slept or whether it was even morning. All around them was a blackness so thick and deep that it appeared to have substance. She didn't think she'd ever seen such complete darkness before. The only light came from the wind-up torch Grim held in his hands - for which she was grateful. She straightened her t-shirt which had managed to crawl up her mid-riff and adjusted the waistband of her jeans so they sat more comfortably on her hips. Grim cast some light her way so she could see where she was treading.

"It's so quiet," he said, when she reached him. "Eerily quiet."

She smiled and hunkered down in front of him. "Well that's a good thing, isn't it? It means there're no cave trolls breathing down our necks."

"Hmmm." His face remained stony and distracted as though he was listening; waiting for something to move or breathe in the oblivion of chambers and passageways all around them. She leant forward and rested her hands on his arms to gain his full attention.

She got it.

He looked at her and managed a smile. Then leaning forward he kissed her gently on the lips, which immediately put to bed all nasty lingering thoughts that had remained from her nightmare. She was down in the pits of an indefinite cave system and yet she was air-fistingly elated by his touch.

"Morning, Libby," he said, his voice rough and delicious just like cinder toffee. She'd had no idea a voice could affect her in such a way. He had the best *come-to-bed* voice she'd ever heard; in fact she'd go as far as to say that it was foreplay in itself.

"Morning, you," she replied, leaning closer and returning his kiss harder; conscious of the fact she hadn't brushed her teeth since the day before but not wanting to stop all the same.

Angling herself over his knees she eased down so that she straddled him, and he instantly responded by putting his hands on her waist and drawing her in closer. There was nothing gentle about his kiss now, his teeth tugging at her bottom lip. She reached her hands up to his face, moving her fingers across the day-old stubble on his jaw. Needing to touch him, to know he was real.

"Do you have to wear those things?" she sighed, breathless, when her knuckles brushed against the sunglasses.

In an instant, his composure hardened and his jaw tightened. His mood suddenly matched the frostiness of his skin.

"Don't," he warned. Hoisting her easily to the side, he jumped to his feet - the moment of spontaneity well and truly lost. "Come on, we may as well make a move."

"That's what I was trying to do," she huffed, sticking her bottom lip out for emphasis.

He ignored the remark and turned away, leaving her to cross her arms with a big harrumph.

Chapter 5

Reeve was already there when Gin arrived, waiting at the foot of Rembrae's throne in The Great Hall with an impatient look on his face as though he was annoyed by her tardy time-keeping. But, in actual fact, she was a whole ten minutes early herself. She resigned herself to the probability that the look on his face was loathing and not impatience at all. This didn't concern her though; there was no love lost between the pair of them - she wasn't overly fond of him either.

She wasn't too surprised to see him there in all honesty. He was punctual at the best of times, and on this occasion she suspected that he'd probably arrived extra early just to suck up to Rembrae, to beg her to let him go back into Sunray Bay alone - or not at all.

Gin's bare feet made hardly a sound on the dusty stone floor as she walked towards the front of the hall. The expansive gloomy room was basking in a burnt-orange glow from a fire that was roaring in the massive open fireplace to her right. It was always hot in The Grey Dust Bowl, no matter what time of year, yet Rembrae insisted that the fire be blazing at all times. The intensity of the heat in the room made Gin's skin feel dry and tight, and she coughed into her hand in an attempt to clear her throat of stuffy air and dust particles.

What little furniture and décor there was in The Great Hall was covered in a thick layer of soot. Four stone pillars, aligned down each side of the room, looked to be made from marble, but they were so grimy it was hard to tell for certain. Standing tall they propped a ceiling which you had to tilt your head back at a ninety degree angle to look up at - but

41

even then, it was so dim in The Great Hall, the ceiling was just a black void. For all Gin knew the room might have risen up to infinity.

As she approached the front of the room, Reeve looked at her through narrowed eyes. Thick rims of eyeliner, smudged around his opalescent eyes, made him look extra moody. His eyes were mesmerising, there was no denying, and she often found herself spellbound - embarrassingly. They were light blue with a dark rim of indigo edging the irises; astonishing and beautiful - the kind of eyes she wished she had herself.

She'd often, unknown to him, watch when he'd go off into The Grey Dust Bowl to collect ashes from the ground. Placing them into a glass pot he'd then mix water from the well into the dusty particles to create a thick black concoction which he would apply to his eyes like kohl. She wasn't sure why he did it exactly, none of the other Blōd Vampyre men did and he certainly didn't need to emphasise his eyes any further. They were dramatic enough of their own accord. But then, Reeve was a strange one and she'd given up trying to fathom why he did anything a long time ago.

He was a beautiful man - a pretty boy, as she often called him. His face was all flawless skin, perfectly shaped eyebrows and high-cheekbones - he was almost feminine looking. Long white hair fell down to his waist in dreadlocks, held back from his forehead and face by a wide black band made of cloth which contrasted stunningly against his pale complexion. He was slender but muscular with it and there wasn't a scrap of fat on him at all. She could picture what his body must be like underneath the tight black clothes he wore (because they left little to the imagination). She couldn't help but notice that he packed an ample trouser bulge and he had a cheeky bum that she wouldn't tire of slapping - had she felt that way inclined about him. He oozed a certain level of self-confidence - and yet, in total contradiction, he was very withdrawn and awkward. She thought *odd* was a good one word description

42

to sum him up. The man was an utter mystery - but a mystery she had no desire to figure out.

Breaking her gaze away from his watchful eyes, Gin bowed low to Rembrae, who sat before them on a shabby-chic throne. The throne was both enormous and elaborate - and it pretty much swamped the Queen. It had ornately carved feet made from a solid gold component, blotched with coppery tones, all four of which sat proudly on the floor like a set of lion or griffin paws. Gin noted that the regal piece of furniture was, unfortunately, one more thing in the castle that had been neglected over the years. Its upholstery was dull maroon and she supposed it could well be vibrant red underneath all of the ingrained particles of dust. She couldn't help but notice, with grave concern, that, not unlike the throne, Rembrae herself was looking rather worn. Her hair looked less vibrant and less - well, just *less*. It was thinning at an alarming degree. And she carried her head lower these days as though it pained her to lift it up straight. At that moment there was a look on her face that was unreadable, but Gin sometimes wondered whether the Queen's expressions could truly be read by any other living creature. Her eyes were like two blue topazes and, despite how aged her body seemed, always maintained something of a sparkle. They were the only part of her that looked truly alive.

"Your Highness," Gin said, as she straightened up. She could feel the weight of Reeve's glare right next to her but she didn't meet it - she kept looking straight ahead.

Rembrae shifted on the throne, her long claws digging into the fabric padding. Her snout was long and pointed (a little *too* long and pointed) and her shaggy white coat hung in wispy, tangled clumps around her belly. She looked like a neglected dog that needed a thorough combing, but Rembrae, Queen of the Blōd Vampyres, was actually a fearsome wolf (who also needed a thorough combing). For the past few years it had been one long moulting season. Rembrae shed more fur than Gin thought feasible, and especially since it never seemed to replenish itself these days. There was always an abundance of white hair floating about the place and sticking to stuff. Funnily enough, Reeve's clothes always seemed to go untouched - which was another Reeve mystery in itself. Gin and the rest of the Blōd Vampyres wore light-coloured clothing, so the hairs seldom showed up. She could only presume that Reeve must have a god-almighty stash of Sellotape for his black to stay so immaculately black.

"Ginnifer," Rembrae remarked, her voice low and grumbling like a big cat purring. "The time has come for stage two."

"Very well, Your Highness."

"You and Reeve will go back into Sunray Bay this evening for the weighing scales. You'll take them from the courthouse and fetch them straight back here to me. Do you understand?"

Before she could answer, Reeve interrupted. "But please, Your Highness, can't I go on my own?"

"Definitely not, you insolent little prick." The answer was so abrupt, Gin's breath caught fast in her throat.

"But I'm a grown man," he argued, squaring his shoulders. "I don't need the back-up of a…a…"

"Of a what?" Rembrae's lip rose, making it clear that she might bite his face off if provoked too much. "Say it, I dare you."

He looked sheepish but finished the sentence anyway. "A…*girl*."

"That's almost funny, Reeve, and do you know why?" Before waiting for him to guess, Rembrae barked, "Ginnifer has more balls than you'll ever possess. Not literally, of course, my dear girl." She looked at Gin in apology.

Gin simply shrugged her shoulders.

Looking at Reeve once again, Rembrae's eyes warned him not to continue his line of whining. "You will be assisting Ginnifer in this matter."

"I will *assist* her? As in, I will be her *assistant*?" he gasped.

Rembrae nodded and snarled - he was trying her patience, as usual. Meanwhile, Gin was smirking. She was quite a lot younger than Reeve - by a few hundred years - yet he was being sent out on the Queen's errand to assist her. Seeing the sheer look of repugnance on his face, she smiled and thought, *Oh Reeve, my little bitch, it serves you right for being such a chauvinistic twat.* If there was one thing she couldn't stand, it was when men had the ridiculous notion that they were somehow more superior.

The Blōd Vampyres, who'd been branded Phoenix vampires by the newly deceased Sunray Bay mayor, Finnbane Krain, (which, incidentally, Gin thought was a much better name since blōd, an old English word for blood, was exceptionally similar to blöd, the German word for stupid, which meant the variance between a dash or two dots was so small and yet it made *all* the difference) were an endangered race. This was because the females weren't interested in procreating. Not because they were sexually indifferent, but mainly because they hugely disliked the sixteen male candidates of their own kind. And also, because the aging process of their race was massively delayed in comparison to any other known species, they were expected to have to rear their young for at least a thousand years. This was more than any of the Blōd Vampyre females, who weren't particularly maternal in the first place, could stomach.

The actual life expectancy of a Blōd Vampyre didn't seem ever to have been recorded, so it was unknown how long they were likely to live - but in non-technical terms, it would be reasonable to describe it as being a bloody long time. Rembrae was the oldest living Blōd Vampyre, so far as they knew, and it was thought she was well over eight thousand years old. She'd spent the latter part of her years in The Grey Dust Bowl, passing on her wisdom to the other twenty-one Blōd Vampyres - who were all classed as her fledglings. She was a well-respected, and much feared, queen.

Strangely, none of her young fledglings knew what she looked like in human form. Many years before, in a time so long ago that none of them could remember, she'd taken on the permanent image of a wolf. She'd never explained why it was she preferred to live life that way and it was something they just accepted.

Apart from Rembrae herself, there were five other female Blōd Vampyres residing in Sun Castle - Gin and her roommates. None of whom had the remotest interest in bearing children. For all they cared the entire Blōd Vampyre race could die out. After all, Rembrae had repeatedly made it clear that motherhood was the biggest misfortune that could befall them and that men were the evil instigators who needed to be supressed.

Despite Rembrae's clear dislike of the opposite sex, there were sixteen Blōd Vampyre men living within the confines of Sun Castle. As long as they showed her utmost respect she said she didn't have a problem with them, and they were forbidden to go anywhere near the Blōd Vampyre girls without prior arrangement.

All twenty-one of Rembrae's fledglings were now of a mature age and she had noted how the men were becoming more and more restless and aggressive. She said there was too much testosterone cooped up inside the castle walls - which Gin supposed meant it was a good job they would all be leaving soon.

Rembrae had only recently grown eager to leave Sun Castle. Gin deduced that it was because they all required freedom, space and fresh blood. They were always under each other's feet in The Grey Dust Bowl and there was absolutely nothing to do. They couldn't even up sticks and move into Sunray Bay, Rembrae had told them that they would perish on the coast. So the day they escaped Sun Castle would be the day they all rejoiced.

"But, remind me again," Reeve asked through gritted teeth. "Why me?"

Rembrae's eyes flickered dangerously and she rose to her feet slowly, the large throne still managing to dwarf her as she stood upright on its cushioned seat.

"Because I said so," she said in a low, throaty growl. The hackles on the back of her neck stood up. "Don't anger me further, *boy!*"

Reeve edged back and bowed his head.

"Apologies, Your Highness, I won't speak out of turn again."

Rembrae eyed him with contempt before relaxing back onto her haunches. She set about grooming her front leg, then after a while, when she was satisfied that Reeve wasn't going to back-chat further, she said, "You're the eldest of the menfolk, that's why this task befalls you. And let's face it, the others have more brute force than you do which will serve me well in the end should anything happen to you along the way."

He sighed, sensing the loathing in her words. Not only was she referring to him being some kind of namby-pamby, she was also letting him know how insignificant it would be if he were to die.

"Off you go then," she ordered, without further ado. "And make sure you look after her well."

This time it was Gin's turn to prickle.

"Oh, Your Highness, I can assure you that I *do not* need him to look after me - I am more than capable of taking care of myself."

Rembrae's face softened and she chuckled, a low sound that was hard to identify as genuine or mocking.

"Yes, I know, my sweet Ginnifer. But if anything happens to you, Reeve will answer for it all the same."

Reeve shot Gin a sideways glance and then bowed his head to Rembrae.

"Of course, *Mother*."

Chapter 6

Thursday, 5:00pm: Courtyard Square, Sunray Bay
Numerous makeshift floodlights illuminated the courtyard, rendering the cobbled area the brightest place in Sunray Bay. Stark artificial lighting reflected against all unblemished stonework that surrounded the square. Most of these structures were authorised buildings such as council offices and the residential homes of some of the most senior court officials. Once a place of stateliness, Courtyard Square now looked like a dilapidated street that was ready for the wrecking ball. Not one pane of window glass was intact and all masonry surrounding the gaping window spaces was tarnished soot-black since smoke had belched out the previous evening. Presently nothing was on fire in the square, but the night was young and there was still plenty of time for that to happen.

In stark contrast to everything else, the actual courthouse stood like a valiant king in the middle of a battlefield. As the tallest, grandest building, it commanded a certain level of respect. With an entourage of armed guards, known as Civilian Court Guardians, who gathered tirelessly around its perimeter, it stood proud and untouched. The Civilian Court Guardians looked like a group of militant angels, in their gleaming white uniforms. Assault rifles were strapped to their backs and they stood silent and watchful, waiting for someone to make a wrong move. They were a select team of men and women who had pledged to serve the courthouse with their lives. Even though Sunray Bay was in the middle of a power struggle there was nothing unusual about them being there - they stood guard regardless of what day of the week it was or what shit was going down.

At the top of the flight of steps that led to the courthouse's heavy wooden doorway, great stone pillars rose from the concrete floor, disappearing beneath the stone canopy that sheltered the front of the building from the elements. Long windows stood at either side of the door but, because of the complete blackness inside, the glare from the floodlights bounced off the panes and made it virtually impossible for outsiders to see in. Numerous additional windows filled the length of the building on both sides, all immaculate and untouched.

A number of people had congregated in the square, including Channel 77's news reporter Dora Storm and cameraman Delbert Sempers. Storm, whose burgundy hair shone synthetic red under the glare from the floodlights, held a microphone close to her mouth and was saying, "Sunray Bay is a wreck of damaged buildings and vehicles but, as you can see, all is relatively calm right now in Courtyard Square." She held her hand out, inviting Sempers to pan the camera out to the scene behind, to validate her words. Glass glittered like jewels across the cobblestones; a reminder that all had not been peaceful in Courtyard Square the night before.

"At present we're unsure as to the exact number of fatalities that have occurred due to this civil unrest, but we do expect that whatever that figures is, it will continue to rise. It's certainly true that disturbances have petered out since the turmoil began during late Tuesday evening but, make no mistake, this definitely isn't the end. Far from it.

"It's been reported that a number of our town's residents have taken to the underground via the sewerage system in order to escape from the violence. For anybody who's thinking of following suit, you are strongly advised not to. Sunray Bay's network of sewers is not designed, and neither is it safe enough, to hold such a large number of people. There's a high possibility that the whole system could cave in on itself, crushing and trapping countless people below ground level. And there are fears that those people who are already residing in the tunnels are at a high risk of contracting potentially fatal diseases. Hepatitis and leptospirosis are just a couple of serious concerns, both of which require immediate medical attention upon infection, and given the crisis situation in our town right now, such treatment might soon be completely unobtainable. Therefore I urge you once again, *do not* go underground.

"The advice is to stay off the streets; to barricade yourselves indoors. Find yourselves somewhere safe to wait it out because the werewolf and vampire situation is still very much underway with some disturbances and untold damage to be expected all through the night once again. The moon is now waning, so it's rather disconcerting to know that there's no easy way to tell what's what out here. The werewolves look like vampires, and the vampires...well, the vampires look the same as ever - like you and me."

Storm started walking, her eyes remaining focused on the camera. She came to a halt when the courthouse itself was looming behind her, satisfied that it was a suitable backdrop.

"As you can see, the courthouse is still intact. I had chance to speak with one of the Civilian Court Guardians earlier and he confirmed that there had been no threats as yet to the building's security. Despite the chaos everyone seems to be respecting the values the courthouse stands for. Does this signify hope for the citizens of Sunray Bay? That even the most ruthless of our residents actually respect the courthouse and its weighing scales enough to leave them alone?" Her face became deathly serious and she edged closer to the camera. "Or are the seemingly fearless and ever watchful Civilian Court Guardians simply enough to dissuade them from criminal damage?"

As it was, right at that moment, she along with everybody else round about failed to notice that a shroud of fog had drifted into Courtyard Square. The air had been so filled with smoke the previous night this particularly small cloud wasn't enough to raise any suspicion. It moved swiftly in a thin wispy mass until it was hovering above the canopy of the courthouse. Creeping downwards, it clung to the walls of the building like dry ice - unseen and blending into the light stonework. Once it had reached the great wooden door it shifted through the tiny gap at the bottom and in seconds the

50

mist had completely vanished. Had anyone been observing, it would have looked as though the courthouse itself had sucked it inside.

Thursday, 5:06pm: The Courthouse, Sunray Bay

Inside the dark foyer of the courthouse the band of fog gathered together into one dense mass. Pulsing and shifting, it began to take shape, its grey form slowly taking on a fleshy tone before solidifying into the figure of a man…

Reeve.

After a brief moment he stood up straight, scrunching his hands in order to get the circulation pumping through his veins once again. He looked back at the door, expecting Gin to arrive any minute.

She didn't.

For a moment he stood, unsure what to do, cursing her slowness. His unclothed body shone an unnatural white in the dimness and the thick ropey strands of his hair hung loose down his back, falling across his face at the front because he wasn't wearing his usual black headband. Standing still, alert, he was completely confident in his nakedness. Although slender, his torso was well-defined and muscular. Pale nipples almost blended into a white chest that was smooth and hairless. In fact, the only hair on his body, apart from that on his head, was neatly groomed pubic hair which trailed up to, and then stopped at, his belly button. His legs were long and shapely, leading the eye to a very firm bottom to the rear.

He stood still, like a glorious alabaster statue; his breathing controlled and his senses searching for any signs that Gin was on her way. Upon sensing nothing at all, he began to fear that something bad might have happened to her - and if so, he worried that Rembrae might actually kill him. In hindsight, he supposed he should have travelled slower to let her keep pace. He'd known she wasn't as fast as he was. But then, it wasn't his fault she was hopeless. All he'd wanted was to prove that he could perform this mission far quicker on his own and that he wasn't anybody's assistant, yet now he'd been left feeling as though he was doing a stint of babysitting that had gone wrong. He threw his head back and hissed, "Where in the blazes are you, *Gin*?"

Chapter 7

Thursday, 5:10pm: Schooners Way, Sunray Bay

"Oh shitting hell." Gin patted her arms and stamped her bare feet on the pavement. She winced as sharp stabbing sensations pricked her skin from the inside out. Pins and needles had a tendency to plague her straight after a fog transformation - and they could last for anywhere up to ten minutes. The irony of it was she hated turning into fog. Reeve had said it was the best way to travel across The Grey Dust Bowl, and she hadn't argued because it was true. It was miles from Sun Castle to the borders of town and fog was less likely to be spotted or attacked - it was imperative that they didn't draw any attention to themselves upon entering Sunray Bay. In bat form, although their white fur and creamy-leathered wings made them look more like sea birds to the chance spectator, up close fox-like faces gave them the distinct look of albino Rodrigues fruit bats - only, Rodrigues fruit bats that were doubled in size. They didn't just pass as the average seagull on the skyline; they looked more like bloody great big albatrosses - which was hardly inconspicuous.

Transformations themselves were a tiring business - and not a particularly enjoyable one either. Hence the reason she looked up to Rembrae with great admiration for her having kept the same wolf image for around three thousand years, which was something that ought to be an impossible feat. Gin had no idea how she managed it, but she believed Rembrae's show of stamina was surely nothing short of godly.

When Gin and Reeve set off for Sunray Bay, Reeve had drifted across the baron plains of the dustbowl quicker. Because his body mass was larger and heavier than hers, she should at least have been able to keep up - but alas, despite her best efforts, he was unbeatable. Much stronger and faster, she hadn't been able to outdo him. She'd tried to entwine tendrils of wispy arms around his fast moving fog, but in the end she'd lost him. He'd left her crawling along in his wake, as he always did. She vowed, in frustration, that she was going to train even harder hence forth to improve her own body strength and transition control. One day she would beat him.

Still rubbing her arms she imagined he'd be at the courthouse already, waiting. She could visualise his otherwise-flawless face scowling; making that expression he always made when she was around. Those lofty eyes narrowed in condemnation. She expected the reason he hated her so was because his mother gave her preferential treatment. Gin was Rembrae's blue-eyed-girl, everyone knew that, and Reeve wasn't even worthy enough to scrape the soot from her throne. Sometimes she felt a little uncomfortable about it, perhaps even a teeny bit saddened. It seemed as though he had tried everything he could to earn his mother's care and love - all to no avail. It wasn't her fault that Rembrae despised him though. In fact it was none of her damn business whatsoever. All that mattered was that she'd been chosen to embark on this mission - and for that she was truly honoured.

Having stolen the deeds to Prospect Point Lighthouse and the blueprints for the weighing scales only days earlier, Gin and Reeve had regained enough energy to sustain a transformation to and from Sunray Bay for the next stage of Rembrae's great plan. The blood they'd drained from the archive workers just three nights ago had helped in replenishing their stamina. It had been a well-deserved treat.

Indulgences of that nature weren't a typical occurrence for the Blōd Vampyres; for the most part they fed from the servants of Sun Castle, seldom venturing into Sunray Bay to feed. Rembrae forbid any travel from The Grey Dust Bowl without her consent, and it would seem she had never ventured to the coastal town herself. Some of the men whispered it was because she couldn't make it there and back on four legs before daylight, and since they'd never seen her transition into anything else they didn't believe she could fly. Of course, these speculations only ever remained as mere whisperings amongst themselves - otherwise Rembrae would have their heads for the impertinence of it all. There were also rumours that she couldn't go to Sunray Bay because of the moondogs, who would rip her to shreds as soon as they got a whiff of her. Gin didn't believe any of the gossip, it made the Queen sound weak and cowardly. Rembrae was better than that. After all she had an escape plan that would amount to much more than visiting or living in poxy Sunray Bay. In the interim if they all had to make do with draining the black foul-smelling clotted blood from the servants she believed it was an inconvenience worth bearing.

The servants were members of the living-dead. They were better known in Sunray Bay as zombies, who feasted on the castle's rat population and provided minimal nutritional value and zero satisfaction to the Blōd Vampyres. Some of the Blōd Vampyres had started to show signs of malnutrition of late and were becoming underweight. Blood was meant to be fresh and soulful, but it was neither of those things when taken from a walking corpse. But apart from the zombies, there was nothing else to feast upon in The Grey Dust Bowl - which was why the need to escape was becoming critical. They'd die otherwise. Gin had faith in the Queen though. And the next important stage of Rembrae's plan for escape was to steal the weighing scales from the courthouse.

The scales were key to everything.

The journey back into Sunray Bay had taken its toll on Gin, and she wasn't confident about the homeward flight. She was exhausted and knew that her only chance was to feed. Human blood would be acceptable, if that was the only option she chanced upon, but modern-day vampire blood would be a preferable and more powerful quick fix. She estimated she was about half a mile away from the courthouse, which she planned to walk on two legs, and in that time she guessed there would be plenty of opportunities to find food.

At the moment she was standing in an empty alleyway all alone, but she knew she would attract attention to herself sooner or later because she was completely naked. Blōd Vampyres could transition themselves but not their clothing as well. They were good, but not *that* good. Even practically-perfect Reeve wasn't capable of such brilliance.

On either side of her a mismatch of buildings flanked the narrow side-street. Red brick townhouses loomed upwards, covering three storeys. Squat buildings which comprised boutiques, cafés and cottages were sandwiched intermittently between them, some proudly bearing their original grey stone masonry, others covered in plaster (some rendered smooth and some textured with a stippled effect), and a few simply white-washed. Some of the larger buildings had thick black Tudor-style beams which, in the gloominess of the streetlights, gave a false perception that the houses themselves were behind bars. One thing the collection of varied buildings had in common was that all of their windows were broken. A lot of them, but not all, shared a display of red spray-painted graffiti. Gin wasn't opposed to graffiti, if it was done properly - but she could tell that this was just the work of an illiterate amateur. Most of the words she couldn't make out, but one streak on the front wall of a small inn called The Laughing Moon was unmistakable: VAMPIRES SUK!

All around her were masses of stagnant shadows, cast by the buildings. Numerous alleyways led away from the side-street and recessed doorways hid in the dark; she couldn't tell where one shadow ended and another began. It was so dark in the openings and crevices she supposed the shadows might even have shadows themselves. As she took a moment to decide which way to go a deep voice crept out from the even deeper darkness like an unwelcome draft.

"Hey, little girl, you lost? Need some help finding your way?"

The rough drawl was both threatening and mocking, which made Gin roll her eyes skyward and sigh heavily with irritation. Squinting her eyes and straining to see into the blanket of blackness to her right she tried to locate the owner of the voice, but in a matter of seconds he stepped out and stood beneath the dull glow of a streetlamp which was some fifty yards away. He was a buffalo of a man; top heavy and extremely tall, with a bushy red beard. She had no doubt he'd make a delicious meal, but he was also a big bugger and she had no doubt that he'd prove to be a difficult challenge for her right now.

Positioned with his legs set squarely apart on the pavement, there was an air of malevolence about him that she could see oozing from his nostrils in dark grey vapours. He glared at her, unblinking, with his lips puckered at the sides in a display of menace.

She allowed herself a small groan when two other figures followed close behind. Their features remained hidden by the immense shadow cast by Buffalo's body. When she failed to answer Buffalo's question, all three of them moved forward in a silent synchrony that was almost impressive. Now closer, Gin could see how they all eyed her seemingly vulnerable, naked body.

"No, you hairy arse rash, I don't need any help," she said. Wafting her hands up and down both sides of her body, she added, "And do I *look* like a little girl to you?"

Buffalo laughed out loud, a sound that held little humour. He looked her up and down once more. "Well, now you mention it…" He tilted his head to the side and grinned a lascivious grin.

"Good," she said. "So now we've got that cleared up you and your friends can piss off. Oh and since you're feeling like such a Good Samaritan, perhaps you could find someone else who needs your charity."

His small dark eyes narrowed in vexation, but before he could respond she said, "Who knows, you might find an old lady who needs some help crossing the road - I'm sure you'd stand more chance of thrilling her than you do me."

He moved his shoulders up and down in agitation, his face murky with anger. She guessed he wasn't used to being spoken to in such an insulting manner. The swirling aura trails escaping from his mouth and nostrils were now black and burgundy tendrils.

"Can't I at least warm you up?" one of Buffalo's sidekicks said. He rubbed his hands together and threw her a wink.

"It's not cold, dick-less."

Buffalo snarled and charged forward. "You will be soon, you lippy bitch."

Instead of moving away, Gin surprised him by stepping forward. He stumbled to a halt just before her, taken aback by her assertive display of confrontation and by the aggressive curl of her lip that showed a complete lack of fear.

"Bet you think you're tough, don't you?" Her fiery words lashed upwards, warming his face with their ferocity.

He remained mere inches away, refusing to back down. His teeth clenched tight, and his fists tighter still. His breath was coming out in short, sharp rasps. Not a result of physical exertion, but because he was now apoplectic. The fury emblazoned in his bulging eyes was roaring hot, appearing to make his face glow redder than his beard and eyebrows. When he opened his mouth Gin noticed he had elongated canines.

Making big eyes at him and smiling, she backed away. "You know, on second thoughts I think I do need warming up."

Puzzled by her change of heart, Buffalo's unruly eyebrows knitted together on the bridge of his nose. "*What?*"

"Well, I was just thinking…" Raising her right hand, she ran her index finger slowly down the lapel of his black coat, maintaining eye contact at all times. "Perhaps you're just what I need after all, big fella."

He watched her, suspicion apparent in fierce eyes that were attempting to penetrate her thoughts to see whether it was truth or scorn in her words. She had the better poker face, and after a few moments he still couldn't decide which. Looking back to both of his accomplices, he received no words of encouragement from them - they simply shrugged their shoulders. When he turned back, Gin opened her mouth and ran her tongue down one of her own perfect fangs.

"Oh..." He moved back in surprise. His expression relaxed with recognition and his full liver-coloured lips curved upwards beneath his wiry red moustache. He nodded his head in understanding and boomed, "Pardon me, angel. Didn't realise you were one of us. You should have said."

She noted that although some of the blood-thirsty malice had left his eyes, the level of lecherousness in them had gone up tenfold. Plumes of aura snorted heavily from his nostrils like scarlet steam rising.

"So...d'ya wanna have some fun?" he asked, his eyes darting down over her body, lingering longer on her chest than should have been polite. "I've got something I'd like to show you." Guffawing he grabbed at his crotch. She winced in repulsion and withheld the urge to head-butt him in the face.

"No, I'd rather have my eyeballs extracted with a rusty screwdriver, thank you very much," she said, her voice unruffled and her stance composed. "And for your information, I'm not *one of you.*"

Her attempt at shrugging off his sexual advances was ignored.

"There's no need to be shy, angel," he said, his voice low and grumbly. His slug-like tongue skirted over his bottom lip. "And don't worry, I'll tell these two to do one." He thumbed over his shoulder towards the other two who were still standing there.

"That won't be necessary," she said, taking a firm hold of the lapel on his thin black overcoat and moving her face so that her mouth was close to his. She grinned when he stopped breathing for a moment, but the cheesy-sweat smell of his matted beard soon wiped the smile from her face and made her want to retch instead. "They're more than welcome to hang around - they're just what I need too."

"Mmm it's like that, eh?" he cackled, eyes glinting. "Dirty little bitch…"

"Not at all, you pervert." Her face was now deathly serious.

"Huh?" Buffalo's smile dropped into a straight line across his face, he couldn't comprehend why she kept blowing hot and cold.

"I'm just extremely hungry, you see," she said.

Locking his eyes with an intense stare, she allowed him to see the full extent of her ill-intent and hunger; wanting him to feel like the fox instead of the hound.

As the realisation registered on his face, his mouth opened in shock. He made to argue but wasn't quite quick enough as she drove her face into the folds of his filthy, obnoxious smelling neck and bit down hard. The painful pins and needles in her arms and legs amplified in an instant as she guzzled his blood, the prickling sensations jetted around the rest of her body. Only this time they felt good - orgasmically good.

When Buffalo's two sidekicks realised what was going on they moved forward to prize her away, but she grabbed them both by the neck and within seconds they were lying unconscious on the concrete floor, their windpipes fortunate not to have been crushed in her solid grip.

Through sheer ignorance or lack of education in their own history, none of the modern-day vampires knew that Blōd Vampyres existed, never mind the fact they were the original vampire super race. Gin's kind had been around ever since the moon had turned white, yet they were mere long-overlooked legends to modern society. They were the forgotten ones - and the unintentional creators of the modern-day vampire, no less. Back in the times when they had lived on Earth they had bred with humans, and it was their off-spring who were to become the half-breeds that were now mistaken for fully fledged vampires.

Within minutes Gin had had her fill of Buffalo. Feeling satisfied, she pushed him away and watched as his heavy body flopped to the floor with a dull thud. A sharp crack followed, when his skull hit the side of the pavement. She contemplated leaving his two unconscious mates alive, but reasoned that it would be bad-mannered to leave good food behind.

After draining their bodies of as much blood as she could manage without being sick, she stood up and wiped the corners of her mouth with her right index finger and thumb. A rusty metal taste surged back up her throat and into her mouth with a belching sound. Patting her stomach she moaned. She felt both gluttonous and bloated - and it was a fabulous feeling. She imagined she might race Reeve back to the castle once they'd stolen the scales. Not confident that she could outright beat him, she didn't dare feel that cocky, but confident enough that she wouldn't be left behind.

Not this time.

She wandered off in the direction of the courthouse feeling gratified and strong. And somewhat competitive.

Chapter 8

Thursday, 10:23am: North Point, Sunray Bay
They'd been walking for at least an hour, everything dark except the glow from the wind-up torch that Grim held. Now and then Libby would hear him rotating the lever to generate more power and, in turn, the beam would shine a little bit brighter for a short while. Not that there was anything more than rock for them to see. He'd offered her the torch when they'd first entered the caves, but she'd declined - preferring him to be up front, leading the way. She kept one hand free, using it to feel along the cave walls to keep balance and bearing, and the other she'd tucked into the back of Grim's trouser waistband. Clamping her fingers down on the fabric she couldn't lose him and the contact of his bare skin against her knuckles was somewhat comforting.

The space around them smelt fusty, like damp carpet, and the darkness was tar-black - altogether it was overbearing. She was beginning to feel pangs of claustrophobia tightening her chest, and it was taking all of her inner strength to remain calm and focussed so as not to voice her concerns, in a hysterical manner, that they might never see the light of day again. Oppressive memories of being tied to the tracks of Sunray Bay's ghost train, just days ago, swamped her mind. And now similar feelings of helplessness churned like acid in her empty stomach, making her feel sick. She'd have been crushed to death had it not been for Grim - she owed him her life. Pity she couldn't have done the same for Rufus, her beloved talking dog. How she'd love to hear his little voice once again - but he'd been stolen from her, killed by Kitty, Finnbane Krain's personal assistant.

Finnbane Krain.

His was a name she tried not to think too much about. The unanswered questions going through her head were almost enough to drive her mad. That he could have been her biological father was just unthinkable, and if all he said *was* true then that made her half-vampire, half-faery. And what the hell did that mean? There were too many grey areas, too many uncertainties, no way of discovering the realities or unrealities of his claims. She'd rather not think about it just yet.

Despite the tropical climate and humidity above in Sunray Bay, the underground caverns were cool. The deeper inside they ventured the more her skin prickled with goose-bumps that no amount of rubbing would alleviate. Having only the clothes on her back, she couldn't even huddle with Grim to warm up - his skin was colder still. Not that she would ever say as much. Hiding his eyes from her was bad enough, if she told him she thought he was as cold as a dead body then he probably wouldn't let her touch him again - and that would be downright tragic. She decided not to express her misery to him and ground her teeth together instead, to stop them from chattering.

"How far do you reckon these caves go on for?" she said after a while.

"No idea," he answered. "Have you had enough already? We haven't been travelling all that long."

"No, I'm alright," she said, wondering if she sounded convincing.

He reached his free hand backwards and squeezed her arm. "We can stop for a break if you like?"

"No, really, it's okay. I'd rather just keep going. The sooner we get out of here the better."

"Not exactly a nice day out, is it?" he quipped. "So bloody quiet all the time, just waiting for something to reach out..."

"Ugh!" Drawing her hand away from the mossy wall of the cave, she wiped her palm down the legs of her jeans. She suddenly imagined horrible creatures with bitey teeth lurking in unseen crevices, waiting to nip her fingers off. *That's just great,* she thought, tucking her hand into the back of his waistband alongside the other one. "I hadn't thought of that."

He laughed. "Chicken."

She prodded him in the ribs. "Not at all. My left hand has been forming quite a bond with your trousers and my right hand was feeling left out, that's all."

"Okay, whatever." He clicked his tongue and she could almost imagine him rolling his eyes and grinning.

They stumbled forth in the gloom for another twenty minutes or so, mostly in silence, until Grim came to an abrupt stop. Libby walked into the broad expanse of his back, her nose taking the brunt.

"Uh oh, we have a problem," he announced.

"Yeah, a broken nose I should think," she replied, stepping backwards whilst inspecting for blood around her nostrils. "Give me some warning next time you're about to just *stop*, okay?"

"Oh, sorry…" He turned to see if she was alright.

She waved him off and peered around to ascertain what the problem was. Not seeing much of anything, she asked, "What is it?"

Flashing the torch ahead, he highlighted the issue.

"A *very* tight squeeze up ahead."

She scrunched the fabric of his vest in her hands, her sore nose all but forgotten about. A nagging, panicky feeling clawed at her nerves when she saw how the cave walls on either side of them narrowed so they almost met in the middle. A thin, vertical cavity was all that remained of the tunnel ahead, and Grim was correct in his assumption - it'd be one heck of a squeeze to get through.

"Do you think it's doable?" She wasn't sure what she wanted the answer to be.

"I reckon you'd be okay to get through," he said. "But I'm not so sure about me. Depends how far it goes and whether it gets any tighter further in."

Libby frowned. As well as being well over six foot tall, his muscular body was solid and thickset. Looking at the gap ahead and then looking back at him, she imagined it'd be like trying to stuff a silverback gorilla into a telephone box.

"Shit," she murmured, her chest constricting the longer she looked on.

"My sentiment exactly," he remarked, his voice gruff.

"What do we do?"

After a few moments of silence, he asked, "Are you *very* claustrophobic?"

She gulped and her eyes opened wide with alarm. "Very." She nodded her head to back up her claim, even though he wasn't looking.

"Shit indeed then."

"Why? What were you thinking?"

"That I wouldn't suppose you'd want to go in there, to see how far it goes?"

She looked at him like he'd gone mad. "Then you supposed right."

"Hmmm, thought so."

Taking a deep breath she held out her hand and said, "Okay, give me the damn torch - I'll go and check it out."

He looked at her in surprise, his face cast in shadow from the low beam of the torch. "Are you sure?"

"Not really, but just give it to me before I change my mind."

"Look, you don't have to," he said. She sensed an element of guilt in his voice, and imagined he felt bad for having suggested she go in without him. "It was just an idea. We can turn back and see if there's another way."

The idea of backtracking for goodness knew how long did not appeal to her any more than the gap. She grasped her hand around the torch and pulled it from his hands. "No. Not unless I find that this way is impossible."

She couldn't believe what she was saying but her thoughts of *Oh shit, what the hell am I doing,* were dashed when he grabbed her by the wrists and pulled her close.

"Only if you're absolutely sure."

She looked up at him, wishing she could see his eyes, and nodded firmly. Feeling brave and impulsive, she wrapped her arms around his neck and pulled him downwards. Tentative, she touched his lips with her own. At first she

65

wasn't quite sure how he'd react, but was thrilled when he kissed her in response. His probing tongue was cold but very welcome against her lips, and she likened his kiss to the effects of menthol; refreshing and tingly in its coldness - and definitely something she'd happily experience every morning and night. The stubble on his face scuffed the skin around her mouth and she brought her free hand around to run her fingers over its coarseness.

His hands worked their way down to her hips, then down further until they rested firmly on her backside. She bit his bottom lip when his grip intensified and then she slid her left hand down over his chest and stomach. Her fingers lingered and stroked the bumpy definition of his abdomen, before slipping underneath his vest. Running her hand back upwards over his bare skin, she delighted in the contact, curling and entwining her fingertips in his chest hair. Just as she thought she wouldn't ever tire of touching him like this, he slapped her hard on the left buttock and said, "Come on Libby, this is neither the time nor the place."

"Spoil sport." Flicking the torch round, she it shone in his face.

Despite wearing sunglasses he batted her hand away to assuage the brightness, all the while smiling impishly. "Well someone's got to keep a level head."

"You're such a tease," she said, deliberately pulling his chest hair as she removed her hand from under his vest.

"And you're not?"

She gave him glowering mock-evil eyes as she stepped away. "You're so gonna get it, mister."

"Is that a promise?"

Feeling frustrated, elated and anxious all at the same time, she walked to the gap in the tunnel and thrust a playful middle-fingered salute back over her shoulder - which, in turn, made him laugh. Clutching the torch, she edged inside the opening and turned back to face him.

"Wish me luck, you torment."

He nodded his head, his smile still visible but lessened. There was a more serious note to his expression. The lightheartedness of his demeanour just moments before was now sullied by - doubt, perhaps? Or apprehension?

"Good luck. Come back if it gets too unbearable in there, we can try another way."

Pushing her back into the cave wall as far as she could, careful not to scrape her face against the jagged wall opposite, she edged herself into the chasm. She left Grim behind, shrouded in the darkness, all the while repeating the mantra *cool, calm and collected*, in an attempt to keep her breathing regulated.

With painstaking shuffling movements she made slow progress into the tunnel, the fact she was creeping further and further away from Grim always at the forefront of her mind. The coldness of the rocky wall seemed to penetrate her body so deeply she thought the marrow in her bones must be chilled. Jagged bits of wall tugged at her cotton t-shirt and bit at her skin. When she reached a point where she was physically unable to turn her head to look back the way she'd come, a frenzied panic clawed its way up from her chest and caught in her throat. Her stomach felt like it was convulsing, and her breaths came out in short gasps as though her lungs couldn't cope with the trauma that her mind was creating. Tears stung her eyes as she fought to control the feelings of blind fear.

She felt entombed.

Afraid to go back the way she'd come, because she couldn't move her head or manoeuvre the torch into the other hand, and scared about venturing further into the unknown, because she had no idea how long she'd be struggling onwards, she whimpered and stood still. Biting down on her quivering bottom lip she refrained from crying out. The last thing she wanted to do was let Grim see how much of a big girl's blouse she really was. Squeezing her eyes shut, warm tears ran down her cheeks. She counted slowly to ten. *I can do this*, she told herself. When she opened her eyes again her sight was blurred, and because it hadn't been wound up in a while the torch's glow stepped down a notch. *Shit, no I can't. No I can't do this.*

67

Her feet felt numb in the flimsy pumps she wore. Earlier she'd been able to feel every single lump and bump through the thin soles but, because she wasn't wearing socks and the temperature kept falling, she couldn't feel them at all now. The rest of her body shivered in involuntary spasms - partly from cold and partly from fear.

Taking a long, deep breath she moved onwards. She had no idea how long it would take for a person to die stuck in a cave - and she had no desire to find out. *Onwards and outwards*, she thought, willing her legs to keep moving. But all of the encouragement evaporated moments later when the torch's light snapped off.

"Oh shit, shitting shit," she cursed, without stopping. She knew she needed to crack on but, as she continued onwards in the absolute darkness, she stepped awkwardly into a pothole and twisted her ankle.

"Ow, ow, ow," she hissed, blinking back tears. Her feet might have felt numb before, but she felt *that*. Leaning over she grasped at her foot, cradling it with both hands to rub the injury. It wasn't until the sharp pain had subsided to a dull throbbing that she realised she had more space. She could actually move about. Gripping the torch's wind up lever between thumb and forefinger, she spun it round fast until the light sparked on. Aiming the beam up ahead, she could see how the tunnel around her was becoming ever so slightly wider, and at the very end of the torch's grainy shaft of light she could see that the cave completely opened up - and what's more she could see natural light.

"*Grim!*" she called out. "It's okay. I can see sunlight!"

***

When he heard her calling back, he let out a huge sigh of relief. It was as though he'd been holding his breath since she'd left, and his chest felt pained. As he ground himself into the tunnel sideways, his vest snagged and pulled to the side. The rough surface grazed his chest, scraping off the top layer of skin. He winced but forced himself further inside.

It'd take more than a scratch to prevent him from venturing onwards - in fact he reasoned that nothing would stop him from getting to the other side.

He slid along in the total darkness, teeth clamped together as he suffered the merciless jabbing and poking and scraping of his flesh. Soon he came to a standstill when his chest became wedged in front of a jutting piece of rock.

"Fuck," he wheezed, instantly regretting the outburst when he heard Libby's worried voice calling, "Are you okay?"

Sucking air in between his teeth, he replied, "Yeah."

Feeling the serrated edge of the stone pressing into his skin he forced himself through until he was no longer lodged, but not before the material of his vest ripped and the skin above his right pectoral tore open. Grimacing, he resisted the urge to swear again.

***

Libby was standing on a deep ledge, the torch now switched off and its nylon handle looped around her wrist. She took in with awed relief the vast space all around her. Beyond the tunnel that she'd just come from the cavern opened out, stretching upwards in a surprising tangle of greenery. Ropey vines hung from up above where brilliant sunlight poured in, their shimmering gold strands reaching down in tassels to a luscious pool of turquoise water below. She breathed in and relished the warmth.

When she heard Grim curse she looked back to the tunnel, and then down at the torch on her wrist.

"Are you okay?" she yelled.

When he called back to say he was fine, she flicked the torch on and made her way back to the gap, to see if she could see him coming yet, but without any warning she came over woozy and faint. White-hot pain flashed behind her eyes, forceful enough to make her drop to her knees. Closing her eyes she rubbed the heels of her hands against her temples, attempting to alleviate the pain. She crawled along

69

the floor, unable to stand upright, and when she opened her eyes again she found that she was on the very brink of the ledge. Looking down, she watched in agonised wonder as the water in the lagoon rippled and stirred. Small waves skittered across the surface and then crashed into the sides, and the water itself had turned black, like ink from an octopus.

"What the hell's happening?" she cried.

As though in answer to her question, the overblown face of her mother appeared on the water's now-calm surface. She looked as ill and frail as she had in her dreams. Libby gasped and blinked her eyes numerous times, all the while clutching the lip of the ledge in order to stop herself from toppling over.

All around her the voice of her mother echoed and boomed, "Libby, is that you? Will you listen to me, sweetheart? I want to talk to you."

There was desperation and pleading in her mother's tone, but as much as she wanted to respond, Libby couldn't. She clamped her hands over her ears instead. The volume of Merilyn Hood's voice made the pain in her head much worse. A thundering tumult of hellish agony. She felt a scream rising from the bottom of her belly and, after her mother had said, "Libby, please listen to me. I need to know that you're okay. There's something I must tell you!" it broke free and rang around the open cave. Shrill and deafening, even to her own ears.

***

Grim battled on, paying little heed to the cuts and scratches on his skin, and when he heard her scream this somehow spurred him on even faster. When he reached the sun-drenched opening at the other side, he emerged disorientated. But as his eyes adjusted to the new light and huge space, he was just in time to see her disappearing over the ledge.

"*Libby!*"

Springing forward he reached his hand out as though to catch her. When he peered over the edge he saw her hit the pool of water that lay around twenty metres below.

Without thinking, he dived in straight after her.

Chapter 9

Just as he was about to go back out into the night to search for his missing partner-in-crime, Reeve noticed white vapours trickling into the foyer beneath the great oak door. Gin had finally decided to grace him with her presence. He sighed with relief but his lips thinned in anger. Crossing his arms, he took on a stern stance and watched as she morphed back into human form. All the while his fingers thrummed petulantly on his upper arms, his black-rimmed eyes narrowed and his jaw pulsed from the effort of clamping his teeth together.

He watched as her lithe body materialised from the thick haze. Her hair hung down in strands that were almost as long as his own, framing a face that looked both flushed and smug. Trailing his eyes further downwards he noticed that her nipples were standing erect and were much darker than usual, and he saw that her typically concave stomach was now ever-so-slightly rounded. His kohl-lined eyes clouded with dark rage.

"You stopped to feed?" he gasped, the disbelief making his eyebrows bow upwards. "No wonder you're half an hour late!"

"It was an unintentional pit-stop," she remarked, shrugging her shoulders in a stoic manner. "Had you stuck with me there'd have been plenty for you as well, but you will insist on racing ahead, won't you?"

He gritted his teeth again, past words and ravenously hungry now he was confronted by her replenished aura - which was radiating from her in blinding white waves.

"So, are we gonna do this thing or are you gonna stand there gawping at me all night?" she asked, purposefully trying to rile him. She loved winding him up.

His face twisted in revulsion.

"*Gawping? At you?*" he laughed. "In your dreams."

"Ha, you should be so lucky. You never feature in my dreams."

"Good!" he huffed, realising how childish they both sounded, yet unable to stop himself. "I wouldn't want to."

Neither pretended to like the other and although Reeve could appreciate Gin's outer beauty for what it was, he found her to be as cold and blank as Hope, and her attitude to be ugly as sin. Still bickering, they moved through the courthouse foyer until they came to a wide marble staircase that was swirled and veined in creams and whites and caramels. It led up to a landing of opulent gold and bronze décor and a crystal chandelier that hung from the ceiling like a cluster of suspended tears, twinkling in the glare of the spotlights outside. A golden balustrade of intricate detail swept upwards on both sides of the staircase, leading the eye to three large pictures mounted on the wall at the top. Both Reeve and Gin fell silent and looked at the paintings.

The man in the centre portrait demanded most attention, his manner both confident and handsome. He had a stern yet honourable face. Sparkling amber eyes belied a certain darkness that shone within, and they were softened further by an underlying smile that subtly touched his lips. Long dark hair fell past his shoulders in sea-sprayed tangles. Two braided sections at the sides were swept backwards, tied together at the back to keep the rest of his hair from falling in his face. His burly toffee-coloured torso was completely bare except for its heavy adornment of tattoos; lines that swirled and curved with the contours of his muscles, creating a beautiful element of symmetry. They even reached high up onto his neck, licking at his jawline like black flames.

To the left was a portrait of another man. The two looked similar, but this one had features that were sharper and less likeable than the first. Undoubtedly he was still good-looking, but he had a certain fierceness to his eyes that conveyed no sense of warmth or empathy. He didn't look like somebody you should trust. His dark hair was pulled back severely and it was impossible to tell from the painting just how long it was. As with the other man, his torso was unclothed and similarly covered in black ink.

The last painting was of a third man. He had the same orangey irises flecked with gold and the same deep Cupid's bow on his full lips as the other two, unquestionably making them all brothers - only this man was a lot squatter in build. His head was shaven right down to the scalp, and there was an element of wild eccentricity emitting from his stare that indicated he was perhaps touched by lunacy. Where the other two men had tattoos covering their torsos and necks, this third man had tattoos covering every bit of exposed skin, including his entire face and head.

"Zephinay, Peroos and Hoof," Gin whispered. "Do you think it's true?"

"Of course it's true," Reeve scoffed, still looking up to the paintings. "Why would you even doubt it?"

"I know." She looked dismayed. "But it's been so long. I…I can't remember that far back. *Can you?* And how could they just *disappear*?"

He rolled his eyes and groaned. "You *know* how they disappeared."

"But *do* you remember? That far back I mean."

He huffed, reluctant to answer. But when he saw that she was staring at him he shook his head and said, "No."

"I find it incredible. Three mighty men such as they were just disappearing. The story never made any sense to me."

"Of course it makes sense. What's so hard to believe? The Turpis Sea is treacherous and unforgiving, each and every time they set out to ride the waves they must have known the risk they took. Nobody was meant to escape the island, don't you get it?"

"They weren't trying to escape. And anyway, the weighing scales - they're a means to escape," she challenged. "That's why *we're* doing all of this."

"Yes, but the weighing scales are relatively modern, there was nothing like that back in the days of the kings."

Gin remembered the story of the weighing scales clearly enough. It hadn't been that long ago when they'd come into being. Godfrey Manning, Sunray Bay's mayor prior to Finnbane Krain, was the person responsible. He'd been a gentle man, with a soft grey beard and a mathematician's mind. Some said he was an actual genius. Preceding his reign, the population of the relatively small island, which was then known as The Isle of the Ignoble Dead, had been kept to a strict limit of 50,000 to prevent over-crowding. These controlled measures were carried out by way of death sentencing, which meant that prisoners and dangerous residents were often put to death. When Godfrey Manning had come along he'd wanted to reverse the process. He believed that everyone deserved a chance to change themselves for the better - and that's when the weighing scales had been introduced. Some said he crafted them with his own hands and others said they were gifted to him by the gods. Either way the population was thereafter controlled in a much more humane fashion. Death sentencing was abolished and redemption was the new means of relief. People oft said he was a god-send. Others said he *was* a god. And others said he was nothing but a naïve fool.

It was Manning who eventually rebranded and reinvented The Isle of the Ignoble Dead - thus creating a more cheerful seaside abode and renaming it Sunray Bay. It was meant to be a positive place in all of its picture postcard loveliness. A place where its people could thrive - instead of feeling like the delinquents they really were. But, genius or fool, Manning only managed to rule Sunray Bay for around forty years before his untimely death. The soul-weighing system that he'd put in place was still used, but his attempt at creating civility was now evidently crumbling away. Rembrae had once said to Gin, "You can sugar a grapefruit all you want, but at the core it'll always be sour." Whether she'd been referring to Sunray Bay, herself or something else entirely, Gin couldn't remember - but the analogy sprang to mind.

"I know all of that," she said. "Why do you always have to be so difficult? Why can't you just admit that the circumstances were highly unlikely? These kings were able seamen who were well accustomed to the Turpis Sea."

Reeve bristled with impatience. "You'll be accustomed to the Turpis Sea soon enough." She looked at him in puzzlement, but when she opened her mouth to respond he cut her off. "Because I'm going to throw you in it if you don't shut up, then you'll see how easy it is to get lost."

He moved away from the grand staircase before she could react, and made his way to the rear of the building. Despite popular belief, the weighing scales weren't situated on the first floor of the courthouse, they were held out back on the ground floor near storage cupboards. He and Gin had studied the blueprints and knew where to find them.

Through a maze of corridors that smelt of cheap carpet squares and furniture polish, they found the room easily enough. An uninspiring, grey door was now all that stood between them and the weighing scales. It looked nothing more than a cupboard door, but they both knew that it was digitally coded and alarmed. They knew what the entry code was from looking at the blueprints, but they had no intention of using it just yet. Keying in the digits would notify the patrol of Civilian Court Guardians that the room was in use - which at that time of night could only mean a break in.

"Well, this is it," Reeve announced.

Gin looked at him and nodded her head.

Together they vaporised, falling to the floor like whirls of steam that was sinking instead of rising. Merging together they became one and filtered underneath the door. Their entwined body of mist poured into the room and then divided back into two separate entities - from which they both reappeared.

"So far, so good," Reeve announced. He was quick to move away from the close proximity of Gin, uncomfortable with their skin-on-skin contact. "This is almost *too* easy."

The weighing room, set out like an office, was comparatively small. A long desk made from solid pine occupied the centre and was set out in a way that the weighing operative on duty would be greeted by whoever should enter the room. But at that hour there was no weighing operative. The weighing scales ran on a nine-till-five basis.

Reeve walked behind the desk and stood to the side of a luxurious leather swivel chair. Resting his right hand on its headrest, he studied the contents of the desk top. Memos, notepads and pens were scattered around in a carefree, but not altogether untidy, manner on the surface. A mug featuring the words *'the right way is the redemption weigh'* was sitting on a coaster - washed-up, but tea-stained nonetheless. And various photographs of two small children (with particularly pointed ears) were propped up at both ends of the desk.

Filing cabinets filled the entire back wall of the room. And to the front of the desk in the right hand corner stood the weighing scales themselves; the phenomenal soul-weighing device; the only known portal out of Sunray Bay.

"Hmmm, this is it?" Gin remarked. "The exclusive weighing room? Not very impressive, is it?"

"No." Reeve actually agreed with her for once.

"And just look at the weighing scales, they're like - well, like *bathroom scales!*"

He smiled at her dumbfounded reaction because, although they'd known what they were coming to collect, he also thought the weighing scales looked more substandard in reality than they did on paper. He stooped and picked them up, studying the needle and dial as he did so. "I wonder why they aren't digital?"

"Or a bit funkier?"

The supposedly precious piece of equipment was simple white with a gloss finish, fairly bulky in size and not in the least bit impressive to look at. Reeve clutched it close to his bare chest.

"Are you ready?" he asked, his voice calm but his heart racing. He was desperate for the mission to be over.

"As ready as I'll ever be." Gin breathed in deep.

"Okay, we do this *quick*," he said. "As soon as I key in the code that'll open the door, we make our way straight to the very back window on the right side of the building. We jump through it at the same time, to lessen the impact. You got that? That bit's pretty important. Then we transition the *very moment* the window pane breaks. Okay?"

"Bats, right?"

"What else?"

She nodded. "And then what?"

He stabbed at the keys on the door's security panel with his forefinger. With a low clunk, the door shifted inwards and the bulb inside the plastic wall-mounted casing above shone white. At the same time the shrill ringing of alarm bells blared out all around them.

"And then we fly," he shouted above the din. "Like shit off a stick."

Gin raised her right eyebrow. "Very poetic of you, Reeve. As ever."

And with that they both ran.

Chapter 10

He saw eddies of white, black and grey. Water rushed into his mouth and up his nose. Spluttering, he drank in even more. Blinking his eyes, everything seemed brighter, even underwater, because he'd lost his sunglasses while plummeting downwards and hitting the water. He'd entered the frothy maelstrom in the same place as Libby. Wrapped in a vortex of bubbles, everything sounded muffled as he thrashed his arms and kicked his legs to dive deeper still.

The further he swam the clearer the water became - and it wasn't long before he spotted her limp body, red hair floating upwards like tendrils of fire. Reaching out he grabbed her arm and yanked her to him, then wrapping his arm around her waist he pulled her back up towards the light. As they broke the surface they both gasped, taking long, greedy lungfuls of air. The water that Grim had swallowed stung the back of his nose and throat, making him cough. Libby, who was now fully conscious, choked and spat out water too. He kept tight hold of her, and she leant heavily on him. He pulled her over to the side and then pushed her up onto a low ledge of rock. She flopped down onto its flat surface with all the grace of a dead fish and just lay there.

Grabbing the rocky ledge, he looked up at her and said, "Are you okay?"

At first she didn't appear to have heard him, remaining on her back looking up to the sky with a dazed expression. But after a few moments she reached over in a gesture to help him from the water.

"Did you hear me?" he asked. "Are you alright?"

"Yeah, yeah," she croaked, shaking her head. "I'm fine."

Her eyes fixed on his and he noticed with relief that her expression didn't turn to one of revulsion as she took in his white gaze. Nevertheless, he still felt uncomfortable and self-conscious under the scrutiny. Ignoring her still-outstretched hand, he broke eye contact and hoisted himself clear of the pool. "What happened?"

"I'm not sure. I passed out?" She shook her head, her face wracked with confusion as she tried to think. "I've no idea what the hell happened. It was nuts."

Grim was reluctant to meet her eyes, but doing so kept his head bowed low and asked, "Do you often pass out?"

"No. Never." Noticing his bloodied chest and mangled vest, she said, "Oh God, look at you. Are *you* okay?"

He shrugged. "Yeah, it's nothing."

"It doesn't look like nothing to me."

"It'll be fine," he snapped.

She knew that what he said was probably true. The two gunshot wounds he'd suffered on Tuesday night were now scabbed over and healing well. *Too* well. This seemingly superhuman aspect, she realised, was just another part of himself that he didn't like to draw attention to - or talk about. The fact that his body was capable of surviving trauma that no normal body would, and could heal itself in phenomenal time, meant that a few scratches would mean jack shit to him. She decided she wouldn't push the issue. Not yet. Her bottom lip started to quiver and her teeth chattered together. It felt as though the coldness of the water had reached her very core.

"Are you cold?" he asked, concern back in his tone.

"Yeah," she replied, rubbing at her wet arms. "Bloody freezing."

"Let's stay here for a while then."

The sun was still beating down into the open grotto and he knew the temperature would be warmer there than if they headed back into the network of caves.

"We don't have to," she objected half-heartedly. "Not on my account."

"No we don't," he said. "But we will."

"Can't we get out that way?" she asked, looking up to the blue skies above them. "Perhaps we're underneath The Grey Dust Bowl by now. We could climb up and check?"

"If only." He smiled, shaking his head. "We haven't been travelling nearly long enough to be there yet."

"Oh." She tried not to be downcast, but her frown was obvious. Grim could see how miserable, cold and worn out she was. She looked vulnerable and distressed as she sat with her knees drawn up to her chest, huddled into a tight ball. He moved over and took hold of the hem of her t-shirt with both hands, all the while managing to avoid eye contact.

"Lift your arms," he ordered, tugging upwards.

"Wha..?"

"Lift your arms so I can get this off."

"Christ, it's all or nothing with you, isn't it?" she said.

"I'm not trying to seduce you, Libby. I'm trying to get you out of these wet clothes so I can hang them up to dry."

"Oh." She lifted her arms and allowed him to remove the soggy top. Smiling, she said, "Well what if I want you to seduce me?"

His face remained unresponsive as he slapped the wet t-shirt over his shoulder. He gently removed her shoes and then set to undoing the buttons on her jeans. "You need to rest, that's what you need."

She allowed him to push her down into a lying position so that he could peel the heavy, wet denim from her legs and by the time he'd laid them out in the sun to dry her eyes had closed and she was drifting off to sleep. He took the opportunity to study her face. Her expression was troubled, he worried that she was overwhelmed by all she'd experienced in Sunray Bay so far. And who could blame her? The poor girl had had nothing but trouble since she arrived - and he had no doubt he wasn't helping the situation. In fact, he didn't know what the hell he was playing at.

He was in combat with vast feelings of guilt and turmoil, unsure as to what, if anything at all, was going on between the pair of them. He cursed himself for having slept with her

81

because he wasn't sure what she expected from him now. And because he wasn't even sure what he wanted himself. But that wasn't to say he hadn't enjoyed what had happened so far. Far from it. He sighed and cursed himself once again.

Her skin was white and her features delicate. She looked as fragile as a china doll. One he hoped he wouldn't break. That'd never be his intention. Bending over, he kissed her lightly on the cheek; her skin was as smooth as it looked.

"I'll try not to mess you about," he said, tucking a strand of hair behind her ear. The statement was as much for his own benefit as it was for hers. A resolve not to treat her like a complete bastard would. Her breathing had become less laboured, her chest rising and falling peacefully, but her forehead was creased and he watched as a tear rolled down her cheek. Wiping it away with his thumb, he hoped he wasn't the cause.

He settled back to relax, resolving to let her sleep until sunset before they journeyed back into the caves. There was an opening right behind them, and now they were on the opposite side of the lagoon he deduced they'd be heading in the right direction. He wondered whether he should get some sleep, but soon decided he wasn't tired at all. Physically yes, but mentally his thoughts were uncontrollable and very much wide awake. So instead he listened to the tinkle of water dripping from slimy-looking vines that dangled from the cusp of blue sky up above and thought about Libby and vampires and black pudding and The Grey Dust Bowl.

A sound of humming from somewhere nearby broke his thoughts and he sat up straight, alert. Tilting his head to the side he listened intently, trying to figure out where the sound was coming from. It was impossible to tell because the noise echoed and bounced off every surface in the vacuous grotto. The tune itself wasn't one he was familiar with, but he could tell it was a woman who was doing the humming - which didn't sit right, given the location. Feeling somewhat guarded he climbed to his feet and looked around. As he did so a head popped up near the ledge by his feet.

It was a woman whose long auburn hair dripped with water. She was looking up at him with a brazen expression on her face. Had she been any further away, he might have thought it was Libby - such was the likeness. On closer inspection this woman was ethereal white, her hair was a shade darker and her eyes, although the same colour as Libby's, were a touch bigger (and surrounded by the longest, thickest eyelashes he'd ever seen). Her lips were the same as Libby's - full, moist and kissable. And they were smiling at him right now, in an alluring manner.

Before he could react in any way she pulled herself up from the water, enough for him to see that she was completely naked, and then she sank back down so she that she leant against the rocky ledge on her elbows, half in and half out of the water

"Who are you?" he asked.

Unfolding one of her hands, she revealed his sunglasses. "Would you like them back?" Her voice was light and sweet, and her eyes were alive with mischief.

His eyes narrowed with distrust, yet he found himself nodding his head all the same.

"Come and get them then," she laughed. And with that, she pushed herself away from the ledge and sprawled backwards into the water, dipping her head back and letting the water gush over her face. He continued to watch without making an attempt to join her. When she realised he wasn't playing, she stuck her bottom lip out and said, "Well? Aren't you coming in?"

With his face stony and expressionless, he simply shook his head. "Who are you?"

"I'm anybody and everybody," she said, laughter lilting her words. Curling her index finger, she beckoned him in. "I can be anyone your heart desires."

He rolled his eyes with irritation. "Good for you, but I don't want you to be anybody and everybody. Just give them back, yeah?"

To his surprise she swam back to the ledge, the light-hearted mischievousness having all but vanished from her face to be replaced by morose doe-eyes. "Very well, there you go." She placed the sunglasses by his feet. "I was only trying to have some fun. It gets lonely down here."

He stooped to pick them up, never taking his eyes off her for a moment, and without inspecting them he put them back on his face and sat down on the ledge. Dipping his feet into the water next to her, he said, "If you're so lonely, why do you stay here?"

"Because this is where I live." Uncomfortable silence hung in the air for a few moments before she said, "Where are you going? Why are you down here?"

Tipping his head to where Libby lay behind, he replied, "We're going to The Grey Dust Bowl."

"Through the caves? That's a funny way of going about it."

"Yeah, but don't bother asking, it's a long story."

She nodded, her passive expression conveying that she didn't really want to know the full story anyway. "You should be careful using these caves," was all she said.

"And why's that?"

"There are treacherous things down here. Things that are older than time itself, and wilier. Very, very wily."

His broad shoulders remained squared and his face unchanged.

"The deeper you go the more chance you have of finding cave trolls too," she added.

"Cave trolls, hmmm?" He smirked, his voice laced with a certain amount of derision. If she was trying to unnerve him, she wasn't succeeding.

"Yes, it's true."

"Have you seen one?"

"Many. They come here to bathe sometimes."

"So how come they haven't killed you before now if they're so dangerous?"

"They never see me."

"Well that's good for you," he said. "But no offence or anything, I couldn't give a shit about cave trolls. This is the way we're going."

84

She shrugged her shoulders. "And that's your prerogative - but I did warn you." Moving close to his legs she smiled, the slight gap between her top front teeth just like Libby's.

"Come on," she said, tugging on his trouser leg. "Come in for a while."

When he shook his head she lowered her lashes. Looking up through them she urged, "*Oh come on.* Come in and play with me."

"No," he snapped, his brow furrowed with vexed impatience.

Signalling to Libby, she said, "She's asleep, she'd never know."

When he still showed no signs of moving, she planted her hands either side of his thighs and drew herself upwards, so that their faces were level. "I *insist.* I want you to come in with me."

"And I want never gets," he said, roughly pushing her shoulder, knocking her back into the water with a splash.

Once she'd regained her composure, her expression changed to one of dislike. "That wasn't very nice."

"I'm not very nice and, besides, you provoked me with your incessant hounding," he growled.

"Just why *are* you going to The Grey Dust Bowl?" she asked.

"It's none of your business."

Her large eyes narrowed to slits and her lips tightened. "There's nothing but vampires there. Vampires and zombies…"

"Zombies?" He stiffened; a feeling of unease crept over his skin like an intrusion of cockroaches. "In The Grey Dust Bowl?"

Moving close to his legs once again, she said, "Yes. Slaves to the vampires, so I hear. Or perhaps *pets* would be a better term. More endearing, you know? After all, somebody's got to love the brain-dead freaks…" Casting her eyes to Libby, a cruel grin snuck to her mouth. "I think she'd know all about that, don't you?"

Grim, determined not to be riled, refused to respond. He sat silent and fuming.

"Or perhaps that's the reason you're going there..." Her eyes grew wide and somewhat knowing. Moving one of her hands upwards, she ran her fingers over the surface of his ripped, water-sodden vest and then prodded one of his blood-clotted scratches with a sharp fingernail. Digging into the raw flesh, she made the wound weep with fresh blood.

"What do you mean?" he asked, unresponsive to her probing fingers.

"I imagine you'd feel right at home with your own kind?" He didn't resist as she lifted his sunglasses. Her dark eyes were cruel and teasing, searching his own, deliberate and slow, so that he couldn't escape her mockery. "I know what you are. You may fool everybody else, but you don't fool me."

When he'd had enough of her taunting, he knocked her hand away. The sunglasses fell back into place on the bridge of his nose, and it took all of his effort not to wipe the facetious grin off her face with the back of his hand.

"Don't get me wrong, I'm sure you'd make a great slave," she said; her face so close to his that he could smell the salty tang of her breath. Her fingers now smoothed over his chest in a sensual caressing motion. "Why don't you stay here and be *my* slave?" Her chocolate eyes flashed jet black for a fleeting moment, and he could have sworn her hair did too.

He jerked his head away. "Get your fucking hands off me."

"Oo did I hit a nerve?" She laughed and backed away, plunging down into the water. With her chin now submerged, she glowered up at him and asked, "Or am I completely wrong? Could it be that you're going to The Grey Dust Bowl to find your late wife?"

"*What..?*"

"Oh come now, you might try and kid yourself, but I can see right through you. You have a feeling she's here, don't you? You can feel it right here." She curled a fist and pounded her chest. "You have an inkling that perhaps you didn't save her soul after all, but you daren't say as much in case saying it out loud will make it true."

He didn't respond; his mouth pulled straight in an angry thin line.

"You know what the sad part is?" she said, feigning a sad pout that made his fists clench. "You might just be right. The Blōd Vampyres have been using zombie slaves for hundreds of years. I'll bet your wife's been grafting for them ever since you killed her. Working her pretty, dead fingers to the bone, while all this time you've been feeling sorry for *yourself*. Wallowing in self-pity, *tsk*," Her eyes glimmered with wickedness and her smile was now a snarl. She nodded in Libby's direction. "Not to mention the fact you've been getting your rocks off. I wonder what poor, sweet Della would make of that?" By now her entire presence was one of dark malevolence. Not a scrap of playfulness in evidence, and her voice curt and spiteful.

"How do you know my wife's name?" he demanded, still resisting the urge to throttle her.

"Truth hurts doesn't it? I know lots of things." Her reply was smug. "And I can tell you where to find your precious Della...but first you have to come in here and swim with me." She held her hand out to him and leant back, letting herself glide on the surface of the water.

"Bitch!" he said, shaking his head. "You're a fucking liar!"

She laughed out loud, a forced sound that pinched at his nerve-endings. Then she dipped her head underwater, vanishing completely. He looked about and watched as air bubbles surfaced near his feet. He closed his hands tight around the lip of the ledge in case she tried to pull him in, and he waited. It wasn't long before the water erupted in an explosion of white waves just in front of him, and as he braced himself for whatever new game she was playing he was staggered to see that it wasn't the red-headed Libby look-a-like before him at all. No, this time it was Della his wife.

87

The beautiful woman he hadn't seen in too long.

The kind woman he'd loved with all of his heart.

The intelligent woman he'd shot in the head with a rifle.

His breath caught in his throat as she studied him with her familiar cornflower-blue eyes. He was afraid to move in case she disappeared. Reaching up out of the water, she placed her hands on his thighs and flashed him a genuine smile. Her blonde hair, darkened by the water, was the same blonde hair he remembered and oft dreamt about.

"Richie," she said breathlessly. "I knew you'd come for me."

He stared open-mouthed as she boosted herself up, using his legs as support. His eyes welled with tears. Hidden tears behind sunglasses. Tears that he couldn't brush away because he wouldn't let her see his eyes.

As she inched her face closer to his, he could see every bead of water that clung to her face with a clarity he'd never quite known. Droplets collected in subtle laughter lines he'd almost forgotten, and in the ridge of her shapely Cupid's bow. The lips he'd kissed at least a hundred thousand times before. Raising his right hand, he cupped her face and stroked her cheek with his thumb.

"Della," he whispered, his chest aching. "Do you forgive me?"

Unspeaking she raised her mouth to his and tilted her head. Parting her lips in readiness for a bitter-sweet kiss, he could feel her warm breath on his face and a familiar salty smell entered his nostrils. He opened his own mouth, wanting this kiss more than anything else. But then he heard a loud *shlapping* noise and she recoiled from him, falling backwards into the water whilst clutching her head. And her eyes - her eyes were furious.

"What the hell are you doing?" Libby was standing with one of her shoes raised high above her head ready to throw, and the other had just landed on the floor next to him.

He watched as Della thrashed about in the water and realised with horror that she'd developed a large, grey fish's tail. She now had long black hair that splayed on the surface

88

of the water like poisonous reeds and her unnaturally black eyes seemed to curse him. He saw that this thing wasn't his wife at all.

"Move away from the edge," Libby ordered.

He leapt backwards just as the mermaid creature reached out to grab his leg. Opening its mouth in a death-warning scream, it exposed needle-like teeth that lined blue bulbous gums. The inhuman, potentially ear-bursting scream rang all around the grotto like nothing he'd heard before. Stumbling further back and never taking his eyes off the creature for a single moment, he said, "I think we'd better go."

Chapter 11

Glass exploded outwards, large shards and razor-sharp glitter pieces spraying all over the pavement outside the courthouse. Gin transformed into a bat but Reeve faltered when a large piece of glass got lodged in his leg. Yelling in frustration, he eased his grip on the weighing scales. They came dangerously close to falling to the ground, but realising his difficulty Gin was quick to take the weight from him. When he finally transitioned, the piece of glass fell away from him with an angry spurt of red. He looked at Gin with what she thought was the closest to a thanks she'd ever get.

With leathery wings beating a furious rhythm they rose up into the night sky, their stealth somewhat diminished because of the shared weight of the weighing scales clutched in their clawed feet. It was by no means an easy ascent.

White-uniformed Civilian Court Guardians now swarmed around the shattered window of the courthouse, cocking their assault rifles into the air and peppering the night sky with bullets. Once Reeve and Gin were out of range they both knew their escape had been down to pure good fortune and not precision or skilful manoeuvrability. This time they were two very lucky vampires indeed to have escaped intact.

Reeve was grateful that Gin had been at his side - though he wasn't quite prepared to voice his thoughts. That would be a step too far. It irked him that the last bit of the operation hadn't gone as smoothly as planned, and he was only too aware of how badly it had almost panned out. If it hadn't been for Gin when that piece of glass had stabbed him...he couldn't bear thinking about it.

It was only when they reached the border of The Grey Dust Bowl that they slowed in their retreat. Gin glanced across at him and, her eyes radiating what appeared to be genuine concern, asked, "Are you okay?"

"Yes." His reply was curt and the rest of their airborne journey was spent in silence. Reeve, beyond disappointed in himself, was trying to ignore the pain in his leg whilst Gin was not in the mood for bickering.

The big silvery face of the moon was now presenting itself high in the sky, highlighting the landscape in greyscale tones and making Sun Castle look as though it had been drawn onto the horizon with permanent marker. The castle's north and south towers stood either side of the battlement's crenellation, whilst the third tower, to the west, appeared smaller because it was set further away on the other side of the courtyard. Built on a triangular base, Sun Castle consisted of three main towers - designed so there was one for each king; Zephinay, Peroos and Hoof.

When they reached the castle they flew straight over the barbican and landed on the fixed bridge, transitioning to human form as their feet touched the smooth stone. Reeve took the weighing scales and gripped them to his chest. Gin didn't argue; there was no chance he'd take the glory.

As they walked through the lower bailey towards The Great Hall a strong waft of ammonia stung their eyes and offended their nostrils. The stables no longer housed horses (the Blōd Vampyres didn't own any), they were used as sleeping quarters for the servants, though sleeping quarters was probably the wrong term. Zombies didn't have a tendency to sleep per se - it was more of a congregational area.

"I wish Mother wouldn't let them stay in the courtyard," Reeve complained. "Why do they have to be *here* of all places? Why not round the back where nobody can see or smell them?"

Gin laughed. "I think the Queen has bigger issues to deal with than worrying about whether the courtyard stinks of piss or not."

"*Really?*" He feigned surprised. "Well she does an awful lot of sleeping - she could at least make the time for a little bit of housekeeping."

"The Queen taking care of housekeeping? Are you serious?" She looked at him and saw that he was. "That shouldn't be *her* job. If you're so bothered, why don't you take charge of the situation yourself?"

"*Me* take charge of anything around here? Are *you* being serious? My mother would have me hanged if I ever asserted any kind of control. Hell, she'd probably give me the second degree if I changed the blasted curtains. And anyway, you talk as though she's above all that…?"

"She's the *Queen*. Of course she's above all that."

"A self-made queen let me remind you. If she was a real queen then I'd be a prince, heir to the throne - which, as it happens, I'm not. Not that I'd want to be. Hers is a crown of pure narcissistic fabrication."

"Ah, that's what this bitterness is about? Because the rest of us don't bow down to kiss your feet and call you Prince Reeve?"

"Absolutely not." His eyes flashed sullen. "A title is exactly that. It doesn't change a person's mind or heart. And neither does it transform a person into some holier-than-thou figure of superiority, as my mother would have us believe. I have no need for such pretentiousness. Shame on the rest of you for believing my mother's claptrap."

Gin's nostrils flared and she jabbed his upper arm with her index finger. "She's spent most of her life here teaching you, me, and the others. That's quite some sacrifice wouldn't you say? Her selflessness makes her a very worthy queen in my books. Who cares, but you, that the courtyard reeks? You're selfish and ungrateful for all she's done for us. Whether you like it or not, she's always been our worthy leader."

"Only because she had no other choice." He sniffed with derision. "Don't confuse her guidance with love or worth. She's using us all as pawns to help herself. Don't be fooled,

Gin. Selflessness is certainly not a word that can be associated with my mother."

She bristled, taking his words as nothing but condescending. "She's shown selflessness as a great leader, you can't deny her that. We needed her harsh guidance and tough love in order to reach our potential. To become what we are today. But you're too sissy to see that. No wonder she despises you."

He stopped walking and glared at her. "She's run this castle like a tyrant, that's what she's done. There's not one Blōd Vampyre in this castle that isn't afraid of her. Furthermore, if I had a son I would never treat him as she does me no matter what his disposition. The bitch doesn't know the meaning of the word love, never mind *tough love.* Don't let the wool hang over your eyes for too long, Gin - you might be blinded by it. Or are you already?"

She laughed without humour.

"Your words have very little bearing. They are contrived - and about as deep as your pretentious, shallow poetry."

He flinched, her words cutting close to the bone.

"You'd never make a great leader like your mother," she added. "You would never deserve the title of Prince because you haven't got what it takes."

He looked at her in hurt disbelief, his voice becoming soft. "Why do you idolise her? And why do you hate me so? Has she been pumping her vitriolic poison into you for so long now you don't even know the answer? Yes, Gin, I have a penis - but that does not mean I'm the monster she makes me out to be. I'm no threat to you or the other girls. As hard as it might be for you to believe, as well as having total self-control, I don't want to fuck everything in sight."

"You're certainly not like the rest, I'll give you that," she said. "The others are growing more and more dangerous, I can sense it."

"You make it sound as though us men are overpowering beasts. There's nothing wrong with the others, they're young men who don't want the responsibilities of family yet, that's all. They don't want to bludgeon you and rape you. They pose no threat at all," he retorted. "My mother has been spewing her feminist bile to all five of you, and you're all ready to believe her. It's sad, Gin. Really sad. And coming from a man's perspective, let me tell you, she's talking nonsense. She's so bitter and twisted about her own life's difficulties - yet you're all too ignorant to see it. Men aren't so different to women, you know. It's not about what's between your legs, but what's up here." He tapped the side of his head with his finger.

"I don't need this lecture, you patronising prat," she barked, her blue eyes blazing ferociously.

"What do I have to do to make you see? Why can't you see her for the demented, damnable oppressor that she is? Don't think for a second that she'll still be your queen once we get out of here. She'd sooner spit in your face than be around you any longer than she needs to be - then you'll know all about tough love." Holding the weighing scales out, he said, "We've done her grunt work. This is her ticket out of here; this is all that's required of us."

"*Her* ticket out of here? You make it sound like she intends to leave us behind."

"To be honest, that wouldn't surprise me at all."

"She's my guardian and my role model. Your spoutings are nothing but verbal diarrhoea. You ought to be ashamed of yourself. Of course she's going to take us back where we belong." Dismissing him with an exasperated shake of the head, she walked on.

He stood still and called after her, "How can we know for certain? Can we really trust her?"

She spun round to face him. "Well if you're such a doubting Thomas, why are you helping?"

A sad smile crossed his lips. "Did I ever have a choice? We are nothing but her slaves. We're no better than the zombies, for heaven's sake. And besides, I want out of here more than any of you. Being trapped in this blasted castle is torture. We live in the shadows of Sunray Bay. Nobody truly knows of our pitiful existence, or if they did they forgot - and *why?* Don't you ever wonder why she's kept us all suppressed? It doesn't make sense, she's holding something back!"

"Then why haven't you left the castle if you hate it so much? You could have lived in Sunray Bay on your own, if that's what you wanted. You could risk dying prematurely if your life here is so hellish - nobody would miss you."

"Don't tell me you actually believe that horseshit about the sun being too harsh on the coast?" He laughed, ridicule making it a dour sound.

According to his mother, the Blōd Vampyres weren't able to live too close to the seaside because when the sun rose in the east over the cursed Turpis Sea, its rays reflected upon the water's surface and made them a thousand times more lethal. She said that no sleeping place, no matter how sheltered, would be enough to protect a true-blood vampire.

"You miss the point entirely," he carried on, when he realised Gin had no intention of answering his question. "Of course the sun is no stronger at the coast than it is anywhere else. Why would you even believe that? Cursed the Turpis Sea might be, but not for us. The sea is not in league with the sun, it's only treacherous for those who sail it. I've never heard such an outrageous cock and bull story. It's something you would tell a child."

"So why are you still here if that's what you believe?"

"I can't believe you're being so naïve. I thought better of you, Gin. Leaving Sun Castle is something I never stop thinking about, but if I left to go and live in Sunray Bay she'd only have me tracked down and killed."

She looked confused. "Why would she want to kill you? You're being paranoid. She doesn't even like you, she'd be pleased if you were gone."

"You don't know the depths of her bitterness, she's twisted and warped. There's no way she'd allow me, or any of us for that matter, to leave and enjoy a better life. She couldn't stand that. Do you think she's told us the entire truth about why we're here on this lousy island in the first place? If you do, then you're more gullible than I ever imagined. Don't you ever wonder why she forbids us to go to the coast, except on rare occasions and to carry out her own missions? Why she keeps us all close to her and pretends to play happy families?"

"No, but I suppose you're going to share your warped insight?"

"I can't," he replied, "because I don't know the answer. But I have a feeling we'll find out soon enough."

"Okay, whatever." She'd heard enough.

"This plan of hers to escape seems to have come about rather suddenly, don't you think? Funny how she never mentioned anything like this years ago."

"I…I don't know. Now is a good a time as any."

"Rubbish! I find it very suspicious. I can only hope that if she *does* plan to take us with her, I'll never have to see any of you ever again. I'll be free to disappear off into some far flung mountain range where none of you can find me. But if she *doesn't* take us with her, then at least she'll be gone. And good riddance I say. The quicker this thing happens, the better!"

This time he strutted off ahead leaving her to watch him with mouth agape. And as she watched him go, she noticed for the first time how badly he was limping. Rusty red prints from his right foot trailed across the cobblestones of the courtyard. The blood was still pumping from his leg wound, soaking his calf and foot.

"I hope you bleed to death," she muttered. But as soon as the words left her mouth she felt ashamed. Hanging her head low, she rushed to catch up.

When they reached The Great Hall a massive fire was built up in the fireplace, as usual, and Rembrae was sleeping on her throne. Flames cast shadows across the dingy walls and the Queen's white fur looked like it was shifting and moving of its own accord, such was the trickery of the low light.

As they reached the foot of the throne, Gin made to cough into her hand but Rembrae's eyes flashed open before she had chance. The Queen's expression was one of satisfaction when she saw the weighing scales in Reeve's grip.

"Well done," she said, her voice low and hoarse. "Both of you."

They bowed their heads, and then Reeve placed the weighing scales on the floor before the throne.

"Now you must rest." They both sighed inwardly, relieved that the mission was accomplished. As they turned to leave, she said, "Not you Reeve, I have another errand for you to run tonight."

His heart lurched and he closed his eyes in disbelief, wondering what new torturous task she could wish to bestow on him now. "As you wish, Your Highness. Can I fetch my clothes first?"

"No, you won't be needing them where you're going."

His mouth went dry at the thought of her expecting him to perform yet more transitions. He felt faint even thinking about it. "Can I at least clean up my leg?"

"Oh diddums, did you scratch yourself?" She cast her eyes down to his wounded shin. "How is it that my son is such a weakling? If you must, you can feed from one of the servants - but don't dally. I've got quite a challenge for you before sunrise. It'll be your chance to prove that you really are worthy of being the son of a queen."

Son of a bitch, more like, he thought, gritting his teeth together. He was sick of proving anything to her. Nothing he did was ever good enough. But too tired to retaliate, he simply bowed his head once again and said, "Very well, Your Highness."

Gin looked at him with something like pity. She could imagine how exhausted he must be, yet she couldn't think of any way that she could help. So she bowed her head to Rembrae and left The Great Hall. Troubled thoughts whirled around in her head and her conscience weighed heavy - something she'd never experienced before.

Chapter 12

They entered the oppressive trail of cave tunnels once again to continue their journey west. Libby's clothes were still damp; denim heavy and stiff on her legs, chafing her skin where it rubbed, adding to her overall misery. She was more troubled by what had happened back at the water's edge though. Mulling it over and replaying in her mind again and again, she couldn't escape the image of the gorgeous blonde woman reaching up to kiss Grim - and him just sitting there wanting her to do it.

She frowned.

Okay so the woman was meant to have been his late wife, the water creature had somehow taken the shape of Della, but that just made it all the more weird - and it made her feel like she was fighting a losing battle. It was obvious where his heart still lay. He was still in love with his wife for goodness sake. *Of course he is,* she thought, *why wouldn't he be?*

She chastised herself for allowing jealousy to consume her with its rancorous poison, and yet the silent reprimand didn't make her feel it any less. She'd known all along that things were complicated with him and she had nobody but herself to blame for the way her heart now weighed heavy in her ribcage. How could she be angry about the fact he still loved his wife? It was natural that he did - even though it hurt her like hell even to contemplate it. Perhaps she should have left him well alone from the very start, he *had* warned her after all. Even Gloria had warned her.

After they'd walked for a good while in uneasy silence, she took a deep breath and said, "Do you want to talk about it?"

"There's nothing to talk about," he replied, sullen.

She suspected he felt foolish for having fallen for the water creature's hoax, he was a proud man and in hindsight the trick couldn't have been any more blatant. No doubt he was also dealing with a shit storm of other emotions, having just been confronted by what he'd thought to have been his dead wife. That couldn't be easy, she truly felt for him.

"But, about what she said…"

"No." The bluntness of his reply denoted that, as far as he was concerned, what the water creature had said was not up for discussion.

She followed his lead through the musty passages, unable to see his face. The height of the tunnel was enough for both of them to stand fully upright, but not wide enough to walk side by side. She fingered the mildewed walls with both hands, groping her way in the darkness, the turmoil in her heart more important than what bitey creatures her fingers might encounter. She didn't dare touch Grim. She didn't know if it was her place to do so anymore. Everything had changed.

"Do you think she's in The Grey Dust Bowl?" she said, not able to bring herself to say his wife's name out loud, but refusing to let the matter lie. She was damned if she was going to give up so easily. He'd been married to Della in a past life, but this was *now*.

"No," he answered, his voice gruff but softer.

"Well what about cave trolls?" she asked, changing tack because she could tell that he had clammed up and she just wanted him to talk - about anything.

"What about them?"

"Do you think they exist? That thing in the water said they do…"

Grim flinched; a growing sourness unsettled his stomach. If she had heard the conversation about cave trolls back at the water's edge then she must have witnessed more than he'd dared to think. On top of the fact he felt dreadful and guilty about all she must have seen between him and - the thing that was meant to have been Della - he now felt sick

99

that she probably knew *what* he was as well. And he couldn't begin to imagine how that must make her feel.

Had it turned her stomach to know she'd been consorting with a zombie?

A *zombie* for fuck's sake.

Though that wasn't strictly true - he wasn't a zombie in the standard sense. He was some sort of mutant zombie because he still had the ability to think coherent thoughts. The truth of the matter was, he didn't know what the hell he was - apart from some sort of soulless, detestable monster.

He wanted to hold her, he could sense her dismay. Everything was such a mess. He wanted to talk to her, to tell her everything. But he couldn't bring himself to say anything - because he didn't know where to start and because he didn't want to come across as pitiful. He didn't want her pity. And so he did what he'd said he wouldn't, he walked on in silence, shunning her like the complete and utter bastard he was. Pleased that he was leading the way so she couldn't see his face, and so he didn't have to see the disappointment on hers now that she knew his shame.

What had happened back at the water's edge had stirred up lots of emotions. Seeing Della again had been incredible, he'd felt uplifted and hopeful - and then, just as quickly, it felt as though his heart had been torn apart by the cruel fingers of reality when he realised that it wasn't her.

He'd told Libby that he didn't believe Della was in The Grey Dust Bowl - but really, he wasn't sure. The possibility that his wife might be a slave in The Grey Dust Bowl was something he could hardly bring himself to think about. If fate *had* led her down that path, she wouldn't even be the woman he remembered. Instead of being intelligent, kind and funny she'd be in goodness knew what state of decay by now. Then there was Daisy. What of his little girl? He gritted his teeth and swallowed the bile that crept up his throat.

If he found them both in The Grey Dust Bowl he would be forced to kill them a second time. He wasn't sure he'd be strong enough to do it all over again. Mercy killing though it might be, it would be no less painful. And how would Libby take it all? Would she understand? Would she be patient and give him time to grieve?

There was some sort of connection between the pair of them now. Not love. He didn't love her. But he liked her - a lot. He enjoyed her company. So long had he been alone he'd just about forgotten how good it was to share a journey with someone else, and sleeping with her had given him the human contact he'd been craving for so long. Simplicities like the smell of her hair and the warmth of her skin had been an indescribable comfort - as well as a massive turn-on. The feeling of being wanted by somebody else was a most welcome one. The way she'd groped his body and clung to him. The way she'd needed him. His heart and mind were still sore and healing though and the thing in the water had just picked at the scabs, making his turmoil bleed again. It would seem he would never find closure.

And none of it was Libby's fault.

His chest heaved with a doleful sigh.

Stopping and turning, he shone the torch upwards so that both of their faces were illuminated. His mouth opened, but it took a while for any words to form. "Libby, I'm sorry. I'm really sorry."

She looked up at him in surprise; unable to respond because the feeling of dread that he might end whatever had started between them was even more uncomfortable than the sodden cold embrace of her wet t-shirt. The idea chilled every part of her. She could do nothing but stare.

"Just, the way things have panned out…" he said.

She could see he was struggling. "Don't worry about it." She smiled, trying to stay strong yet biting the inside of her lip to curb any tears that might be unleashed. "Neither of us knew what would happen."

He smiled back at her; a small smile that relayed no joy. He wanted to pull her close and hold her tight, until his mind stopped reeling - which he realised might take forever. But he didn't dare. There was an emotional barrier preventing him from reaching out. So instead, he took a deep breath and said, "I'm ready to talk about stuff. You deserve to know the truth."

She gasped. A smile, marked with relief, brightened her face and her warm chocolate eyes sparkled with hope. She took his fingers in her hand and squeezed, gently encouraging him.

"First, I just want to say thanks."

Stroking his fingers with her thumb in acknowledgement, she said, "Thanks for what?"

"For being here. For persevering." His expression was one of immense awkwardness. He almost certainly wasn't a man who liked to bare his feelings. "I know I'm not the easiest person to get along with. But…"

"But what?" She raised her eyebrows, spurring him to finish the sentence. She could see he was having a hard time saying what he wanted to say, but she wasn't going to let him off without saying it. She wanted to hear everything.

Rubbing his forehead, he looked down to the floor for a few moments and said, "But you've kept me sane."

"I've kept you sane?" She laughed. It was hardly the declaration she'd hoped for, but still, it was something. "You'd class yourself as that?"

He laughed and squeezed her hand. "See, that's what I mean. You've always got some smart arse answer. You've made this journey more interesting than if I'd been on my own."

Her heartbeat quickened. Was he saying there was still a chance?

Before she could respond, they heard movement up ahead in the tunnel. She tightened her grip around his fingers when a deep, scratchy voice boomed, "Well, well, what do we have here then?"

Chapter 13

Thursday, 7:56pm: Prospect Point Lighthouse, South Pier, Sunray Bay

The sea was calm, a black mass playing host to thousands of diamonds. The horizon was clear, nothing untoward lurking on the surrounding stretches of the Turpis Sea - just as she liked it.

Standing on the main gallery with her back to the unlit lantern room, Morgan gripped the metal railings and squeezed tight. She closed her eyes for a moment and thought of her late husband, Finnbane Krain, as the soft wind massaged her skin and played with her hair. She hadn't cried once in the three days since his death.

Theirs had been a marriage of convenience but, still, they'd grown rather fond of each other in their own inane way. Yes, she'd threatened to kill him on several occasions - but then, he'd threatened her similarly. Sometimes they'd driven each other to distraction, which was no bad thing since it oft served to stoke their lust for one another. Following a fight their lovemaking had been at its primal best, and so for this reason alone she knew she'd miss their habitual bickering and bantering. Even down to the mundane things, she knew she'd miss him. Like the way he'd kept the place spotless, for one. His obsessive compulsive nature would be a huge loss. She wouldn't have anybody to keep on at her about being tidy. Finnbane had often, endearingly, called her a *messy cow*. Yet, despite all of this, she found it hard to grieve. Not because she didn't care, but because something else had been set in motion since his death - something that was much bigger and more powerful than all of the feuding vampires and werewolves put together.

Something that unsettled her deep within.

The past few mornings she'd read her tea leaves with great trepidation, and each time they'd forewarned of the same thing…

Something ancient was shifting.

Something dangerous was impending.

Something from her deepest past was coming back - and that *something* would cause her a whole world of terror. She paced the floors of the lighthouse all day long, unable to eat, unable to sleep, because something that she'd tried to put to the back of her mind for thousands of years was now stirring her consciousness and feeding her fears - reminding her of the very reason she was bound to the lighthouse. It was safe to say that she, the most powerful witch in Sunray Bay, was scared shitless.

She'd kept vigil on the main gallery since sunset. Ever watchful of the horizon, searching for movement and guarding the lighthouse because her life was at stake. Clutching at the chipped metal rail, she fed it through her hand and walked round the platform until she was looking out across Sunray Bay.

So much had changed in the past few days. The brash and gaudy seafront, consisting of B&Bs, cafés, ice-cream parlours, arcades and souvenir shops, had been all but annihilated. Sunray Bay's short-lived cheery mask was now replaced by a darker malevolence that had represented the town in the days prior to Godfrey Manning. No amount of cheerful, self-promoting tea-towels or sugary fare had been enough to tame its residents. Morgan could remember the days before Manning well, but the fire and the hooliganism and the cold-blooded killings along the shore weren't what disturbed her thoughts.

She watched tall red-orange flames framing the entrance to the lighthouse's very own south pier. Kitty, her faithful familiar, maintained a roaring inferno there each night in order to dissuade would-be trespassers from stopping by for a spot of looting and maiming. Prospect Point Lighthouse was all Morgan had - *nobody* would interfere with that, she'd make certain of it. She'd defend it with her life.

A band of smoke traced the line of the bay. She eyed building tops to see what was burning, but her mouth went dry when she realised that this smoke was drifting with purpose. And what's more, it was heading straight in her direction. She gasped, gripping the railing in both hands to steady herself. Other memories in the deep recesses of her mind roused and tried to take shape. She worried that this purposeful smog and the tea leaf prophecies might somehow be connected.

Chapter 14

Flames lashed the air along the mouth of the pier like fiery whips. Reeve held back. The ferocious heat weakened his resolve, preventing him from advancing further. Lingering in the air, he surveyed the surrounding area. He was determined to reach the lighthouse before his energy levels sapped altogether, but the feeling of desperation threatened to skew his judgement. He couldn't recall ever having felt so drained in all his life - which was saying something.

Getting to the lighthouse uncooked wasn't even the pinnacle of his problems - he had no plan as to how he'd go about persuading Morgan, the witch, to turn on the lighthouse's lantern. He'd never met the woman before and he had no idea as to the extent of who or what he was dealing with, but if rumours were correct he was inclined to think that getting to the lighthouse would be the easy part.

He wasn't sure of his mother's logic, why she'd seen fit to send him on his own to Prospect Point Lighthouse, or moreover *why* the lighthouse was now integral to her plans. Thanks to him and Gin, she was now in possession of the weighing scales, and that, he'd thought, should have been the end of it. But now she was telling him that the next step towards the great escape was to light the lighthouse.

He did indeed wonder whether she'd sent him on a suicide mission.

Shifting to the left he crept over the water to give the fire a wide berth, and it was as he edged closer that he saw the fabled witch herself standing at the top of the lighthouse - watching him.

As Gin would say, he thought, *oh shitting hell.*

Regardless of his twitchy resolve, he seeped onto the metal gridded platform of the gallery, as far away from

106

Morgan as he could manage, and transitioned back to human form. He clung onto the metal railing for support as he did so, heaving and panting, feeling physically sick. All the while, not even attempting to hide his pained expression, he watched the witch. She studied him as well, and it was with pleasant surprise that he saw she was ball-achingly stunning. Shiny black hair fell way past her shoulders in a mass of mussed, loose curls. Her watchful eyes were tantalising, like dark chocolate coins unwrapped from their golden wrappers, ready to indulge. One of them watched him from beneath a black net veil that fell across the left side of her face from a black pill-box hat that sat on the side of her head. A clingy black dress accentuated the curves of her body and also complemented her skin, which was quite simply made for sun-worshipping, and her full lips were drawn back over plastic-white teeth in a hostile scowl.

"Wait! Wait," he said, holding out his hands and hoping to regain more of his composure before a physical fight might ensue. "I haven't come to hurt you."

"Who are you?" she asked. Her voice was cool, but her body language denoted all the ferocity of a cornered rat. "And what the hell are you doing? I don't recall inviting you into my home. You have no business being here."

"Reeve. My name is Reeve," he answered, his chest still rising and falling heavily with each laboured lungful of air. He pushed heavy strands of hair away from his eyes and stood up straight. "And, with all due respect, technically you don't own Prospect Point Lighthouse anymore, so an invitation wasn't necessary."

Her eyes narrowed in angry wonderment. "You have the cheek to come here and question the ownership of *my* lighthouse? Who the hell do you think you are? I've lived here for more years than you could know."

"You don't have the deeds though, do you?" he said. "Otherwise you'd know that they're no longer in your name."

"Not that it's any damn business of yours, but the deeds *are* in my name. My darling late husband didn't even share

ownership, so don't come here talking tripe about deeds."
Looking him up and down, she said, "If you weren't such an
intriguing and delectable creature, I'd kill you now."

"Well I'm sorry to be the bearer of bad news." He
blushed. "But I'm guessing you don't know that the deeds
were stolen from the archives earlier this week…?"

Her eyes were unsettled with fury and the hem of her
gown thrashed in a gust of wind that was so sudden he
couldn't help but wonder if she'd summoned it for effect.

"My mother has them now," he explained. "Which is
what I'm trying to tell you. Theoretically, *she's* the new
owner of Prospect Point Lighthouse."

"Your *mother?*" she asked. "She being who exactly?"

"Rembrae. Queen of the Blōd Vampyres."

And there it was. Yes, she remembered that name. In fact,
the mere mention of it made her cringe with a revulsion that
ran through her bones like the teeth-squeaking nausea of
biting down on a woollen sleeve.

"So the Blōds are still alive then? I thought you must
have died out years ago, you've certainly kept a low profile.
And don't be absurd, you ridiculous fool. Just because she
has the deeds does not make her the legal owner. Prospect
Point Lighthouse belongs to me. It always has done. Tell
your mother that she may as well tear the deeds up and use
them to wipe her backside." A look of knowing passed
across her eyes, fleeting like a shadow. "Or maybe not. If I
remember rightly your mother is a dog, isn't she? She'd be
better off lining her doghouse with the deeds. I presume she
is still in the doghouse?" She laughed, a sinister sound that
made Reeve wonder whether there was a riddle in there
somewhere.

"Dog is certainly one way to describe her," he replied.
"Though, personally, I'd be more inclined to use the word
bitch." He was surprised when Morgan laughed. "But that's
by-the-by, let's go back to discussing ownership. You're
correct, the deeds probably are worthless scraps of paper. I
mean, who really cares? Nobody would care less if winged
unicorns were to fly down and stake ownership of the

108

lighthouse. But worryingly, on your behalf, who's going to stand up for you? Look out there, look at Sunray Bay. Now that you don't have the back-up of Krain and his legion of modern vampires, how will you hold your fort against all of that? I doubt your fire will keep them at bay forever." He nodded his head towards the promenade. "The residents of Sunray Bay are helping themselves to whatever they like. As the saying goes it's a case of finders keepers - and it's with great regret, or not, that I must warn you my mother *has* made Prospect Point Lighthouse her own."

Morgan made a sound of outrage and lunged forward. With speedy reflexes he held his hands up to his face to prevent her from clawing his eyes out, and as her nails scratched down the backs of his hands he was quick to add, "Don't get me wrong though - it wasn't my intent to piss you off. I'd be more than happy if you were to carry on living here. I'm merely my mother's dogsbody, relaying her messages of spite and malice."

She backed down, her eyes quizzical and trying to weigh him up. He let his hands fall away from his face, happy enough that things weren't about to get more physical and confident that his eyes were safe for the moment.

"I have no fight with you. I didn't come to harass you, and besides I'm sure you're a much nicer lady than my mother."

"Don't try to butter me up. Tell me why you're really here," she said, casting her eyes to scan the horizon. "I don't believe you came to talk about deeds and ownership, or even to threaten me with eviction, because I can't understand why your mother would possibly want the lighthouse. No, there's another reason for all of this, isn't there?" Her eyebrows arched upwards as she met his gaze again, her expression one of serious threat. "And if you've come for what I *think* you've come for then let me tell you you're playing with fire, boy."

"You're right." He dipped his head in a slight bow of apology. "I've done enough bush beating and unnecessary rambling. Ownership and deeds are only secondary to the reason I'm here. The primary reason I'm here is to turn this thing on." He reached out to his left and patted his palm against one of the glass panels that sheltered the lantern room.

In response her features glowered in angry shadow. "Why?"

"My sincere apologies," he said, feeling somewhat foolish. "But I have no idea. I'm just the errand boy."

She ran the tips of her fingers over the same pane that Reeve still rested his hand on, her nails, painted some shade of dark, *plick-plicking* on the glass. "It's absolutely out of the question. Nobody turns that light on. *Ever!*"

He shrugged his shoulders. "Look, I'm sorry but I have to turn it on. My mother can be quite the bad-tempered old snark, and I've no desire to be at the end of her tether when she reaches it."

"Believe me, I'm even more of a bad-tempered snark and I'm almost at the end of mine. I won't let you do it."

"In that case, it's a pity. If you won't stand down, you're going to have to die."

"Oh, is that so?" She tipped her head back and laughed. "You've been ever the gentleman until now. What happened that you now dare threaten to kill me?" She leaned forward, encroaching on his personal space and daring him to make a move.

"Sorry, I must learn to explain myself more clearly otherwise this tongue of mine might get me into a whole load of trouble one day. Just to clarify, I wasn't making the threat personally." He stood his ground, shoulders squared and head held high, hoping she couldn't sense the fact that she made him nervous. "See, if you won't let me turn the light on, *my mother* will want you dead. She's highly unreasonable like that. I should know. So whether I turn it on, you turn it on or she turns it on, she won't rest until it's done. Therefore, may I suggest, it would work in both of our favours if you'd just accommodate the request?"

If the witch was unnerved, she didn't show it. In fact, she was sniggering behind her hand.

110

"Rembrae, Queen of the Blōd Vampyres, Dog of the Desert wants me dead, is that so?" Her dark eyes danced black and confident. "She and whose army?"

"Er…her own."

Her eyes narrowed as she waited for him to explain.

"There are twenty-two Blōd Vampyres in total, so please don't take my warning lightly. If you won't allow me to switch the light on now…"

She threw back her head and laughed once more; a sound so shrill and sudden that it made him flinch. "Okay Reeve, I'm beginning to like you. I tell you what, why don't you try switching it on? Save your mother's fearsome army the trouble of having to kill me."

He swallowed hard, sensing trickery in her tone. She ran her hand down the side of his face, raking faultless skin with her nails.

"What's the matter? Are you scared?" she asked, with a wicked grin. He shook his head, but remained frozen to the spot.

"If you like…" she said, eyeing his mouth as he wet his dry lips. "I'll put you out of your misery, how's about that?" She patted his cheek when she saw the look of alarm that flashed across his face. "Don't worry, cutie pie, I'm not going to hurt you. I just wanted you to know that you're wasting your time." Slapping her hand on the pane of glass, she said, "It doesn't work, you see. Hasn't been switched on in ooo…" she puffed out her cheeks, "…nearly forever. I'm actually quite astounded that you - sorry, *your mother* - would think me stupid enough to leave a light bulb in there. I mean, *seriously?*"

He studied her face and sensed no deception residing there.

"Try it if you like," she urged. "I give you my permission to try turning it on."

He shook his head. "No. Actually I believe you."

"Clever boy." Casting her eyes downwards, she said, "In that case, now we've got all of that silly business out of the way, how would you like to turn me on instead?"

He breathed in sharply as she pushed him back, the metal railing now digging into the small of his back and her face inches from his own. As she traced her finger along the definition of his chest and then around his left nipple he remained still, trying to fathom what his next move should be.

"Well?" she urged. "What do you say? You're already halfway there…"

He shook his head, indecisiveness taking hold.

After a few moments of further teasing with her wandering fingers she nuzzled her nose into his hair, right next to his ear, and whispered, "Go back to where you crawled from, boy. And tell your mother I'm here and waiting. Whatever her reason for wanting to bring the kings home, let her know that I won't let her do it. Come what may, that light is staying *off*. Do you understand?"

He made a stern face, trying to ignore the fact she was now twirling her fingers amongst his pubic hair, intermittently brushing them against his manhood.

"Tell her yourself," he gulped.

Her eyes twinkled with a maniacal glee as she touched his nose with her own. He could feel her warm breath on his mouth like a ghostly kiss, tantalising. Hovering close so that their lips were almost touching, she waited until he took a long breath and then kissed him gently. He sighed and closed his eyes, and she drew back and pushed him hard.

Crying out, he toppled over the railing and plummeted down towards the waiting black sea below. All the while the witch watched and laughed, and then she blew him a kiss. He almost found himself grinning. Morgan was a trickster and a seductress of the highest order, and he'd fallen for her charm…

Just as his mother had expected.

Chapter 15

The torchlight revealed the owner of the scratchy voice to be some grotesque creature with a long, slanted forehead which hung over sunken eye sockets - the eyes of which could not be seen for shadows. Its nose was bulbous and covered in warts or cysts, and the creases of its nostrils were glistening with mucous. Rubbery lips seemed to flap about wetly of their own accord, slaver glistening down into the folds of its jowls. Libby caught glimpses of its teeth, all spaced out and the colour of dead leaves. The only saving grace was that they were all rounded and seemed to be as herbivorous as any cow's teeth.

The creature's skin was varying shades of beige with moles and warty skin tags all over, some of them like great hanging nodules of meat and others like black crusty scabs. Its black hair was scraped back from its face in thin, balding strands, and fuzzy bits too short to be tied back sprouted from its temples, meandering down to moth-eaten pork-chop sideburns. Thickset shoulders, upper arms and leg muscles gave the creature a squat, rectangular shape, and contrary to what Grim had said earlier, Libby decided that it *had* to be a cave troll. She stood wide-eyed, frozen to the spot, only vaguely aware of the fact she was squeezing Grim's left forearm, her fingernails digging into his skin.

"Who are you?" Grim demanded. His voice sounded unperturbed, but Libby could feel how tense he was.

"Name's Leif-Mestler," the creature said in a voice that sounded like it belonged to someone who'd smoked cigarettes their entire life. He scratched at a random cluster of whiskers on his chin, looking in no way threatening.

"Are you a cave troll?" Libby asked.

"Well that's bloomin' charmin' that is," he said. "S'ppose some might say so, girly, but it's quite an uncouth term, don't you think? And any road, no I'm not a bleedin' troll."

Her face flushed pink and she said, "Oh I'm sorry, I didn't mean any offence."

"Ah that's okay." Leif-Mestler sighed, waving his right hand dismissively. "Been called worse than that before so don't you be worryin'." Clapping his hands together, looking somewhat upbeat, he said, "So, what brings you to these parts, girly? It's not often we have visitors." Fingering an angry-looking mole on his chin, he looked thoughtful. "Fact o' the matter is, I don't remember the last time we *did* have us some visitors down here."

Libby cast a sideways glance at Grim, whose stance had not yet relaxed. Clearing her throat she said, "The Grey Dust Bowl." Gripping Grim's upper arm tight, she tried to explain, "Me and my, erm…my…Grim here, we're going to The Grey Dust Bowl. I'm Libby, by the way, and as I said this is Grim."

"Oh, I see." Leif-Mestler shrugged his shoulders and nodded. "Fair dos, I s'ppose."

"Are we heading in the right direction?" Grim asked.

"Oh aye, that you are, laddy." Leif-Mestler looked back over his shoulder and pointed into the darkness. "You're a canny way off yet - but you're on the right track."

"Right then." Grim placed his hand on Libby's hip and said, "We'll be off."

As Libby made to step past Leif-Mestler he thrust a woven basket into her face, making her jump.

"Whoa, hang fire there, girly," he said.

The basket was filled to the brim with some sort of unidentifiable clumpy matter that smelt of damp clothes. She winced and backed away from it, stepping on Grim's foot and elbowing him in the stomach.

"Before you go gallivantin' off," Leif-Mestler said. "I'd hoped you might consider joinin' us for some lichen pie first. Eh?"

114

"Lichen?" Libby asked, her mouth twisted and nose wrinkled in distaste. "Isn't that fungus? A bit like mushrooms or something?"

Leif-Mestler shook the basket in front of her again, making its contents move about."Near enough," he laughed.

"I'll pass on that," Grim said, not bothering to hide the look of revulsion on his face.

"You dunno what you're missin', laddy." Leif-Mestler plucked a large wedge of lichen from the basket and plopped it into his mouth. His teeth ground down around its yellow-ochre flesh, making Libby cringe. The smell of the cave creature and the smell of his basket of lichen was the same damp she'd smelt all day in the caves, only much stronger and concentrated. She imagined having some of the lichen in her own mouth and almost retched at the thought.

After a couple of chews, Leif-Mestler swallowed with an exaggerated gulp and said, "At the very least, won't you stop by and say hello? The others'll be over the moon when they realise we've got company."

"There are more of you?" Libby squeaked.

"Of course there are, girly," he laughed. "Why wouldn't there be? It'd be a sad thing if I was left down here all on my own self."

Libby smiled, a nervous gesture that made the corners of her mouth twitch. "Okay, I suppose we could spare a little while."

Grim's hand tightened on her hip and she could almost hear him saying, *what the fuck are you doing?*

"Great!" Leif-Mestler patted the mounded mass inside of his basket.

"Though no lichen pie for me either, thanks," she was quick to point out.

When he gave her a look of offended bewilderment, she stuttered, "I have a very, erm, a very sensitive stomach, and, well, the last thing I need right now is a gyppy tummy."

Leif-Mestler's lips wobbled as he laughed and rubbed at his own stomach, "Aye, I s'ppose you're right, girly. Lichen is only for the hardiest of digestive tracts. If you don't have a constitution made out of steel, then this little bugger might give you a touch of the squirts."

"*Nice*," Grim muttered, his right eyebrow rising above the top of his sunglasses.

"Sounds like a good enough reason not to have any," Libby said.

"Indeed," Leif-Mestler replied, still chuckling. "Now, if you please, follow me and I'll take you to the squirrel den."

"The *squirrel den*? Don't tell me you have squirrels here too?"

"Oh no," he replied, waving his hand and looking at her as though she'd just asked the most ludicrous question. "We don't have no squirrels down here. Squirrels need trees and nuts. There's no trees or nuts down here. Squirrel den's just the name for the main communal cave. It's where we hang about and socialise, that's all. Nothing squirrely or bushy about it in the slightest. Sorry."

"Oh okay. Well how many of you are there in the squirrel den?"

Leif-Mestler blew out his cheeks and his now visible beady black eyes looked upwards as though he was trying to calculate the number in his head. "Hmmm hundreds I s'ppose. Can't say I've ever counted. But I do know there's only thirty of us professional lichen hunters, and that's me included." His chest swelled, as though it was a proud accomplishment.

"Lichen *hunters*?" Grim asked.

"Oh aye." Leif-Mestler wore a grave look on his face. "Lichen is a very tricky little blighter indeed. If it's not the right shade of brown, did you know it can be fatal when consumed? And, as you well know, it's bloomin' well dark down here."

Grim looked unconvinced.

"Do *you* know your russet from your sepia? Or your sienna from your chestnut?" Leif-Mestler challenged. When Grim shook his head, he said, "My point precisely. We'd all of us be dead if you were a lichen hunter."

"Wow, fascinating," Libby said, feigning enthusiasm and desperate to get moving once again. Standing around in a smelly, confined space talking about fungus wasn't her idea of fun.

Failing to note the sarcasm in Libby's response, Leif-Mestler nodded his head in agreement. "As well as the lichen itself being a mite tricky, very few are willing to venture this far from the squirrel den."

"How come?"

"All this way out we have to be careful of water wraiths."

"Water wraiths?"

"Yes, that's what I said."

"Well…are you going to tell us what they are?"

"Mischievous bloomin' spirits who live in the water, that's what they are."

"What do they look like?"

"They can look like all different kinds of things. Feed off a person's thoughts and emotions they do, know what I'm sayin'?"

Libby felt Grim bristle beside her. "Yes, I think I do as a matter of fact," she said.

"Why?" Grim asked, his voice rough and blunt. "Why do they do it? What do they gain from it?"

"To lure you to the water's edge, then they drag you in and drown you. It's said they feast on thoughts, but I've also heard that they feast on flesh."

Libby shuddered. "I believe we've already had the privilege of meeting one."

Leif-Mestler looked from Libby to Grim and then back to Libby, scepticism marking his brow. When he was satisfied she was telling the truth, he said, "Then you're bloomin' lucky to have escaped, girly. Not many would have done, I can tell you."

"I'm not quite sure lucky is a word that would fit into my week so far, though I appreciate what you're saying," she said. "The water wraith told us that vampires live in The Grey Dust Bowl, is that true?"

Leif-Mestler's sloping brow lifted. "Yes, that's right. The Blōd Vampyres. They're the original vampire species and they live in Sun Castle these days."

"Sun Castle? I've heard of that," Grim remarked. "I thought nobody lived there. It's so remote, why would anybody want to?"

"It didn't used to be remote," Leif-Mestler said. "It was a lush haven of greenery once upon a time."

"What's so special about these Blōd Vampyres?" Libby asked, now more fearful of what lived in The Grey Dust Bowl than what its terrain used to be like.

"Nothing's special about them if you don't like that kind of thing. I'm not so keen myself. I much prefer lichen."

Libby huffed. "But what makes them original? You must know…"

"Oh I don't know, girly. As far as I know, vampires who aren't members of the Blōd Vampyre clan are sort of part-human. That's the way I understand it anyways," he muttered.

"So these Blōd Vampyres, do they have slaves?" Grim asked.

"Slaves?"

"Yes, *zombie* slaves."

Leif-Mestler wiped his nose across the back of his hand and shrugged his shoulders, "Oh I don't know, laddy, I'm just a lichen hunter of the Sun Watch, I wouldn't have a clue about anything like that."

"The *Sun Watch*?" Libby asked. "What the hell's that when it's at home?"

Leif-Mestler's eyes twinkled like glassy black buttons and with a renewed vigour, he said, "Perhaps I can tell you the story of my people over some lichen pie and hot moss tea?"

Libby looked at Grim, and he back at her. He was frowning, which made him look no less attractive.

"Okay, then," she replied, grabbing Grim's hand in hers. "Lead the way, Leif-Mestler."

Chapter 16

Thursday, 5:30pm: Market Square, Sunray Bay
Journalist Dora Storm stood facing the news camera, her trademark black gem-encrusted microphone held in her left hand. "...of course, this isn't the first revolt Sunray Bay has ever seen," she was saying. "And you can bet your arse it won't be the last."

Her long glossy hair shone claret under the glow of a nearby streetlight and her make-up was applied so perfectly it could almost be reasonable to assume that her smoky eyes and red lips were natural. With the aid of a push-up bra, her small cleavage was hoisted upwards and inwards beneath a black sleeveless chiffon blouse that tied around her neck in a big pussybow. A full-coloured sleeve tattoo snaked its way from her left wrist up to her shoulder - a myriad of vibrant rainbow colours pieced together to make tigers, skulls, love hearts and naked ladies.

Storm was new to Channel 77. The channel's bosses had managed to tempt her away from rival channel Sunray Bay Today with the promise of a hefty pay rise. It was money that Channel 77 couldn't exactly afford but, since they expected Storm to be something of a sensation, they saw it as an investment. They had new projects lined up for the young journalist, intending to make her a household name. A pin-up of sorts.

With a petite figure, just over five foot two, a pretty face, an infectious grin and a voice pitched high enough to be playful without being annoying, it was hard to imagine that Storm had been a serial killer in her past life...

As the bass player in an all-female nu metal band called *Aspiring Angels*, she'd always come across as the shy one amongst a group of otherwise boisterous, potty-mouthed girls. Her reserved nature had given the outward impression of reticence, perhaps even fragility, which had subsequently

119

led her to be dubbed *the sweet one*. This was all just a ruse though. There was nothing sweet about Dora Storm.

She was a vengeful grudge-bearer whose conscience was about as heavy as a snowflake, her heart just as cold. And there was nothing that irked her more than people who assumed friendship, or tried to rekindle past relationships, simply because she was a member of a reasonably successful band. These people often included ex-boyfriends and school bullies, every one of them trying to wangle limelight, fake-friendship and drugs from her. All of which she'd happily obliged them with - feigning friendship for a short while, allowing them to think they'd fooled her, and sharing cocaine with them too. Eventually, when she couldn't stomach the charade any longer, she'd lace their lines with strychnine - resulting in each of them getting their own little bit of limelight on local news bulletins and in newspaper obituary sections.

Storm hated free-riders and exploiters more than anything else in the world, and she got away with her murdering spree for as long as three years - until karma drew back its lips and bit her on the arse with great big teeth of irony. At the age of just twenty-four, Storm died of a drugs overdose in a nightclub called *Poison*. Consequently, for her sins, she was transported straight to Sunray Bay.

"Just over twenty years ago," she said, talking to the camera that Delbert Sempers directed at her, "following the death of the dearly loved mayor and revolutionist, Godfrey Manning, the whole town fell into a similar state of disrepair. It wasn't until two months later, when Finnbane Krain was elected as the new mayor that things settled down again and peace was restored. Now, however, with the unexpected death of Finnbane Krain, we appear to be seeing history repeating itself - but in a much more rapid and destructive manner. It would seem that what Sunray Bay needs is another man, or woman, like Manning to come along to resurrect it from the bowels of despair before it's too late. The town needs a leader who has the same emphatic

120

views as Manning, someone who can drive us forward onto the straight and narrow once again.

"How long must we wait until a new leader is assigned? And who will step up to the challenge, if anyone? After all, some fear the role of governance in Sunray Bay is a cursed one. Could it be more than mere coincidence that both Finnbane Krain and Godfrey Manning succumbed to untimely deaths...?"

Storm finished her broadcast on that cliff-hanger and turned to look at the open space of Market Square behind, scanning for other potential stories, but there was nothing but a couple of petty brawls underway. In the doorway of the red-bricked indoor marketplace, three masked youths were attacking a thickset older man, their fists flying and feet stamping, accompanied by grunts of anger. The older man tried to cover his head and face with his arms, whilst clutching a carrier bag that was rammed full with goodness knew what.

And then there were three men having a dispute beneath the statue of Godfrey Manning, in the centre of Market Square. They threw accusations at each other, every now and then someone pointing a finger of blame. When one, who sported blue denim jeans ripped in unfashionable places, prodded his finger deftly into the chest of another, who wore tight leather trousers and a toothless grin, the quarrel stepped up a notch and blood spilled onto the cobbles. All the while Godfrey Manning's statue looked straight ahead, the kindness in the laughter lines around his eyes and the volume and length of his beard making him look a lot like Santa Claus cast in bronze.

"Come on," Storm said to Sempers, unfazed by the fighting. "Let's go to the seafront, see if anything big is kicking off there."

Sempers nodded his agreement and followed behind as she strutted off.

"Oh and Sempers..." She stopped and waited for him to catch up.

"Yeah?"

"If you point that camera at my tits one more time, you're a dead man."

Chapter 17

Thursday, 8:02pm: Prospect Point Lighthouse, South Pier, Sunray Bay

Before the black gelatinous-looking sea could claim him, Reeve managed to will the strength to transition. He skimmed across the calm surface, clipping the water with cream wings. Beating them furiously he rose upwards, and in a battle of stamina he climbed the heights of the red and white lighthouse once again until he was level with Morgan. She smiled, evidently somewhat impressed by his display of recovery. In return he flicked his wings in her direction, spattering her face with sea water. When she reeled backwards laughing, he blew her a kiss and retreated to the shoreline.

At the shallows of the shore his bat's body exploded outward and his naked human body slapped down hard onto the wet sand. He lay for a while on his belly, panting and letting the sea wash over his feet and legs. The salt water stung where he'd been injured earlier, but the wound was beginning to scab over. His senses were dulled but still he winced with pain from the pins and needles that coursed through his limbs like thousands of immobilising electrodes beneath his skin. Clawing his fingers through the sodden sand, he lay with the right side of his face embedded. He feared he might not be able to make it back to Sun Castle before sunrise. He was so weak.

Listening to the sound of the Turpis Sea's gentle sing-song of waves breaking the shore, it reminded him of a siren trying to snare sailors. He wondered if it would try to lure him before long, and whether he'd even put up a fight. Probably. His would have been a pitiful existence if he gave up now. And when he thought about what Morgan had said, how lighting the lighthouse lantern would see the return of the lost kings, he wondered what devilment his mother was up to now. His curiosity was roused.

"Hey mister, are you alright?"

The voice cut through his thoughts like a hard, wet slap to the face. He flipped himself over and looked to the sea. A girl crouched in the water, her long hair falling loose and wet over her shoulders and her eyes wide. When he didn't respond, she said, "What are you? I saw you just...I saw you..."

He shook his head. "I'm irrelevant." The words hissed out, it was painful even to talk. "Who are you? Why are you swimming at this hour?" He propped himself up onto his elbows so that he could see her better.

"I'm Priska," she said, standing up so the water lapped around her thighs.

"That's a strange name."

"I'm a strange girl," she replied, shrugging her shoulders. "Besides, it's not as strange as *Irrelevant*."

He smiled. "So what are you doing in there?"

"It's safer in here than it is up there." She nodded her head in the direction of the town and walked towards him, her limbs dredging through the water as though they were as heavy as bags of dry cement. "You ask as though *I'm* the crazy one." She laughed, looking him up and down. "Yet it would appear you've come to do a spot of skinny dipping. At least I've got my clothes on."

Now standing at his feet, he could see she wore a dark coloured maxi dress that clung to her ample body. Her hair hung down to her waist, equally divided down the middle by a severe centre parting. Because of her smooth skin and fresh eyes he put her at around nineteen.

Extending her hand towards him, she smiled. The sweet-lipped offering was intended to be a token of friendliness, but it didn't escape Reeve that it was a little too forced. Nevertheless, he reached up and took hold of her hand, allowing her to help him up onto his feet. He stood around a foot taller and when he looked down into her eyes he saw an edginess there that she couldn't quite hide. Her dilated pupils flitted about, as though she was scared of him - or up to no good.

"Are you alone?" he asked.

She nodded her head and looked down, but when confronted by his nakedness she looked up to his face again, flustered and blushing.

"Look I have to go, Priska. It's been a long night. Are you sure you're okay here?"

Her eyes looked startled, growing wider still. "Where are you going?"

"Home."

After a moment's hesitation, she held out her hand and offered him a shy smile. "It was nice to meet you, Irrelevant."

He returned the smile and accepted her handshake. "You too, Pr…"

She twisted his wrist and kicked his ankles at the same time, managing to swipe his legs away from underneath him before he knew what was happening. She pinned him to the floor with his arm twisted up his back. Sand stuck to his lips and grit got into his mouth. Her knee was digging into the small of his back, but he put up no struggle. He just lay still.

"Don't try anything silly," he warned, his voice amicable enough despite the fact she had her fingers locked into his hair and was digging her nails into his scalp.

"Oh yeah, and what you going to do about it?" she sneered.

"You'll only get hurt," he said. "I promise."

"Well from where I'm sitting it looks to me like you're the only one hurting." Swiping his hair to the side to reveal his neck, she smoothed her fingers down it and bit her bottom lip. "Besides, I won't hurt you for much longer. It'll all be over soon enough."

"I take it you call yourself a vampire?" he asked, unfazed by the threat.

"I *am* a vampire." She bent his arm even further up his back and he wondered whether the bone might snap.

"You don't know the meaning of the word." He forced a laugh.

"Oh yeah? I'll let you decide for yourself," she hissed, raising her knee and jabbing it into his kidneys. Baring teeth that didn't look particularly sharp, she then bit down onto his neck and guzzled the blood that sprayed forth.

In an effort that made him cry out in blinding pain, he transformed into fog. She gasped and sat upright, her knees falling heavy to the sand where his body should have been. She wafted her hands into the haze before her, and gasped in horror as she breathed it in through her mouth and nostrils.

He coursed through her body, seeping into her veins and absorbing the highly nutritious blood that flowed through them. All the while she scratched at her skin and screamed, but only after he'd consumed every last drop of blood within her did he relent - by which point she was lying face down in the sand without a pulse. Wisps of fog erupted from all of her pores and orifices with such force that flesh and bone exploded outwards onto the surrounding beach.

Transitioning back to his proper form, he lay down on the sand amongst dismembered body parts. Sinewy muscle tissue stuck to his skin and he could feel grains of sand in crevices of his body that felt most unpleasant. Nevertheless he lay star-gazing for a short while, allowing the new blood to work its magic inside his ravaged body, all the while very much aware of his pulsing erection. The heightened arousal brought about by fresh blood was like no other. He lay listening to the sounds of the Turpis Sea, a grin on his face, knowing that she wouldn't snare him that night.

Eventually he made the return journey to Sun Castle when the sky turned battleship grey and he knew the sun would not wait for him. Even though he felt physically uplifted, he dragged his feet along the cobblestones of the courtyard, dread weighing heavy. He expected his mother would go berserk upon seeing him. *Perhaps I should have surrendered to the Turpis Sea,* he thought. Casting a glance upwards, he saw two figures sitting huddled together on the battlement wall, silhouetted against a lighter sky.

Gin and Lilea.

In his absence it seemed they had stolen his favourite spot. He felt a pang of jealousy. Not because they'd spent the remainder of their evening sitting on his merlon with his Hope, but because they had one another. Gin and the other Blōd Vampyre girls were all very close, yet he had nobody. Not one single person to consort with.

By the time he stepped inside The Great Hall, he felt emotionally burnt out - so much so, he didn't even care that his bare feet were filthy with dirt. When he stood at the foot of Rembrae's throne he looked as dejected as a scolded child, head bowed low and shoulders stooped.

"I'd begun to think you weren't returning," his mother said, her eyes burning like blue ice.

"That is what you'd hoped."

"What took you so long?" she ignored his accusation. "And why does Prospect Point Lighthouse still lie in darkness?"

"I spoke with the witch. You knew that she wouldn't let me turn on the lighthouse lantern. You sent me to my death. You hoped for her to kill me so that you wouldn't have to. So that you'd be free of me once and for all."

"Such an imagination. A poet's imagination. If only you could put it in place where your courage lacks."

"Therefore you meant for me to kill Morgan?" he asked.

"I meant for you to turn on the lantern, by whatever means necessary."

"If only I could believe you, Mother," he chided. "Had that been the case, you wouldn't have sent me in the state I was in."

"Excuses, excuses," she said, her tone emphasising her spite. "Tomorrow I shall send your brothers to the lighthouse. They will show you how it's done properly."

"They'll have a job."

"Oh?"

"Not to mention whether or not they'll find willpower enough to resist the witch's bedroom proposals," he said, a smug grin daring to reach his lips. "But they'd better make

127

sure they find a specialist hardware store on the way. The lantern hasn't got a bulb in it."

Rembrae pounced to the floor before him, the hackles on her back raised and her lips pulled back over browning gums. Her head stooped low and Reeve was wise enough to back away.

"Why do you want to see the lost kings return to Sunray Bay, Mother?" he demanded, his voice confident - yet inside he was a quivering mess.

"Inquiring minds that are undeserving do not get answers." She snapped her teeth, making him jump sideways to avoid them. "Now get out of my sight."

He turned to leave, happy to obey her command for he was sick of the sight of her.

"Oh and Reeve, make sure you're well rested tonight."

He stopped and turned, raising an eyebrow.

"You'll be in charge of sourcing that light bulb tomorrow." She smirked, her face radiating a level of smugness that made him feel like he might tip over the edge soon. Clamping his fists so tight that his fingernails broke the skin on his palms, he thought, *you can fuck right off, Mother!*

Chapter 18

The squirrel den was an enormous open space, a naturally-formed hall of stone. The walls were a cosy taupe colour and they stretched up to dizzying heights, pitted with large holes that petered out towards the top. Dancing, milky light poured from many of these holes, and Libby expected they were living spaces. A cluster of long, thin stalactites hung down from the centre of the ceiling, like a chandelier of jellyfish arms, and chunky stalagmites sat on the floor with their pointed ends snapped off and sanded down to create fixed pieces of furniture.

Low murmurings of what she presumed were voices hummed and echoed all around them but, apart from Leif-Mestler, no Sun Watch cave dwellers could be seen. It would appear they weren't as over the moon about their company as Leif-Mestler had suggested they would be. She felt no sense of threat, however, and reasoned they might just be shy creatures. After all, Leif-Mestler was a fearless lichen hunter, a warrior no less in his own eyes, and according to him there were only twenty-nine others who shared the same title - the rest of the Sun Watch were perhaps less brave and more wary.

The smell of damp was much less evasive in the vacuous space of the squirrel den, which lent her a small sense of relief. The overpowering reek of mildew in the closed-in tunnels had further added to her feelings of confinement, whereas here she felt less hampered. It was warm and had an inoffensive lived-in smell.

"Rest yourselves, if you like," Leif-Mestler said, pointing to a stalagmite-come-chair, its broad surface ample enough to seat a dozen people. "I'll be back in a jiffy."

Libby sat, but Grim remained standing. They both watched as the lichen hunter walked off, disappearing into an opening in the wall about ten metres away. Fire torches mounted to the wall flickered orange outside the chamber, but a more intense white-yellow glow emanated from inside.

Pulling her feet up onto the platform of the stalagmite, Libby hugged her knees close and looked at Grim. The stubble on his face looked a shade blacker in the low light, and the hair on his shaved head was beginning to grow through dark, almost covering the large tattoo on the side of his head. Most of his exposed skin was ingrained with dirt, which made her wonder whether they'd get an opportunity to bath or shower. She was long overdue a good soak and she'd love to scrub him down.

The scratches and scrapes on his chest were dark scabs now, healed and almost ready to fall off. His black vest was torn and dishevelled, and through one of the tears she could just about see the rounded pink scar of the bullet wound that Jarvis Strickler had given to him just days ago. She had no doubt that the one a little further down on his chest would be in a similar state of repair. Kitty, Finnbane Krain's personal assistant, had shot him through the heart. She wondered if it was just as scarred physically as it was emotionally.

"What do you reckon?" she asked. "Shall we stay or shall we make a break for it?"

He moved over and sat down next to her, his cold arm brushing against hers. "Make a break for it? You were the one who wanted to come."

She watched as he scoped the squirrel den, his head moving around as he took it all in. His body was tense next to hers. He was always so tense.

"There're probably hundreds of eyes watching us," he said, his voice low and gravelly. "I don't think we'd get very far."

Before she could answer, Leif-Mestler emerged from the glowing cavern and walked towards them, whistling a rather tuneless tune on his great rubbery lips. He was followed close behind by a woman who could only be described as another Sun Watch cave dweller. She was certainly no stunner. Her top lip was barely there and her bottom lip drooped down so much it touched her chin, and large teeth that were the colour of popcorn kernels stuck out of her mouth at a forty-five degree angle. Her hair was thicker than Leif-Mestler's but it was pulled back in much the same way and her beige skin was covered in similar warts and moles. She wore a fawn-coloured sarong tied around her waist, covering her bottom half down to her ankles. Her top half was completely bare, so her long breasts hung to the sides of her potbelly, quivering with each step she made, and her belly button looked about as big as a pool table pocket.

"Having said that," Grim said. "I don't much fancy staying either."

Libby dug him in the ribs with her elbow.

"Welcome, travellers," the woman said, her words hard to decipher because of the awkwardness of her lips.

Libby stood up and pulled Grim to his feet. "Thank you," she said, offering a shaky smile. "I'm Libby. And this is Grim."

Grim tipped his head in acknowledgement, but said nothing.

"I'm Feryl-Belcher," the woman said. She paused to lick her teeth. "The Sun Watch's chief chef."

"It's a pleasure to meet you," Libby said, cringing at the cliché but unsure as to what else to say.

"Will you both be stayin' for dinner?" Feryl-Belcher asked. "The pantry's plenty full. Leif-Mestler an' the rest have stocked it well this week. How 'bout a pot o' hot moss tea to start with?"

Grim shook his head and Libby said, "No thank you. We won't impose on you for too long."

"Don't be daft, girly," Leif-Mestler chided. "You could only be imposin' if you were unwelcome and since that's not the case then you can hardly be imposin' now can you?"

Libby shook her head. "Okay then, we'll stay for a short while. But how about some water instead of hot moss tea? A cup or two of water would do just fine."

"*Water?*" Feryl-Belcher looked at Leif-Mestler for validation that she had heard correctly. Her bottom lip had folded upwards and her small eyes seemed to shrink further back into the blackness of their sockets. Leif-Mestler roared with laughter at the chef's quiet outrage, his own tiny black eyes sparkling in the low light like beetles when he tipped his head back.

"It's alright. The girly's got an iffy belly, that's all," he said, patting Feryl-Belcher on the shoulder. "Don't be so touchy, she wasn't insultin' your abilities in the kitchen or nowt like that."

"Oh God, no I definitely wasn't," Libby echoed, mortified at the thought of having just offended the chief chef.

"Just give her some water, eh? I think that'd be best all round," Leif-Mestler said, throwing Libby a conspiratorial wink. "Nice plain and simple water."

Feryl-Belcher nodded, but her expression remained dubious. "I think I've still got some gastropod tonic in the kitchen if you want me to go see?"

"What's gastropod tonic?" Libby asked, already afraid of what the answer might be.

"A Sun Watch speciality for curin' digestive problems and the likes."

"Yeah, but *what's in it?*" Grim asked, his whole demeanour showing impatience.

"Nothing but grey slugs and spring water." Feryl-Belcher shrugged her rounded, sloping shoulders. "Doesn't look too clever, I'll admit to that, but I have to use the grey ones else it don't work properly. Have to stew their mantles for 'bout three hours till they're nice and tender, then grate the foot fringes on top and leave to simmer for another half an hour. Blitz it all up and there you go."

Libby's face drained and she thought she might have turned grey herself. Thankfully, Leif-Mestler jumped to the rescue and said, "The water'll be fine, lass. These are folk with delicate innards, remember? Let's not force things on them. But since they don't want nowt to eat, make sure you

132

put plenty on my plate, eh?" His brown tongue slobbered over his already-glistening lips.

"Suit yourselves, but I'm tellin' you, there's nowt better for stomach complaints than my gastropod tonic."

Libby smiled weakly. "I'm sure there isn't."

Feryl-Belcher clomped back to the kitchen to fetch some water, her arse cheeks like two large sofa cushions rubbing together as she went. Once she was out of sight, Leif-Mestler said, "Wait right here. I'm goin' to fetch my two little 'uns. They'll be right made up to meet you. They've never seen a human before." When Libby looked slightly bewildered, his eyes narrowed and he asked, "You *are* both human, aren't you?"

She looked at Grim and he back at her. When she saw one of his eyebrows poke above his sunglasses she imagined he must be thinking *how the fuck are you going to explain that one?* So she nodded her head and replied, "Yes we are. Absolutely."

"Good." Leif Mestler chuckled and clapped his hands to together. "Right then, I'll just go and fetch them. Be back in a tick."

As soon as the lichen hunter was out of sight, Grim put his hands on Libby's shoulders and said, "Okay, we meet the kids and then we leave." He was wearing his usual look of dogged determination, the muscles tight across his jawline.

"But what's the hurry?" she said. "They seem okay after all, and they might put us up for the night. Just think, we could get a decent night's sleep without worrying that something might eat us."

"How do you know they won't?" He nodded his head in the direction of the cosy-looking chamber they presumed was Feryl-Belcher's kitchen.

"Nah." She shook her head. "I don't get that impression at all."

"You don't? Oh well that's comforting to know," he said. The derision in his tone stung like gravel rash.

"Sarcasm is the lowest form of wit you know."

"Yeah? You should know."

"Ouch. Are we bickering already?"

He shook his head and sighed. "No, I just don't understand why you're keen to stay. I mean what the hell are these things? And *slug soup*! For fuck's sake, what's that about?"

She shrugged her shoulders. "I don't know but they seem nice enough, I mean we're meeting the family already. And Feryl-Belcher offered us *gastropod tonic,* not slug soup. I think it's a wonderful show of hospitality." She winked and a smile crept to her face. "Besides, I thought it'd be nice to spend some time together, you know?" She grabbed a handful of his vest and pulled him close.

At first he remained stony, but then his mouth curved up at the left in a lopsided grin - something he tended to do when he was partially amused, and a trait that she found downright gorgeous. When he nodded his head in *okay* she wanted to kiss him, but as she stretched up her eyes went blurry and she fell forwards into his chest. For no apparent reason her head was swimming as though she'd drunk a whole bottle of wine. She could feel his hands gripping her upper arms, steadying her and keeping her from falling. He was calling her name, yet try as she might she couldn't focus on him, and his voice faded fast until all she could hear was a nauseating buzz like the white noise of a bad radio signal.

As quickly as it had begun, the buzzing stopped. Everything went quiet and her eyesight came back with clear precision. But instead of Grim standing in front of her, there was now a woman. A woman she'd never seen before.

Gnarled hands, like bird claws, gripped her arms where Grim's had been, and a cloying smell of lavender clung to the back of her throat, making her want to cough. The woman was around the same height as Libby and her face was disconcerting in its closeness. Libby wanted to push her away. She could see orangey face powder sitting thick and unblended on her old skin and her eye-liner looked like black crayon, crude and heavy. The woman's eyes were squeezed shut, creating so many crows' feet that Libby imagined a crow had done a worm-dance on her face. Her mouth was moving, but no words came forth between thin lips and aged teeth. Her chestnut hair was pulled back from her face, failing to conceal reddish splodges around her hairline that were the remnants of hair dye.

"Who are you?" Libby demanded, trying to shrug the woman's hands off.

The woman's eyes popped open, her watery blue stare intense and probing. Libby felt something spark within. Some sort of connection, like an electric current jolting her brain. But before she could say or do anything else, she slumped forward and fainted. And then everything was black.

Chapter 19

Libby awoke on a lumpy mattress of piled blankets. Dark scratchy blankets that made her skin itch and took away none of the harshness of the hard, uneven floor. The dull ache in her hip where it dug into the ground was disregarded when she found her head to be resting on Grim's bare chest and her left arm draped across his torso. Feigning sleep for a while longer she enjoyed the feel of him combing his fingers through her hair. She wondered how long he'd lain awake. Despite how cold he was she loved being so close to him and breathing in his musky smell, even the feel of his chest hair tickling her cheek. She listened to the unhurried rhythm of his heart beating whilst feeling happy that he'd stayed with her while she'd slept.

Eventually she cracked open her eyes again. She could see that they were enveloped in a mid-grey gloom, the chamber doorway lay near their feet and a faint light from somewhere beyond was casting a glow.

"What happened?" she murmured. "Where are we?"

"You passed out again," he said. His fingers stayed resting on her head. "So we spent the night with the Sun Watch folk."

She twisted round to look up at his face and was instantly dismayed to see that he'd slept in his sunglasses. That is, if he'd slept at all.

She gasped and then in an excited whisper she said, "Oh I think I can remember! You were there and then you - weren't. Yes, and then there was this woman. An old woman with really bad make-up and coloured hair. She looked at me and then…I don't know. I'm not sure."

Grim's fingers resumed a lazy combing motion through her tangled hair.

"It was strange, she didn't just look at me," she continued. "It sounds funny, and I can't really explain, but she *really* looked at me. Like there was some sort of link between us, as though she was trying to delve into my mind. And she did, she made the link, I'm sure of it because I could *feel* her there."

His face remained serious and he swept a stray strand of hair from her face. "The Sun Watch think it's the water wraiths."

Her face crumpled in doubt. "But, it was so real…"

"I know," he said, his voice and expression harsh. "I know exactly how real it feels, and I think the quicker we're out of this place the better."

Shifting her to the side, he sat up and reached for his tattered vest. Pulling it over his head, he said, "But first, I think you should take Feryl-Belcher up on her lichen pie."

"*What?* Why would I want to do that?"

"You haven't eaten in ages and that's not good for you. We have a long journey ahead - you need some strength."

"What about you…?"

He shook his head. "When I said I'd tell you everything, I will - but not right now. All I will say is that I don't need food as often as you do." In seeing her look of anxiousness, he said, "I'll have some of the damn lichen pie too, if it'll make you feel any better?"

She smiled and play-punched him on the arm. "I appreciate the sentiment, but I'm not that much of a bitch. I wouldn't put you through it."

He grinned and stood up, stooping low so as not to bang his head on the ceiling. She lay on her back, propping herself up on her elbows, and watched him move to the doorway.

"Hey, did I miss the kids?" she asked.

He laughed; a sound she enjoyed a great deal.

"Yeah, you missed a real treat. Flamespoon-Mestler and Mensha-Mestler were fucking adorable. You'd have loved them."

137

"Oh that's a shame," she giggled. Cocking her eyebrow, she asked, "Anyway, where do you think you're going?"

Still stooped by the doorway, he looked bemused. "To see what morning's like out there with the Sun Watch folk."

The sound of his coarse voice tantalised all of the erogenous nerve-endings in her body and she lurched forward, grabbing the waistband of his trousers. Yanking him back towards her, she said, "Don't you want to see what morning's like in here with me first?"

His cheeky lopsided grin appeared.

"Actually that sounds much better," he said, allowing himself to be pulled back, falling to his knees before her.

With quick hands she pulled his vest up and over his head, unable to get enough of his ripped body beneath. Pressing her palms against his icy, rock hard chest she savoured the skin on skin contact and met his probing tongue with her own. As he curled his fingers beneath the hem of her t-shirt she pushed him hard, urging him to lie down. When he obeyed and lay on his back, she straddled his torso. Without asking permission, she removed his sunglasses and cast them aside. Then as she pinned his arms to the ground above his head, her warm brown eyes glowing with fiery determination, she said, "You're all mine."

An hour later, in the communal area of the squirrel den, Libby was sitting on a stalagmite seat, watching as Grim blew into the contents of a stoneware dish that Feryl-Belcher had given to him. He took a cautious sip and then seemed to take a while savouring the taste, his face unreadable.

"It's alright, it's actually really nice," he said after a while.

She was cupping a similar looking bowl in her own hands, steam rising from it in swirls of not-very-pleasant-smelling wisps. She eyed him, doubting the sincerity of his declaration, but before she could call him on it Feryl-Belcher, who had just returned from the kitchen with another bowl for Leif-Mestler, asked, "Are you feeling better today, Libby?"

Lowering her head and feeling a little foolish for the scene she must have caused, she said, "Yes, thanks. Sorry for giving everyone a scare. I suppose it must have been down to exhaustion."

"Yes." Feryl-Belcher nodded her head in agreement. "You need to build your strength else you won't last much longer in these caves. I've never known the water wraiths to demonstrate their power this deep. You must be very weak. Go ahead and get that hot moss tea down your neck, then you'll be feelin' much better before you know it, I swear."

"Thanks." Libby smiled with all the genuineness of a poker-playing snake. The mere look of the green liquid churned her stomach and every time she blew into it the cloying steam almost made her gag.

"It's nice to see you're getting an appetite, girly," Leif-Mestler observed.

She raised the bowl to him in silent cheers then put it to her lips and took a long swig. Once inside her mouth the bitter, foul-smelling slime served only to offend her taste buds. It tasted like vegetable soup that was months past its best-by date. Her initial reflex was to spit it out, which made Grim laugh aloud.

"Is everything alright?" Feryl-Belcher asked in alarm.

"Oh yes, it's just…it's just hotter than I expected, that's all."

Grim nudged her with his elbow before downing the rest of his tea in one mouthful. She nudged him back with her shoulder and gave him the evil eye. As she sat cradling the hot moss tea, taking tentative sips every now and then, she watched with interest as other Sun Watch people started to appear from holes at ground-level.

"Is that where they live?" she asked, directing her question at Leif-Mestler.

"Yes." He nodded his head. "Families of up to twenty can fit into some of the hollows in here. There are more livin' spaces other than these ones surroundin' the squirrel den though. It's a complex cave system and we make the most of our space."

139

"What about all those?" She looked up to all the hollows in the cave wall. "Do people live in those ones right up there?"

"Good grief no," he chuckled. "Those are storerooms for stuff. You know, clothin' and tools and other supplies."

Some of the Sun Watch people sat down on nearby stalagmites and some wandered into Feryl-Belcher's kitchen.

"What are they all doing?" she asked.

"They'll be off to work shortly," Leif-Mestler said. "They're the Sun Watch dayshift. Nightshift will be ending soon."

"You never did tell us what the Sun Watch is," she said. "Presumably you don't watch the sun?"

"Oh no, not exactly," he replied, his small eyes twinkling with humour. "We're much too far underground for that, but we *do* have essence of the sun."

"Essence of the sun?" she remarked, tilting her head to the side. "What on earth's that?"

"Exactly what it sounds like, girly, *essence* of the *sun*." He laughed. "And we're its protectors. It's a hefty role which gives us numerous responsibilities. We have to stir it up every now and then to keep it vibrant and flowin'. But more importantly we must guard it to ensure that nothin' untoward happens to it. You know, so that nobody tampers with it or extinguishes it, that sort of thing."

Libby was lost for words, so Grim asked, "Are you saying you have a part of the actual sun down here?"

Leif-Mestler nodded his head. "In a roundabout kind of way, yes, I s'ppose so."

"What does it look like?" Libby gasped.

"Probably how you'd imagine it - a pool of liquid fire; orange and yellow and red. It's really quite beautiful."

"But…why is it here - and *how?*"

Leif-Mestler chuckled at her enthusiasm. "It was entrusted to us a very, very long time ago by Blain, the god of the sun."

Her eyes widened in wonderment. "Are you being serious?"

"Deadly." His face grew serious to show as much. "If anything should happen to the sun's essence, the sun would be lost to these lands forever. Sunray Bay would be cast in complete darkness, save for the moonshine."

"But you live down here in darkness," Grim said. "Why should you care about the sun and what happens up there?"

Leif-Mestler nodded his head, understanding the logic in Grim's train of thought.

"We're servants to Blain and it's his wish. We do it because he commands that Sunray Bay is always to be found by the sun. These lands are cursed, you see, and without his gifted essence actin' as a magnet to draw the sun in, the light would be lost forever."

"That's pretty cool," Libby remarked, putting her dish down on the surface of the stalagmite next to her. "Can we see it?"

"Oh no, I'm afraid not," Leif-Mestler said, waving his hands and shaking his head. "Aside from the fact we have heavy security in place, it'd be much too hot for your skin anyway. It's as hot as lava it is, it'd melt you like candle wax."

"How come you can go near it?" Libby challenged, feeling a little duped.

"My skin isn't like yours, girly. We've been evolvin' for thousands of years. We're just not the same. Tough as old boots this skin, see..." He pinched at the skin of his forearm as though the action would prove how hardwearing it was.

"Well since we can't see this sun's essence and since we don't want to be taking up much more of your time, can you point us in the direction of The Grey Dust Bowl?" Grim said, shuffling his feet. Libby could tell he was itching to be on his way.

"For sure, of course I can, but I'm not sure you'll find much adventure there - that is, if that's what you're looking for."

"I wouldn't exactly say we're looking for adventure. We're looking for *anything*," Grim said. "There's got to be more to this shithole than Sunray Bay and the dustbowl."

141

"Neither of us has a soul," Libby explained. "And there's very little point in hanging around in Sunray Bay unless you have a soul to redeem. So the way we see it is that we may as well venture outwards and see what we come across."

"Well why don't you stay here with us?" Leif-Mestler suggested. "We're a civilised bunch, and you'd be most welcome."

Libby and Grim shook their heads in unison. As kind as Leif-Mestler's offer was Libby already felt suffocated by the caves. She was craving sunlight and fresh air.

"We really appreciate your generosity," she said. "And who knows, perhaps we'll come and visit again sometime and tell you all about our adventures."

Leif-Mestler smiled. "I'd like that very much, girly."

They used a hot spring nearby to wash themselves down - it certainly wasn't the bubble bath she'd been dreaming about, but Libby felt refreshed nonetheless. Leif-Mestler's wife, Tattian-Mestler, mended the tears in their clothes and Feryl-Belcher made a hamper of food and drink for them to take on their journey. Leif-Mestler then guided them through the tunnels towards The Grey Dust Bowl.

Libby found the deeper they went the warmer it became and after around just forty minutes of walking she was drenched in sweat. Eventually, when she'd begun to lose all hope of ever finding her way out into the open again, Leif-Mestler stopped and pointed to a crevice.

"This is where I leave you. Take this route and you won't be affected by the heat of the sun's essence too much. You'll surface in The Grey Dust Bowl at a safe enough distance from Spewin' Mouth too."

"What the hell's Spewing Mouth?" Libby asked.

"A large openin' in the ground, a big chimney I s'ppose. It's where the ash from the sun's essence belches out, a sort of release point for heat and soot."

"Oh."

"As I mentioned yesterday, The Grey Dust Bowl wasn't always as it is now," Leif-Mestler said, upon seeing the look of apprehension on her face. "It used to be lush and green at

142

one time. A tropical paradise, some might say, but the ash spurtin' from Spewin' Mouth has taken its toll."

"That's a shame," she said. The idea of surfacing in a lush haven sounded much more appealing than surfacing in a gigantic ashtray.

Leif-Mestler shrugged his shoulders. "A small price to pay though, wouldn't you say?"

It dawned on her what he meant. Without the sun's essence the sun wouldn't shine down on Sunray Bay therefore no greenery would grow. Yet with the sun's essence the ashes were spreading far and wide, destroying the greenery. In one way or another, the area that made up The Grey Dust Bowl was never destined to maintain an idyllic setting. In fact the whole island was destined to become bleak and barren - the sun was killing Sunray Bay, whichever way you looked at it. She sighed and wondered just what the hell she and Grim were hoping to find beyond Sunray Bay, apart from soot.

Chapter 20

"What will happen to them once we leave here?" Lilea asked, resting her elbows against the rough stonework of the keep. She was peering down into the lower bailey area, wisps of her white hair dancing in the breeze like spider trails. Gin followed her gaze to where a couple of zombie servants were extracting water from the courtyard's well.

"I dunno," she replied. In honesty, it wasn't something she'd considered or even cared about.

"I feel sorry for them," Lilea said, her voice hushed. "They're lost shells, stuck in some sort of unimaginable nightmarish limbo. Every one of them soulless and mindless - they hardly know what they're doing and I'd dare to bet they can't remember anything about their past lives either. It's tragic. They've been bound to an eternity of wandering and roaming aimlessly. They simply exist for the sake of it, not one of them looking for anything in particular. Could you even contemplate that? They don't *strive* to be anything better, they don't *seek* anything."

Gin looked at Lilea, her expression one of bafflement.

"Whoa, you're beginning to sound like our resident poet, Reeve. Has Sun Castle been oozing compassion lately or something? If so, why did it miss me out?" She shook her head and laughed, but Lilea didn't share the joke - instead she frowned.

"Well, what would you have done with them?" Gin asked, when she saw that her attempt at lightening her friend's mood had failed.

"I don't know," Lilea sighed. "Just *something*."

Gin put her arm around Lilea's shoulders and guided her away from the east wall, leading her instead to the opposite side of the keep where the moon hung low like a shiny button on the waistband of the skyline.

"Before we leave for good I'll make sure I put them out of their misery, just for you. Okay?"

Lilea looked up at her and smiled, her elfish face glowing and waiflike under the spell of the moon. In one quick leap, she jumped up onto the keep wall and dangled her short legs over the side. Gin joined her, her own long limbs managing the wall more easily and gracefully.

"It's such a peaceful night," Lilea said, after a few moments had passed. The light wind flowed in and around her white chiffon dress, blowing the scant material inwards and then outwards, making it look like a ghostly jellyfish. "Do you think Rembrae has plans for tonight?"

Gin breathed in deeply. "I'm really not sure, Lil. It depends..."

"You mean it depends on what happened with Reeve last night?"

Gin nodded but she didn't answer. She remained quiet for a while, angry with herself. She'd only just teased Lilea for her compassion towards the servants and yet here she was feeling sorry for Reeve. It was something she could barely admit to herself - but it was true. Compassion was a weakness, Rembrae said so, but she couldn't help the way she felt. The best she could do was to hide her unwelcome twinges of empathy.

Turning her head to the side, so Lilea couldn't see her troubled face, she spotted the silhouette of Reeve in the distance. He was sitting in his usual spot near the north tower, his mass of white hair shining radiant down his back. She imagined that he'd be looking out over Sunray Bay whilst writing poetry, his long gentle fingers guiding pen across page to make sorrowful verses in impossibly neat handwriting. *Silly bloody man,* she thought, scowling in his direction.

"Are you worried about him?" Lilea asked.

"Don't be absurd," she snapped. In realising that her response had been a little too harsh, she softened her tone

145

and said, "Reeve's affairs are nothing to do with me. I can't help that the Queen makes harsh demands of him. That's just the way life is, I suppose, and life's not always fair."

She picked at a loose bit of thread on her harem pants for a while, and when she realised Lilea was still studying her, she added, "Besides which, he's a *boy*." And with that she scrunched up her face in mock distaste.

Lilea forced a smile, trying to hide her own feelings of uncertainty. A lot of things were changing lately and it was all too much, too soon. Gin's *couldn't give a shit* attitude that she'd once possessed, especially in regards to Reeve, had suddenly been replaced by a different kind of attitude altogether. A quiet and thoughtful brooding.

The previous night they had watched as Reeve had returned to Sun Castle. After he'd trudged crestfallen across the courtyard, Gin hadn't said another word - despite her chatty disposition prior to his arrival. It was obvious she'd been worried sick. Lilea just wasn't sure at all what was going on in her friend's head.

As though she was all too aware of Lilea's thoughts, Gin said, "Why are we even talking about *Reeve*? Let's enjoy the night."

"Okay, what shall we do?" Lilea was more than happy to change the subject. "A game of cards with the others?"

Gin gave her a sullen look and shook her head.

"I'm sick to death of that same pissing game Mord likes to play every single night."

"Well, how about…transition control? We could race each other? I bet my wolf could beat your bat to Spewing Mouth and back…"

"In your dreams," Gin laughed. "But no, I've had quite enough of transitioning for the moment. I do it so often these days I fear I might take on a permanent transformation like Rembrae. Only, instead of getting stuck in wolf mode I'd probably wind up being fog!"

Lilea giggled and rolled her eyes. "I very much doubt it. You're such a drama queen, Gin. But okay, if you don't want to play cards and you don't want to practice transition control, then what do you want to do?"

Gin sighed and shrugged her shoulders. "Tae kwon do training?"

Lilea shook her head. "No way, you kick my arse every time."

"I'll let you win."

"Then what would be the point?"

"Let's just sit and watch the world go by then," Gin huffed.

Lilea's eyes sparkled and she jumped to her feet, balancing on the ledge of the west wall on her hunkers. "How about hide and seek?"

This time Gin rolled her eyes, though she laughed at the same time. "The age of us and you suggest we play *hide and seek?*"

"Aw come on, we have to stay young at heart somehow," Lilea chided. "And that's why you love me, and you know it, because I stop you from being a grumpy old cow."

Gin tried to look offended, but she couldn't keep up the pretence. "Oh alright, I'll play your childish game," she laughed. "But you're on first." She flashed her friend a mischievous wink.

"No way," Lilea retorted, her bottom lip pouting. "It was my idea. If it had been left to you, we'd be sitting here twiddling our thumbs for the rest of the night."

Gin crossed her arms in protest, but said, "Okay, go on then. I'll count to one hundred and then I'm coming, ready or not."

Lilea reached out and pinched Gin's small waistline, making her yelp with glee, then she sprang to the floor and was climbing down the wall of the keep before Gin could retaliate.

"No shape-shifting mind!" Gin called after her. The command was met with silence so she wasn't sure whether Lilea had heard or not - or whether she'd merely pretended not to hear. Gin looked up at the moon and started counting, "One…Two…Three," her voice barely a whisper.

She grew bored by the time she reached just fifteen, so she stopped counting and concentrated instead on the infinite stretch of The Grey Dust Bowl ahead. Chalk-white moonlight shone down, making the whole area look like the pitted surface of the moon. She wondered what The Grey Dust Bowl looked like during the day, expecting it would be quite severe under the harsh light of the sun, which in turn brought her to think about what creatures might crawl out from under their rocks during daylight hours (much in the same way as she crawled out from her hiding place as soon as the moon ruled the sky). Reptiles most likely. And perhaps the flock of jackdaws that sometimes flew in from the west. Reeve had once written a poem suggesting that they were borne of the soot from Spewing Mouth. She'd told him it was a stupid idea but secretly it had captured her imagination. She'd only seen them once or twice, the black birds seldom visited Sun Castle during the night.

Nothing usually did.

Even people from Sunray Bay didn't venture to the castle - it was far too remote and difficult to access. So she was very much amazed when she noticed the outline of two people, way out in the distance, walking straight towards it. Forgetting all about Lilea and their game of hide and seek, she sat up straight.

"What in the buggering hell...?"

Chapter 21

Friday, 3:24pm: The Grey Dust Bowl

The ascent up the rocky incline was nothing but hard work. A constant gruelling challenge - even for Grim. It was hot and airless, and Libby's mouth was so dry that her throat had begun to hurt. In places the tunnel became tight and unbearably enclosed, which made carrying rucksacks full of foodstuffs a struggle for both of them. The slight weight of the food parcels in Libby's rucksack now weighed heavy on her shoulders, feeling more like a bag of breezeblocks, and the bulk of the liquid containers in Grim's rucksack meant that he got wedged between rocks frequently.

On numerous occasions Libby had needed Grim's voice of reason to calm her down. At one point she'd refused to budge another inch, tears of frustration rolling down her cheeks and her chest rising and falling too quick as she'd begun to hyperventilate. Grim had reasoned with her, stroking her hair and telling her that they'd soon be out in the open - which made him something of a convincing liar because although he had no way of knowing how far from the exit they were his words had had the desired effect. She'd resumed the steady climb upwards, holding his hand and allowing herself to be goaded onwards.

Feeling the burn in her thighs and buttocks with each laboured step, she knew beyond doubt that she'd be stiffer than an over-starched shirt collar the next day. And the soles of her pumps were wearing dangerously thin, so much so she reckoned she'd be shoeless within the next day or so.

She flinched when Grim squeezed her hand, grinding her knuckles together uncomfortably, but before she could complain he announced, "Thank fuck for that, we've made it!"

Craning her neck she peered around him to see for herself. She expected to see bright light beckoning up ahead - instead she saw insipid light casting lazy shadows. *Ugh great,* she thought, *night time and more bloody darkness.*

When the opening was directly above them, Grim took off his rucksack and threw it up over the ledge. When they heard it clatter to the ground, he urged Libby to shrug off her rucksack and then he threw that up as well. Planting his hands on the craggy rim of rock above, he heaved himself upwards, scrabbling his feet against the wall opposite for extra momentum. Veins bulged in his forearms as he pulled himself clear of the opening. Resting on his knees he reached back down and beckoned for her to grab his hands, hoisting her out as easily as if she weighed no more than a dressmaker's mannequin. When her feet touched the surface of The Grey Dust Bowl, she smiled and took a deep breath.

A warm breeze caressed her skin and the moon above, with its accompaniment of stars, highlighted the vast amount of open space all around them. Her eyes pricked with tears of relief. Grim moved over and wrapped his arms around her shoulders, holding her close to his chest. She buried her face in his vest and breathed in his smell. When she felt him kiss the top of her head, she closed her eyes and sighed. His embrace was as cold as ever, but somehow it warmed her core. She wrapped her arms around his waist and squeezed him tight, and they stood like that for a while as they silently commended each other for having made it through the North Point cave system intact. It hadn't been an easy feat for either of them.

"So, this is it then?" she said finally, raising her head to take in the scene around them in more detail. "The infamous dustbowl?"

Grim dropped his arms and hooked his thumbs into the belt loops of his black trousers. "Yep, this is it. I hope you weren't expecting something better."

She was actually overwhelmed by it. As the caves had been claustrophobic, this was at the opposite end of the spectrum. The Grey Dust Bowl was a wide open space, stretching forth in all directions - perhaps perpetually in some - and there was nothing but blackness and greyness. She suddenly felt very insignificant.

"How do we know which way to go?" she asked.

"See that over there?" He pointed to a dark outline skulking on the horizon. "I'm guessing that must be Sun Castle."

"Oh yeah." She nodded, straining her eyes to focus on the structure that was sitting in the shadows like a predatory chameleon. A feeling of dread coursed through her body, making her shiver despite the warm air. The shape of the castle looked like something right out of a fairy tale - and under the light of the moon, not a good one either. "So we head in the opposite direction, right?"

He shook his head. "No, I think we should go there."

"We should go to *Sun Castle?*" Her voice was incredulous. "But isn't that where the Blōd Vampyres live? Leif-Mestler said so, and the water wraith..." Breaking off mid-sentence, she realised that going to Sun Castle was something he needed to do. She'd heard the water wraith proclaim that that's where his late wife might be. Nodding her head, even though she felt more than uncertain about it, she said, "Okay, why not?" Her voice was strained as she struggled to keep the fear from rising.

"There might be other resources," Grim suggested.

"Feryl-Belcher gave us as much food and drink as we can carry..."

"Some of which you've already used," he answered. "And besides, I've been thinking, we could do with something to shield you from the sun. You'll burn otherwise."

She couldn't argue with that.

"I suppose you don't need such frivolous things as sunscreen and parasols?" she said.

"No, I don't." He draped his arm across her shoulders, pulling her close, and she slipped her arm around his waist, sliding her thumb into the back pocket of his trousers. "If you like, I'll tell you everything while we walk."

151

"Everything about *you,* you mean?" she said, hopefulness making her eyes wide. "About your past…?"

"Yeah, unless you don't want to hear it."

"No. I mean, *yes*. Of course I want to hear it. I'd love to know all about you."

He looked sceptical and uncomfortable, but as they made their way through the ashes of The Grey Dust Bowl towards Sun Castle he opened up and told her all about his life prior to Sunray Bay. He told her that his real name was Richie and that the *D* tattooed on his head represented *Della* and *Daisy*, his wife and daughter. He told her how he'd once been a police officer, how he'd lost his younger brother to a car accident and his home to a flood, and how he'd been on the verge of a nervous breakdown. He told her about the holiday cabin that he and Della had owned, and he mentioned the last holiday they'd taken there - the holiday that had changed everything. When he clammed up she urged him to tell her what had happened there.

"It was unreal," he said, his voice quiet and gritty. "We were winding down, enjoying a few beers on the porch one night. It was warm and summery and I was actually starting to feel like my old self again. I'd decided to stop wallowing in the self-pity that had been suffocating me like some big fucking pillow pressed to my face, because the time away with Della and Daisy had made me realise how bloody lucky I was. I mean, so what if we were on the bones of our arses because our house got flooded - we still had each other and *that* was the important bit. I also realised that I had to stop treating my brother's death as my own bad luck. It was so selfish of me. It was *his* bad luck, not mine - he'd had his whole life ahead of him, yet I still had mine. I realised I owed it to him to carry on living mine to its fullest potential. It's what he would have wanted.

"It was as though something had changed in me that day, finally it all made sense, you know? Like there was this light poking holes through the dark fog in my head. It felt great - and then…" He stopped talking and gritted his teeth.

"And then what?" she asked, worried that he wouldn't continue.

"And then the whole wooded area surrounding the cabin was besieged by zombies. I mean *zombies,* can you believe it? What were the chances? I wouldn't have seen it coming in a million years. There were hundreds of them." His breathing had become ragged with anger. "They got to Daisy first. One of the evil bastards near enough ripped her throat out with its teeth... I'll never forget. And then it attacked Della."

He fell silent and she waited for him to continue. When he didn't, she squeezed his waist and asked, "So what happened?"

"What happened?" he laughed, a humourless sound thick with scorn. "I did what no husband or father should have to do. I killed them. Shot them both."

Again he went quiet. She allowed him some time to gather his emotions, but after a lengthy amount of time elapsed it seemed he'd said enough. Tears welled in her eyes, for the sad story itself and for the anguish that his voice betrayed. She couldn't even pretend to imagine what it must have been like for him.

"So what about you?" she said, needing to know how it ended. "I mean, what happened?"

"I killed as many of the fuckers as I could," he said. "I don't remember a lot of it, it's all a blur. A red blur. Eventually though, when I knew I didn't have long, I killed myself."

"I don't understand," she said, coming to a halt and turning him to face her. "What does it all mean? What does that make you?" Her eyes were marked with confusion. "You aren't a zombie..."

He sighed and shook his head, rubbing his forehead as though it would help in the search for an answer. "I'm not sure. I don't know what the hell it makes me. By rights I should be cabbaged - just like one of them. Slavering and groaning and looking like shit. But I...I don't know what happened..."

153

"Were you definitely bitten?"

He raised an eyebrow, a sardonic *yes*. "Several times, I *should* be a zombie."

"And yet, you're not."

"But I do have some traits," he said.

"Like what?"

"My skin, just in case you hadn't noticed, doesn't get warm," he said, his bitter tone expressing his shame on the matter. "And…and my…my…"

"Your eyes?" she finished for him.

He simply nodded.

"Okay," she said, realising his discomfort. "Let's focus on the positive things then. What traits do you have that *aren't* zombie-like? I bet there are more of those."

"Well for one, I can *think*. I can tell which shoe goes on which foot, I know when to take a piss and I can find my arse with both hands in the dark."

Libby rolled her eyes.

"Stop being modest, I get that part - I think we can safely say you're definitely not brain-dead, but what else is there? I have to admit, I don't know much about zombies."

Although visibly uncomfortable with the entire discussion, he answered her question anyway, "Well instead of gradual decomposition my body doesn't change at all. In fact, it works almost in reverse. It has the ability to fix itself in the event of an injury - and that also applies to fatalities."

She moved her hand up and traced her finger around the pink scar on his chest. He took hold of her hand and laid it flat to his chest where she could feel the slow *whump* of his heart.

"I'm not normal, Libby."

"Who is?" she said, trying to sound nonchalant for his sake.

He surprised her by moving his sunglasses so they rested on top of his head. The dilated black pupils of his otherwise zombie-white stare engaged her own.

"I'm like a goddamn machine," he rasped. "I haven't been able to find any sense of peace since I got here because even when I wanted to cease to exist my body wouldn't let me.

"I killed myself at the cabin hoping that it was before the virus had taken hold. I convinced myself I'd beaten it and that the reason I was in Sunray Bay was because I'd murdered my wife and little girl - which is reason enough, I accepted that. But you know what? It's bollocks. The amount of time that elapsed after the first zombie wound I obtained would have been enough to turn me a dozen times or more. No question. So the blunt truth is, I just don't know what I am - and I've never met anything else like me. I'm like some sort of mutation."

She cupped his face in her hand whilst searching his eyes deeper, seizing the opportunity *really* to look at him while he was unmasked. She tried to define where his irises should be, but there was no faint line or colour difference at all. The white was complete.

"Thank you," she said in a whisper. "For telling me."

"Are you pleased you know now?" he asked. "Or do you wish you'd never asked?"

She struggled to find words that would sound sincere, to let him know that she was overjoyed that he'd opened up to her, and when she faltered too long, he said, "Do you still want to come with me, knowing all of that? Do you still want to know me?"

For the first time since she'd met him, she detected worry in his tone.

"Of course I do, you bloody idiot," she said, gripping his fingers and entwining them in her own. "I *want* you."

"What?" He took a step back, his face not belying the bewilderment there. "*You want me?* I don't know what to say…"

"So don't say anything, just shut up and kiss me."

He obeyed and gave her the most lingering kiss she could have hoped for. When he drew away from her again, she said, "You know, I never thought in my wildest dreams that I'd find a …that I'd find a zombie so incredibly sexy."

"Yeah well, until this week I've always hated vampires..."

"Hey that's *vampae* to you, mister - the faery part of me is most important and don't you forget it. The vampire in me is so miniscule I can get all the sustenance I need from a veggie burger."

They were so engrossed in each other they didn't notice the *swoosh-swoosh* flapping of wings until the sound was right upon them. When they turned around to see what made the noise, they were both shocked to see a naked woman crouching on the ground nearby in the darkness, watching them.

"Great, we're in the middle of bloody nowhere and still we manage to run into some potential-crazy. And a naturist one at that," Libby said. "Will this place ever stop surprising me?"

The other woman eyed them like a predator might its prey. Her cool eyes were made-up with black paint and there was a black band smudged diagonally down her right cheek like some sort of war paint.

"Are you a Blōd Vampyre?" Grim asked.

The woman rose to her full height, pulling her long white hair to one side so that it covered her right breast and tapered down past her belly button. She ignored his question and, said, "Who are you and why are you heading towards Sun Castle?"

"We just want to use it as a stop-gap," Libby said. "We mean to travel across The Grey Dust Bowl so we want to rest up and get some fresh supplies."

"It's been a long time since Sun Castle was visited by the general public," the woman said, her voice as curt as a whip. "And it's not a tourist attraction." Crossing her arms over her chest in a manner of authority, she moved closer. "But, since I'm not entirely unreasonable, come - I will give you a guided tour."

Before Libby had time to register what was happening, the woman's body shrank and morphed into what she could only describe as being a flying Chihuahua. It rose up and

156

swooped off into the distance. Libby turned to Grim, her face still full of wonderment. "Do we follow?"

"Yeah, I reckon so."

"She kind of creeps me out though. What if there are hundreds of them?"

"Well we'll find out soon enough, won't we? This is how life is going to be from now on, we don't know anything about anything here. Besides, stop being so pessimistic - they might be as friendly as Leif-Mestler's lot."

"Somehow I seriously doubt that," she said. "I reckon that woman wouldn't even know how to say the word hospitality, never mind know how to demonstrate it."

Chapter 22

Jungle green blades sway in the wind. He knows what colour they should be even though right now they look more black-green. Nonetheless, they're just as juicy and sweet and fabulous for running fingers through. The air is a shiver off being cold, fresh enough to be invigorating. Mole-coloured mountains are white-capped behemoths along the horizon. They surround him three hundred and sixty degrees, standing bold like guardians. This is a vast area full of opportunities and places for him to investigate. There'll be no more boredom and no more confinement - this is just the beginning.

His new beginning.

For now he lies on his back looking up, caressing the grass between his fingertips and sometimes hovering his hands just above it, enjoying the tickling sensation on his palms. The sky is still the same black he's always known and the moon is still the same moon it's always been. This familiarity holds no sense of sentimentality, because he has no emotional attachment to the life he used to lead and he'd sooner the sky be blue and the moon be replaced by the sun. But he can't have it all. He'll settle for black and silver instead of blue and gold.

He digs the heels of his boots into the supple soil of the earth and all at once he feels content. It's a good feeling. Contentedness is something he never thought he'd know - but against all odds, he does.

Finally.

He's listening intently to the night sounds all around him, because here, in this place, there are plenty of animals and birds. It's not barren, this new home. It's teeming with life. And he watches and listens as nocturnal mammals scurry about, snuffling and busying themselves with night-time duties and frolics. They all act oblivious to him, their observer, readily accepting him into their realm.

Slowly he turns his head because he hears somebody approaching. And then he sees her standing there. Her face is cast in velvety shadows. He can't see her features clearly, but he knows that astounding beauty lies there. Her hair is long and wavy, radiant red. It's the colour of a zealous twilight sky, and it's dancing like flames in the breeze. She stands signalling for him to go to her, so he waves back and jumps to his feet quickly, because he won't make her wait. He can't wait. He won't disappoint her.

She's wearing a pale gown but he knows it's not white; he hates white. No, she's wearing gold because she's fit to be a queen, his queen, and because it's a declaration that she's blessed enough to be able to walk in the light of the sun. All of which she's about to tell him. She'll relay stories of budding flowers, of vibrant skies and of rainbows; a colourful world that he can see only through her eyes. He is happy to live it through her eyes. But as she opens her mouth to speak, no words come forth. They never do. And this is where it ends...

Friday, 6:49pm: The Battlement, Sun Castle, The Grey Dust Bowl

Reeve drew his foot back and kicked at the wall in frustration, the heel of his cowboy boot making a satisfactory *thwacking* noise on the stone.

"Why can't I ever *hear* her, Hope?" he whined.

Knowing he'd never get a response from the faceless etching in front of him, he didn't wait for one. He climbed on top of the merlon to his right and looked out across The Grey Dust Bowl towards Sunray Bay. More than anything he wanted to scream his anguish into the night, as though by ridding his lungs of all the air inside them he might release his pent-up frustration like a load of bad toxins. He wanted everyone else to know how dismally fed up he was. He was sick of suffering in silence, yet he didn't make a sound. He held it all back and ground his fingernails into the palms of his hands instead.

He needed to demonstrate patience for a little longer, then the other life he dreamed about would be his for real. The mountain range, the fields and the animals, they'd make up his new home. He'd have so many choices, so much freedom - and he'd also have the woman in the golden gown. That is, if she ever transpired. This part of the plan made him feel anxious. What if he couldn't find her? He wasn't sure he could live as a solitary creature for much longer; he imagined he might die of loneliness.

Could a person die of loneliness?

It was too scary a thought and just as well that it was disrupted by the sound of Gin's voice down below in the bailey.

"...two of them, a man and a woman. They're coming here now!" she was saying in an excitable tone.

What? he thought, *visitors coming to Sun Castle?* It was a ridiculous notion, and one that didn't make sense. Nobody ever visited the castle. Why would they want to?

He stood and watched as the other four Blōd Vampyre girls congregated around Gin, their voices now a hushed mumble so he couldn't quite make out what they were saying and their hands gesticulating. Scanning the terrain between the castle and Sunray Bay, he found himself even more bewildered when he failed to see anybody approaching. *What on earth is she talking about?* he wondered.

Crouching low, he remained on the merlon for quite some time. He watched as Gin, Lilea, Mord, Brinda and Van scattered about the drawbridge. Gin made her way outside, positioning herself on the bridge itself, whilst the others loitered in the shadows at either side of the inner entranceway. Perplexed by their behaviour, he watched and waited in silence.

It was some time before he eventually heard the sound of unfamiliar voices. Looking straight down, he saw movement at the corner of the north tower. Focussing on the shapes he

160

saw that it was two figures making their way alongside the curtain wall towards the drawbridge, a man and a woman, just as Gin had said.

The man, who was tall and muscular, wore sunglasses - bizarrely. Reeve presumed he must be blind. And the woman was slim in build and, although young, he could sense a great weariness about her. If his eyes weren't mistaken she had *long red hair*. His breath caught in his throat and his heart quickened. She wasn't wearing a golden gown but he did allow himself to imagine for a brief moment that she might be his own real-life Hope.

Chapter 23

Friday, 6:38pm: The Grey Dust Bowl

"Can I ask you a question?" Libby said, hitching her rucksack further onto her shoulders because it kept sliding down her arms.

Grim eyed her from behind sunglasses that were back in their rightful place. "Do I have a choice? I'm surprised you didn't ask anyway. When do you ever wait for permission?"

She grinned and he grinned back.

"Okay, what is it?" he asked.

"I was just wondering…what colour were *Richie's* eyes?"

If he was bothered by the question he didn't show it. He carried on walking, his expression unchanged. "Why should it matter?"

"It doesn't." She shrugged. "I was just curious."

"Sorry, they're pretty horrific aren't they?"

"No," she said. "They're part of you. They're part of Grim - and I like *him* very much."

"Thanks, you're kind of sweet, you know?"

"I do try," she said, batting her eyelids and giving him her most mischievous smile.

Sun Castle drew close at a painful level of slowness. Libby had had to work extra hard to keep up with Grim's long steady strides, but he'd slowed down when he realised she was struggling. Looking down at her dust-covered pumps and filthy ankles, she said, "Who'd have thought it, eh? A zombie and a hybrid faery."

Grim looked at her in amusement. "Yeah, it is a bit nuts, I suppose."

"Imagine what our folks would say."

"Hmmm I don't think mine would get over the zombie bit, never mind anything else," he said dryly. "Mind you,

162

technically I think I'm past the stage of taking girls home to meet the folks."

"How old are you?"

"Thirty-one."

She grinned. "Gloria was wrong then."

He looked at her and she could tell that his curiosity was piqued.

"Gloria? What was she wrong about?"

"She said that you were a good ten years on me *at least*."

"Oh, is that right?" he laughed. "So how many years do I have on you?"

"Nine."

He eyed her with suspicion. "Why were you and Gloria even discussing my age?"

"Because I asked her how old you are, of course."

He remained quiet for a few moments and then asked, "So what else did she say about me?"

"Not much really," she said, shrugging. "Although she did say you're hard work."

"Really?" When he saw her thin-lipped look of *don't even deny it*, he sighed and said, "So she must have been right about that at least then, huh?"

"Too bloody right." She laughed, knocking his bare arm softly with her fist, then looking down to her feet once again she said, "She also said you'd break my heart."

He didn't answer. When she looked up to see if he would respond she saw that he was looking straight ahead, his jaw set firm. He had no intention of disputing the claim. After a brief moment of awkwardness, she said, "You know, my dad would think I'd been smoking my own socks if I told him about us, but I think after the initial shock of discovering you're a zombie, he'd actually like you."

"Yeah?"

"Yeah, he's an open minded bloke - sound as a pound. But as for my mother, I'm not so sure. I don't really know what to think about her anymore."

"Don't be too hasty to judge her based on what Krain told you," he said, turning to look at her. "Even if all he said is true, and he really was your biological father, your mother was probably only trying to protect you by not telling you. I mean, what good would it have done for you to know the truth when Dennis Hood was the only dad you needed?"

"I suppose so, but…"

"Just try to remember your upbringing for what it was. Knowing the truth would have accomplished nothing except for to taint what mattered most. Try not to be overly harsh on your mother, we all make mistakes."

"I know what you're trying to say but…I feel as though she deceived me."

"Being a parent can be a strange thing at times," he said, his tone more clipped. "Most parents will do anything to protect their own children - even if it's morally wrong."

Yes, you'd know all about that, she thought with sadness, imagining the look of torment haunting his eyes right now.

"Be thankful for what you had," he said. "And don't over-analyse things."

They walked in silence for the rest of the way, his mood so brooding she could almost feel the dark weight of it. She gave him some time to his thoughts, and she spent some time sorting through her own until they reached the castle.

The sheer height and scale of its stone walls dwarfed them, especially when they crossed down through a dip that had once been the castle's moat. She bent her neck to look up at the tower that was looming over them and thought if it wasn't for the Blōd Vampyres, she'd have loved to investigate the place inside and out.

"Wow, this is pretty impressive," she said in an awed whisper.

"Yeah, it's a bit surreal," Grim said.

But as much as it was impressive, there was a certain eerie ambiance that hung in the air like a stagnant smell. The hairs on her arms and the back of her neck tingled, and she wondered what ghosts the walls kept inside. It didn't seem right that this grand building was standing in the middle of nowhere. It was as though it could have just risen from the ashes themselves because it was miles away from

164

civilisation. She tried to picture what it must have been like when it was surrounded by plants and trees and settlements but it was a hard task because the greyness of the place made it look no more than a giant gravestone. She inched closer to Grim, a subconscious act that made her feel safer.

Just before they rounded the curtain wall, Grim sighed and said, "Hazel."

"Excuse me?"

"My eyes. *Richie's* eyes. You wanted to know. Well. They were hazel."

She was taken aback.

Trying to envisage him with hazel-coloured eyes she couldn't seem to do it, and in a way she was glad. She accepted him for all he was now. White eyes or hazel eyes, it was all irrelevant.

They turned the corner, sticking close to the castle wall. The barbican, a great hulking structure, sat to their left, and up ahead was the drawbridge. Standing on top of it, watching them, was the white-haired vampire they'd met earlier. Even at that distance, Libby could sense that the woman's fixed glare was cold and calculating. Her hair was now pulled up in a messy up-do and she reminded Libby of a lioness; watchful, dangerous and hungry. No longer naked the vampire wore a white bikini top, embellished with clear jewels that glittered under the moon's vivacity, and a pair of loose white harem pants that sat low on her hips and billowed down in heavy-looking folds of fabric to just below the knee. Her hands were placed firmly beneath her waist in an authoritative no-nonsense manner. Libby didn't trust her one bit.

"Greetings once again. And welcome to Sun Castle." She wore a self-righteous smirk, thus amplifying Libby's paranoid feelings of potential trickery at play. "Come, I'll take you to our Queen," the vampire said, gesturing with her hands for them to venture into the castle grounds ahead of her.

Libby looked to Grim for validation that he still thought his plan to camp out at Sun Castle was a good one, though she suspected it was too late to back out now anyway. He tipped his head once and then started across the drawbridge. She clutched at his forearm, feeling more than a little vulnerable, and fell into step beside him. They passed underneath the dark metal prongs of the portcullis in the stone archway, which sat aloft looking like giants' swords poised and ready to strike. As they entered the courtyard she didn't get much chance to take it all in because she was soon aware of shadows moving at either side of them. The shadows emerged from the gloom, presenting themselves as four women, who then formed a semicircle and proceeded to block the exit behind them. None of them said a word, but the air of silent threat they exuded was enough to make Libby's stomach feel sickly with dread.

The vampire who had greeted them moved forward. Taking the lead, she said, "Come, have no fear, we will escort you."

Libby and Grim allowed themselves to be herded across the cobbled courtyard until they reached a big open doorway in the main section of the castle. The lead vampire stepped inside and invited them to follow. The already warm air from outside seemed to intensify once inside and it harvested a smell of dust and age that made Libby think of Ancient Egyptian tombs - cementing her idea that the castle was like a gigantic grave-marker.

The first thing she saw in the massive room was shadows leaping and flitting all around the stone walls. Candles burned in wall-mounted sconces and a raging fire blazed inside a hearth that was plenty big enough to be a dragon's mouth, its orange tongues flicking upwards. All of the naked flames were catalysts for the spirited shadow play upon the walls. None of the light rose high enough to highlight the ceiling that was a blackened emptiness too high to see. Above the fireplace was a large gold-framed picture - but the painting itself was so grimy it was impossible to see what the subject matter was.

They were led to the other side of the room and when the white-haired vampire in the harem pants came to a stop, she moved to the side and Libby saw a white wolf curled up on an antique throne, its ice-blue eyes open and vigilant.

"Your Highness," the vampire said, bowing her head to the wolf.

"You're the Queen of the Blōd Vampyres?" Libby said in surprise.

"Indeed I am," the wolf snapped. "So know your manners."

"But you're a…*wolf*," she proclaimed. Remembering her manners, she added, "Your Highness."

"Yes, your eyes do not deceive you. I'm Rembrae. Queen, guardian and eldest of the Blōd Vampyres."

"When you say eldest…?" Libby said, already enthralled by the talking wolf.

"Let's just say you'd be hard pushed to meet anybody older or wiser than I am," Rembrae replied. Putting her two front paws onto the stone floor, she slithered the rest of her body off the throne until she was standing on all four paws on the ground. Libby didn't miss the look of pinched pain on her face as she moved.

"But how come you're a wolf?" Libby asked. "None of the others are."

Rembrae laughed, a growly noise that rattled in her throat like loose chains. Her large paws padded silently on the floor as she moved closer and Libby felt cold sweat prickle her face when she caught a glimpse of thick black claws, sharp enough to gut a man.

"Would you prefer that the others were wolves?" she asked. "It could be arranged."

Libby looked at the four white-haired vampires who stood behind her and Grim. When they bared their teeth and sneered at her she shook her head and tried to sound unfazed. "Not particularly."

Rembrae reached her snout towards Libby's hand and drew deep breaths, sniffing loudly. Libby shuddered with every warm, damp puff that the wolf exhaled onto her skin. She fought the urge to pull her hand away. Instead she stood still, hoping the wolf didn't mean to amputate her hand.

When Rembrae drew back, her shrewd eyes narrowed. "Such a strange concoction, child."

"Oh?" Libby raised her eyebrow and feigned ignorance.

"Partially human, no doubt about that," the Queen said, wrinkling her nose. "You also have hints of modern-day vampire - but not much. Tell me, do you have the power of smell?"

"Of course."

"Tell me then, what does a human smell of?"

Libby's brow crumpled. "Well that would depend entirely on the person you're smelling. Some people don't adhere to high standards of personal hygiene, you know? Deodorant, perfume, soap...that kind of thing."

Rembrae laughed. "Such a superficial answer, child. Your vampire make-up must be so infinitesimal it's hardly worth a thing, otherwise you would have risen above the obvious to tell me the real answer."

"So what is the real answer?"

The wolf licked her lips and looked thoughtful. "Rusted metal with a hint of camomile. A smell that's neither sweet nor sour - but a distinct smell nonetheless."

"I hate to imagine what I smell of right now," Libby said, remembering the sweaty climb out of the caves.

"You smell sickly sweet," Rembrae said. "An interesting cloying aroma which for the moment eludes me. Pray tell me, what are you?"

Libby shrugged her shoulders, still assuming ignorance. Until she knew what being a faery entailed, she intended to keep the information out of public knowledge in case it could be used against her. Only Grim knew about it, and she was determined for it to stay that way. "I don't know what you mean."

The wolf's eyes blazed with antagonism, but instead of disputing what Libby said she diverted her attention to Grim instead. Inhaling the air all around him, as she had done with Libby, she took several moments before saying, "How strange, you are nothing. Nothing at all."

"That's ridiculous," Libby argued. "How can somebody be *nothing*?"

Without answering Rembrae returned to her throne and climbed back onto its cushioned seat. Her face looked weary as she said, "Take them to the dungeons, Gin."

The lead vampire bowed her head. "Very well, Your Highness."

"Let them bide there until the girl learns to show respect. And fetch her back to me when she learns how to tell the truth."

Grim made to resist but the four vampires behind swamped him at once, one of them hissing in his ear, "Try it and we'll break your arms and legs."

"There's plenty of back-up about the place," Rembrae added. Her head was now balanced on her two front legs and her eyes were closed. "Don't try anything rash."

Disgruntled, but not foolish, Grim let the five white-haired vampires steer him and Libby from the great room. As they stepped across the threshold, the Queen called out, "And don't drink from them!"

"Your Highness?" The vampire called Gin turned and looked to the front of the room where the wolf was still curled on the throne.

"I want the girl alive, at least until I know what she is."

Gin nodded her head. Slapping Grim hard on the back, she asked, "What about him?"

"He's nothing, and a person who is nothing is dangerous. I don't trust him one bit. Keep him locked up indefinitely."

169

Chapter 24

"Did I ever teach you that eavesdropping was acceptable and that sneakery was some kind of proud art form?"

"Actually, yes, you did."

Reeve stepped out from a recess at the rear of The Great Hall to reveal himself. He'd been stooping in empty darkness at the bottom of a spiral stone staircase. The now-unused staircase had been trodden by servants many moons ago when the kings had thrown banquets - it had been their unobtrusive passage into the kitchens above - now it was Reeve's spying place.

Rembrae nodded her head and chortled; a nasal noise that sounded like she had inhaled fluff and wanted to sneeze. Her eyes were alight with hostile mischief. "Yes I did, didn't I? But, did I ever teach you that practising it on me was appropriate? Funny, I don't recall that."

He frowned. She was impossible - there was no hiding anything from her. "No, Your Highness, you are correct. You did not."

"No," she said. "I thought as much." She let the threat of her tone hang in the air for a while, to serve as a warning, before saying, "Go. Get out of my sight. You have a light bulb to source, may I remind you. I want it sorting before the night's out."

He bowed his head and then turned to leave, but after he'd walked only a few steps he spun around and started towards her instead.

"Mother?" His voice rose toward the end of the word, indicating he was asking a question.

Her head was dipped, sagging as though her neck couldn't support the weight of it and her stony-blue eyes watched him, yet she didn't respond. As fearful as he'd always been of her, at that moment there was an element of frailty about her that gave him courage. The wolf was dying. He could see that now. Her body was failing, and behind the wrath of her gaze there was something else - fear. Suddenly he wondered if her plans to leave Sun Castle and The Grey Dust Bowl were somehow related to her ill-health. *But what does it all mean?* he wondered. Did she mean to run from Death itself? And did she truly mean to take him and the other young Blōd Vampyres with her?

"Who is the girl?" he asked, as bold as he had ever been.

"What's it to you, you impertinent little prick?"

He shrugged his shoulders and refrained from turning his head away, unwilling to back down from those eyes that skilfully dissected him and succeeded in making him feel uncomfortable.

"I'd just like to know."

"You'd just like to know?" she echoed. "And why would that be?"

"Because I've…" He cleared his throat. "Because I think I might have seen her before."

"Oh?" Rembrae's head shifted up, her voice spiked with intrigue. "And where is it, pray tell, that you think you've seen her before?"

He fumbled with the cuffs of his sleeves for a moment, pulling them down over his hands so that only his fingers protruded from the ends. Ethereal digits that he had imagined wrapped around the wolf's throat countless times before.

"In my dreams."

"*In your dreams?*" She cackled with laughter, her whole body convulsing with the effort. Then her face grew serious and she growled, "Are you mocking me?"

Reeve held his hands up. "Of course not, Your Highness."

"So tell me about these dreams of yours. What kind of dreams are they?"

171

He stood tall and spoke with conviction, "They're dreams in which I'm far away from here. I'm happy and I'm free."

"And what does all of that have to do with the girl?" she asked. She scratched at her neck with a hind paw, sending a flurry of loose fur into the air. "Do you think *she* could make you happy?"

"Maybe," he answered. "Yes."

"And do you think that I should encourage these dreams of yours? That I should cheer your foolish notions of happiness and - *romance*?"

He nodded, feeling small and hopeless once again under the weight of her scrutiny; her contempt was both obvious and stomach-roiling.

"Why ever do you think I would do that?"

"Because you're my mother?" he suggested, in a near whisper.

She roared with laughter, her eyes ferocious and cruel, and with that he had his answer. Having had enough of her ridicule, and before he humiliated himself further with tears of frustration, he turned to leave. When he reached the door, she called out to him, "Go and dream more of your soppy dreams, Reeve, but I command you to stay away from her. There's more to that girl than happiness and romance. I'll expect you to visit me later when you've done your chores."

Fuck you, Mother, he thought. *My dreams are only ever happy because I'm far away from you - and you can find your own damn light bulb!*

Swallowing hard, he left The Great Hall without another word and instantly made a resolution to take matters into his own hands. With or without his mother's consent, he was going to meet the girl.

Whisking through dark passages he was as nimble as a cat and as light as a whisper, he knew how to tread on his cowboy boots so they made no *cilik-cilak* sounds on the stone floor. A master at being covert, he used the shadows as though he owned them. His mother was the only one who could detect his presence. He imagined that was because she could hear the beating of his heart from miles away, having probably attuned herself to its rhythmic pump at the time when he'd been growing inside her womb so she could know her enemy. It wasn't hard to picture her sitting there with a swollen belly, listening to it, feeling it, learning it - and hating it, so deep was her loathing for him. Only the image in his head was of a wolf, whereas she'd been a woman when she'd given birth to him. He couldn't imagine his mother as a woman - she was nothing but a callous bitch with a dog-sharp bite.

Upon reaching the well of the stony staircase, which led down to the dungeons, he halted when he heard voices coming upwards. The unmistakable, animated chatter from Gin and the other Blōd Vampyre girls skittered out from the darkness, becoming louder as they grew closer. Ducking into an empty alcove, he held his breath and watched and waited. It wasn't long before they all bounded into sight; a blurring of white hair, white skin and white clothes. A gaggle of ghosts. Without blinking or swallowing he kept his entire body frozen, pressing it to the wall. They knew he shouldn't be in that part of the castle, he had no business there, so if they saw him they'd think he was spying on them. And a showdown with five Blōd Vampyre girls who would undoubtedly accuse him of being some kind of sex pest was the last thing he wanted. So he remained as still as a statue until they had disappeared from sight, lingering for a few moments longer just to ensure they had definitely gone.

When he stepped from his hiding place he bolted down the steps, forgetting to control the clamour of his footsteps. The metal-on-stone sound flew all about his head in the hollow cavity. His heart thumped with anticipation as he neared the bottom. Skipping the last three steps, he jumped down into the long gloomy passageway of the castle's dungeon. The nearest wall-mounted torch flickered amber but the rest remained unlit, making the tunnel a pit of uncertain darkness. The dungeon's cells weren't typically inhabited these days, but in the first cell to his left sat the girl and her companion. Both were sitting on the floor, basking in the orange light, and both were looking pretty cheesed off.

173

The fire from the torch amplified the redness of the girl's hair, giving it all the allure of the sky just before the sun comes up - the sky at its most dangerous. It hung way past her shoulders, untidy and natural. He wanted to touch its warmth.

Lost for words he stood staring, wondering if hers was the face that could fill in the blank one from his dreams. He knew he should introduce himself, but he didn't know how. He wanted to impress her somehow, but instead he was rendered speechless.

Chapter 25

"What do you want?" It wasn't intended to be a rude, or even snappy, question. She was too worn out to be snarky. She wasn't alarmed by the man's arrival; she and Grim had heard him coming down the steps like a herd of horses. Then he'd just stood gaping at them. Thick white hair meandered down to his waist, held back by a black fabric hairband that covered most of his forehead. He looked similar to the female vampires who'd just locked them up, but where they wore white he wore black.

He didn't answer her straight away, but when he did he bowed his head and said, "I'm Reeve, er, Prince of the Blōd Vampyres."

His voice was deeper than Libby would have imagined.

"You're the wolf's son?" she said, tapping the toes of her shoes together as she stretched her legs out in front. "Has she sent you down here to torment us some more? Because if she has then you can tell her to piss off."

To her surprise he laughed and his stance relaxed a little.

"No, I haven't come to torment you at all. In fact, Rembrae doesn't even know I'm here." He edged closer, a warm smile serving to make his face even more stunning. "Though, if you insist, I'll certainly relay your message. Nothing would give me greater pleasure."

"So what do you want?" Grim grunted. His back was resting up against the wall and the look of thunder on his face made him look nothing but dangerous.

Reeve ignored the question and carried on looking at Libby. "Who are you?" he asked.

"Well, since you're being civilised, and since you're the only one who's even bothered to ask so far, I'm Libby. And this is Grim."

"Libby." He repeated her name, a pleasant smile lingering on his lips. "I like that. I like that a lot."

Her eyes narrowed and she looked at Grim with vague apprehension.

"Look, Prince of Darkness," Grim said. "Did you come down here just to exchange pleasantries and talk utter shite? If not cut to the chase and stop frigging about."

Reeve looked at Grim, a look of irritation now marring his friendly smile. Nonetheless he bowed his head. "It's a pleasure, of course. And, please, it's Prince of the *Blōd Vampyres*, but no matter, you can just call me Reeve. Let's not bother with titles and formalities. They're so stuffy, don't you think?"

"You're doing it again," Grim said.

"What?"

"Frigging about."

Reeve edged closer to the cell. "What if I told you I'm here to free you?"

Libby sat up straighter. "Well are you or aren't you?" she said. "Don't be talking in riddles."

He traced a finger down one of the cell's iron bars, his intense blue eyes following it. "I need to be sure of something first."

"Okay. What?" she said.

His hand gripped onto the bar at waist height and he dropped his gaze to the floor. "I can't tell you."

Libby groaned. "Well how can you find out what you want to know if you won't even tell us what it is you want to know?"

"It's just - I don't know how to put it."

"This night isn't going to get any easier is it?" she groaned, covering her face with her hands. "But then, why would it? This whole bloody week has been a complete nightmare."

Grim grunted in agreement, his arms resting on his knees as he studied his hands in the gloom.

"Please, come with me." Reeve stretched his arm through the bars and offered his hand to Libby.

"*What?* But why?"

"I want to talk to you."

"You already are."

"No. Well, yes. What I mean is - I want to talk to you alone."

Before she had time to answer, Grim jumped to his feet and grabbed Reeve's outstretched hand. He yanked it hard, pulling it round the wrong way so it was palm-facing-up. Reeve cried out.

"What the fuck are you playing at?" Grim snarled.

"I wasn't talking to you," Reeve said through clenched teeth. With a speed that neither Libby nor Grim saw, he punched out with his free arm and hit Grim firmly below the jaw, sending him spiralling backwards. Libby rushed to his aid and glared at Reeve.

Reeve held his hands up in surrender. "He started it."

"What is it you want from me?" she said.

"I want you to spend the night with me," he said, resting his forehead against the bars. When Grim growled and made to charge at the bars again he realised the wrongness of his words. "Oh no," he said. "Not like that. I wasn't suggesting, er…you know, anything like *that*." His face flushed a delicate pink. "What I *intended* to say was that I'd like for you to spend the night *talking* with me. Nothing uncouth, just a little friendly tête-à-tête. It'd be a fully-clothed night of civility, I promise."

"But why?" Libby asked.

"I can't say."

"Look, if it's anything to do with what your mother was harping on about…"

"No, it's not. As I said, she doesn't know I'm speaking to you."

"Suppose I oblige - what then?" she said. "Will you let us go?"

Reeve nodded. There was something about his manner that made her believe he was telling the truth.

"Alright, let's get on with it then," she said. "You can talk my head off all you like but I can't promise you I'll stay awake. Oh and I'll warn you now - I can be a right stroppy cow when I'm tired."

"Libby…" Grim began to protest.

"It's okay," she said. "I'm a big girl, I'll be alright."

"You don't have to do this."

"I know I don't have to, but I don't fancy hanging around here for God knows how long either. Give it a few more hours and I'll be going stir crazy. I think I'd rather pop out to negotiate our freedom, then we can be on our way."

He didn't agree, but he didn't try to stop her either.

"Don't miss me too much" she said, giving him a playful prod in the ribcage.

"Just watch what you're doing," he replied, scowling. Moving to the bars, he gripped two in his hands. His knuckles turned white. "You," he said to Reeve. "Lay one finger on her and I'll break every fucking bone in your body."

Reeve's eyebrows rose. He stood his ground within swiping distance of the bars and said, "An unseemly bastard, aren't you?"

"You don't know the half of it."

Chapter 26

Friday, 8:22pm: The Dungeons, Sun Castle, The Grey Dust Bowl
The tall flame of the torch leaped and jerked fitfully. He didn't think it would be long until its mesmerising fiery dance came to an end and it smouldered and stank of black smoke instead. But for now it provided ample light, enough to see all around the cell. Not that there was much to see. It was a rectangular space of about ten feet deep by fifteen feet long. Stone walls surrounded him from behind and to the sides, and the bars in front offered a view of the stone wall opposite. The low ceiling was made of stone as well, and it was only around five inches taller than him. He felt boxed in.

Now he found himself alone, he removed his sunglasses and rested them on top of his head. He rubbed at the bridge of his nose with his thumb and forefinger, feeling two slight grooves where they'd lain. His world was usually shrouded in a veil of darkness, so to watch the bright orange flame opposite, unhindered, was somewhat refreshing - even though it highlighted the fact he was locked away in a miserable dungeon cell. Alone. Well, not completely alone. He could hear *scritchy-scratchy* sounds of movement close by. He couldn't see what it was - which was probably no bad thing - but he suspected it might be rats. Or bloody great big spiders.

He thought about Libby and of what she must think of him now - and of what she *really* thought of his zombie eyes. He wondered if she was a good liar or if she genuinely wasn't bothered by them. He hadn't yet decided. Either way, he felt a twinge of regret that she'd had to see them. It had been unavoidable though, he couldn't have prevented it; even though he hadn't yet made peace with them himself he knew he couldn't have slept with her whilst wearing the

179

damn sunglasses - that would have been on a par with fucking in his socks. *And my God, what a twat I'd have been doing that,* he thought.

In his small murky prison cell, the feeling of solitude bothered him more than the feeling of confinement. Libby had reminded him lately of what it was like not to be lonely. And it was a good feeling. Too long had he pigheadedly trudged on alone. And now here he was, alone again. She'd left him to go off with the Blōd Vampyre - the one with the rock-star get-up who looked like he'd have no qualms about fucking in sunglasses. In fact, he imagined that Prince of The-Tightest-Trousers-Ever was probably trying to charm her socks off right now. His fists clenched and his lips tightened. He had no intention of sitting about the cell waiting for her to come back. No chance. He was a do-er not a thinker.

Clutching at the bars he pressed his face into one of the gaps between, scoping the corridor both left and right as far as he could. A thick bunch of gunmetal keys, which included the one to open the door of the cell he was in, was hanging on the wall at the foot of the steps - much too far away for him to even contemplate reaching them. Not even if he removed all of his clothes, tied them together and then aimed a canny swing did he stand a chance in hell of snagging them.

"Fuck sake," he muttered, tapping his thumbs on the metalwork in agitation. How did he hope to get out of this one? *Think, damn it, think,* he urged himself. Picking at the paintwork and rust patches with his fingers, he studied the bars themselves. He and Libby were at the mercy of the Blōd Vampyres, it would seem. This thought made him well up with a deep anger and frustration that threatened to explode out of him. He'd endeavoured never to put himself at the mercy of anybody or anything ever again, not after…

Well, not after Richie.

His thoughts then drifted to Della and Daisy. He twisted round and slammed the ball of his hand against the back wall of the cell in restless fury. Bits of stone crumbled to the floor in a shower of cream coloured powder and the scurrying noises roundabout stopped dead for a moment. Richie screamed at him from beyond the murky pall of his subconsciousness, begging him not to let go of the past lest he forget about his wife and daughter. Grim didn't want to forget them, he simply wanted to lay them to rest - Richie included. He wanted them all to have peace. And he wanted to find peace for himself, so that he could move on and live a life more bearable. The past was beyond reach, there was no going back. No chance of a happy reunion. In light of this, he wanted to explore the possibilities of what Libby could mean for him.

But, all the while, Richie wasn't convinced.

He breathed in deep and growled like a bear.

Grim or Richie, who would prevail?

Either way, neither one of them would stand for no action. Sucking in air between clenched teeth, he braced himself for impact and ran at the bars. If he couldn't reach the keys to free himself in a sensible manner, then he had no other choice but to become a human battering ram. *And if I raise all hell in the process,* he thought, *then that's just dandy.* He'd gladly take the big red fella on. In fact, he'd skewer the smarmy bastard with his own pointed fork if it came to it.

As the bars resounded from the force of his body blow, he readied himself to charge again. He was a raging mass of muscle and fury ready for anything, an unstoppable force that would kill everything in his way.

Chapter 27

"This is my own quiet spot," Reeve told her.

Libby looked out at the stretch of greyness beyond the two merlons he'd pointed to. They were standing on top of the battlement and it wasn't until she recognised Sunray Bay in the distance that she realised how far she'd come in a matter of days. Her mind skimmed over all the things she'd seen within that same matter of days that she never would have thought could be true.

But now it was her world.

She shivered at the notion.

"Are you cold?" he asked, touching her shoulder with a look of concern etched onto his face.

She shook her head, feeling somewhat melancholy - and, yet, strangely safe. Reeve gave off no trace of threat that she could detect.

"Please, sit down," he said, pointing to the wall. His voice was rich and frothy like a latte.

Nodding, she moved to the nearest merlon and made to climb up onto it. He held out his hand and, as she accepted his genteel offer, she noted how firm and smooth his hand was in hers. For some reason she imagined he'd be cold, but to her surprise he was as warm as any normal person should be.

Once she was perched on the merlon she dangled her feet down the side of the outer wall and lent forward to look down. She wasn't fond of heights and neither was she afraid of them, but the sheer drop made her take a sharp intake of breath.

"It's a contradiction, isn't it?" he said. In a flash he was sitting next to her, his thigh touching hers.

"What is?"

"That…" His outstretched arm traced along the line of the horizon, drawing her attention to the scenery beyond. "This view. It's horribly stunning, beautifully grim."

Beautifully grim. Her thoughts instantly wandered to Grim. She wondered if he was worried about her. Whether he'd sleep while she was gone or whether he'd fret, unable to rest. Secretly she hoped the latter.

"Hmmm." She nodded her head in agreement. There *was* something captivating about the harshness of The Grey Dust Bowl. It was like nothing she'd ever seen before. A black beach without a sea. Instead of grains of sand it had flakes of ash that crumbled underfoot. The light breeze moved the surface ash around in swarms of insect-looking waves. She dreaded to think what it would be like in high winds. Her shoes and the hem of her jeans were deeply ingrained with black soot from walking in the dustbowl thus far; she wondered if by the end of her journey the blackness might be embedded in her insides.

After a few moments of mutual silence, she braved a glance to her left. He was sitting so close she could feel his hair tickling her bare arm. When he turned to face her she could see darker bands of colour circling his pale irises. Oddly, she thought the black eye-liner surrounding his eyes suited him. It lent a harshness to his otherwise gentle complexion, which was smooth and poreless and almost feminine-looking. His face was a striking work of symmetry, and she was shocked at how beautiful he really was.

At around the same height as her, he was very lean with light muscle definition showing through the fabric of his black top (which he wore like a second skin). Broad shoulders and a tapered waist gave him a triangular body shape. He looked like a gymnast, all lithe and fit. In a display of equal brilliance, Libby found his mass of chunky white hair nothing short of fascinating. There was just so much of it and it splayed right down his back, tailbone long.

She watched as his eyes boldly searched her own face, lingering on her eyes for a while then tarrying about her

183

mouth. He smiled, as though he knew how spellbinding she must find him, and her eyes widened in shock when she saw how pointed his canine teeth were. He was an arresting creature and she just couldn't take her eyes off him, try as she might. And the more she looked, the more she was stupefied that she couldn't find anything flawed about him. Nothing at all. There were no scratches or scars or blemishes that she could see. And it was because of this searching for a fault, *any* fault, she found she just couldn't look away. His perfection was hypnotic.

"So tell me," he said at last, his voice thick and warm. "Who are you? And where did you come from?"

She finally broke eye contact and looked away, concentrating hard on the horizon instead. "I already told you, I'm Libby."

He laughed, a hearty sound with no hint of reproach. In fact, she found that he had a very calming effect on her overall. Sitting with him on top of Sun Castle was one of the most tranquil moments she'd had since arriving in Sunray Bay - which was odd.

"Yes you did. But *who is* Libby?"

Shrugging her shoulders she looked down at her hands and tried to think of an answer. She wasn't sure who Libby Hood was herself anymore. Picking distractedly at the already-chipped red polish on her fingernails whilst she thought, she suddenly felt embarrassed about how her once-tidy hands were now thick with dirt. Black was embedded beneath her nails and in the grooves of her knuckles. Ashamed, she stuffed them underneath her thighs and sat on them.

"She's just a poor sod who died. Aren't we all?" she said, without enthusiasm. "And all she has left is the clothes on her back and a strange will to survive."

A sudden and robust breeze ruffled through her hair, lifting it up and whipping it in his face. He made no attempt to move. Instead he just closed his eyes and smiled, his seashell-white lips closed, concealing predatory teeth. When Libby tamed her hair and pulled it to the side, his neat eyebrows furrowed (making them no less neat) and he said, "What about, er, what's his name…Gimp?"

She cocked one of her own eyebrows, warning him not to go further down that line of insult. "His name is *Grim*," she said. "What about him?"

"Who is he? What is he to you?"

"It's complicated," she said, her voice curt.

"I take it he isn't blind?" he quizzed. "I mean, the way he leapt at me like that…"

"*Blind?* Why would you think…oh. The sunglasses? No. He's not blind."

"So what's that about?"

"It's complicated." She shuffled about on her backside, the stone wall beginning to feel as much a pain in the arse as Reeve's probing questions about Grim. "Let's talk about something else."

"Okay." He brought his feet up and hooked the heels of his boots on the edge of the wall. Leaning back and resting on his hands, his face was beyond her peripheral vision. "Where are you from?"

"You mean, before I died?" she asked, without turning to look at him.

"Yes, where did you live before you passed on to this dreadful place?"

She smiled, that was one thing they agreed on.

"A little place called New Town," she said, looking into the distance at Sunray Bay. She imagined that if it hadn't been destroyed she'd be able to see the lights of Prospect Point Fun Fair twinkling now - especially the slow dancing ones of the ferris wheel. Recalling the cafés and the shops of the seafront, and the seediness of Knickerbocker Gloria's and the nightclubs in the backstreets, she decided that Sunray Bay and New Town were nothing alike. "You've probably never heard of it though?"

Nobody tended to have a clue where New Town was, even people who lived in the same county. It was an insignificant little village in the north of England that didn't even have a cash point or a Chinese takeaway. As far as

185

Libby was aware, its original name was Newton but over the years it had mutated into New Town - whether to jazz it up to make it sound a little more up and coming or just through sheer laziness of the tongue, Libby couldn't be sure. But she *was* sure that Reeve wouldn't have heard of it.

As expected, he shook his head. "Is that on Earth?"

She gave a small hiccup of laughter and looked at him in disbelief. "Of course. Where else?"

He sat forward again, dangling his feet over the edge. His pupils dilated with quiet excitement, the paler part of his irises now the same width as the darker rim. "Excellent. Do you know it well?"

"New Town? There's not much *to* know."

"No, I mean Earth. Do you know Earth well?"

Casting him a bemused look, unsure as to whether he was being serious or not, she said, "Not half as much as I would've liked. I mean, I did a little bit of traveling here and there - but I'm certainly no David Attenborough."

"David who?"

"Never mind." She rolled her eyes. "So where are you from?"

"I'm from Earth too."

"So why the hell are we getting so excited about me being from Earth when you are too?"

His face grew thoughtful, his lips pursing and his blue eyes narrowing in their black outlines. "Because I don't remember what it's like," he said in a near whisper.

"I don't understand. How can't you remember?"

"I was forced to leave Earth many, *many* years ago..."

"Really? How many years is many, *many* years ago?" She looked dubious.

He made a weary puffing sound through his mouth and then looked up to the stars. "It's hard to say *exactly*."

"Well just guesstimate. I won't penalise you if you're a year or two out, you know," she said. "I'm not marking you on precision."

His eyes lit up with merriment. "Okay. Somewhere in the region of three thousand years.

"Three thousand years? Shut up!" Whistling in wonderment, she didn't know whether to feel sceptical or impressed. "So that must mean that's how old you are too?"

His shoulder brushed against hers as he laughed at her response. "That's still relatively young for a Blōd Vampyre, I'll have you know. And besides, I'm even older than that. I'm probably just past the four thousand year mark."

"Flipping hell, that's not young in my books," she laughed. "But fascinating all the same."

"Not really," he said, indifference ruining his smile. "It's been tragically boring for the most part."

"*Boring?*" she exclaimed. "But you must have seen so much!"

"Yes, but my brain can only store so much at the forefront. Most of my memories from earlier years are so fuzzy around the edges they've become impossible to access, let alone define. I dare say, half the time, I'm not even sure I know the difference between *true* memories and mere fantasies - you know, stories that I've elaborated and glorified in my own head. I'm almost certain that my clearest furthermost memories have been dressed up with a good splash of romanticism, and, likewise, the worst ones worsened with a dose of despair. I find perception of bygone days is not a trustworthy thing for a Blōd Vampyre - but, of course, my mother, the all-knowing-all-seeing despot, would no doubt tell you differently."

"That sounds sort of…I don't know, *depressing?*"

Reeve laughed, but the cheerfulness didn't reach his eyes. She suspected she was right.

"So you will have been around a thousand years old when you died?" she said.

"No." He shook his head. "I'm not dead yet. I was sent here - *forced* to leave Earth."

"But why? And who by?"

The moon was almost above them now. Its white face, speckled with blue craters that were the same colour as Reeve's eyes, illuminating everything roundabout and

187

making the grey ashes on the ground below them glow Prussian blue.

"I was ordered here, along with numerous other Blōd Vampyres, by Casiphia our moon goddess. We're her people, and at that time she saw fit to relocate us in order to keep The Isle of the Ignoble Dead…well…*ignoble*."

"Isle of the Ig*what* Dead?"

"Back then the island wasn't split up into different sections as it is now. There was no Sunray Bay and there was no dustbowl either - it was all known simply as The Isle of the Ignoble Dead."

"The Isle of the Ignoble *Dead* - but you weren't dead…" she said. "I don't get it. Why did she send you?"

"Casiphia is creator of all nocturnal peoples and she considered us to be her most powerful resource. Fundamentally, we were supposed to be her revenge." Looking up to the moon, he said, "She can be the most graceful and elegant of ladies if treated with respect, or so I hear, but when she feels disparaged she can be the most cold-hearted, hot-tempered bitch you're ever likely to encounter. Even worse than my mother."

Libby copied Reeve and looked up to the moon, wondering what a moon goddess herself looked like. "Who scorned her?" she asked.

"It's quite a long story," he said. "Would you like to hear a shortened version for now?"

She nodded her head, eyes wide with expectation. She loved mythology and folklore.

"Her husband, Blain, the sun god, fathered three illegitimate sons with a clerk of his called Xanthe. It's said that he was all-out smitten by her exquisite beauty and gentle nature. Casiphia, who is beautiful in her own right, was oft said to be too busy to make time for him. I mean, sometimes a whole month would go by before they would even see each other. So for many years Blain and Xanthe were lovers. They kept the affair secret, and Casiphia was none the wiser. However one day when Casiphia was walking in the gardens

188

of Gemma, she chanced upon the Chattering Daws of Koo She and they told her everything."

"Who are the Chattering Daws of Koo She?"

"Jackdaws," he said. "Jackdaws who like to gossip. They have no allegiance to the sun and no allegiance to the moon. In fact they have no allegiance to anybody or anything - they just like to make their mouths go."

"If they have no allegiance then how could Casiphia be certain they were telling the truth?"

"Ah but the Chattering Daws of Koo She must always tell the truth when eye contact is made. Casiphia looked right into their eyes when they told her of Blain's adultery. Legend would have it that such was her fury, that's what turned their eyes silver."

"So what did she do? About her husband and Xanthe, that is."

"Well she was more than a little bit angry, but rather than unleash her wrath upon either of them directly, she sought instead to wound them even more deeply. So she killed their three sons."

"Wow, that's harsh - I mean, to take it out on the children…" Libby cringed.

"By this time they were no longer children," he explained. "They were fully grown men."

"But still…" She shrugged her shoulders. "Innocent parties nonetheless."

He nodded his head and pulled his mouth to the side in a *yeah, I suppose so* kind of way. "Anyway, Blain resurrected all three of them and hid them here on this island, but it wasn't long before Casiphia found out. She swore they would never be anything but dishonourable bastards and that they would forever walk in her shadow. She vowed to shine the light of her moon down upon them endlessly."

"But the moon doesn't shine here endlessly," Libby argued.

"Indeed, daylight reaches here because Blain injected some of his sun's essence into the very core of the island. It acts like a lure, drawing the sun to it each day - it's his only

189

connection with his sons. So that's when she gathered her most powerful night-walkers and set us here - we were supposed to extinguish the sun's essence."

Libby remembered all that Leif-Mestler had told her about the Sun Watch in the caves below The Grey Dust Bowl; her mouth was slightly agape in fascination. "So how come you didn't?"

"It just never happened, it was written off as being an impossible task. My mother said that all of the other elders that were sent here died whilst trying to do it. She was the only surviving elder - left alone to take care of me and the other twenty young fledglings."

She studied his face. "Why do I detect doubt in your voice?"

He shrugged his shoulders, his arm resting against hers. "You do? Perhaps it's because I doubt everything my mother tells me."

"I take it you two don't get on very well."

This time he laughed raucously, dimples in his cheeks making him look boyish.

"She detests me vehemently," he said, between breaths. "And me? I don't like her and I certainly wouldn't trust her as far as I could throw her. Actually, that's not true - I trust her even less than that."

"That's sad," she said. When he didn't say anything further, she asked, "So what happened to Blain's and Xanthe's sons? Are they still here?"

He pointed out to the horizon. "Zephinay, Peroos and Hoof are somewhere out there - lost to the Turpis Sea."

She couldn't make out the sea, the horizon was a black band. "How long have they been gone?"

"Countless years. They disappeared not long after me and my kind arrived here."

She sat up straight, a thought occurring to her. "*Sun Castle* - is this theirs?"

"Yes, we moved here when they failed to return from their seaward voyage. Before then we lived in caves further west of here. When the ash from Spewing Mouth began to spread, the people of Sun Castle and its surrounding settlements moved further towards the coast. Sun Castle was left to rot - so we claimed it as our own. But now, my mother has other plans."

"Oh?"

"She wants to light the lighthouse lantern to guide Zephinay, Peroos and Hoof home."

"But why? Surely they'd kick you out of their castle if they came back?"

"She doesn't care about Sun Castle. None of us do. All we want is to go home."

"Home?"

He laid his hand on top of hers. The contact made her jump as though he'd given her a static shock. "Yes, Libby, we're going home. We're going back to Earth."

Chapter 28

"Why do you think they were coming here?" Lilea asked.

Gin lay on the oak table amidst strewn playing cards and pots of burning incense. Thin trails of blue smoke wisped upwards to hang in the air, filling it with a musky bitter-sweetness. Her eyes remained closed as she inhaled deeply, her face peaceful. She was so relaxed and still, she looked like an alabaster figurine set on top of a tomb.

"I've no idea," she said, her voice low and unconcerned. "They're a strange pair though. Hopefully Rembrae will remember what it is the girl smells of."

"It was an odd smell, I thought," Lilea said, kneading her thumbs around the silken skin of Gin's temples. "Not offensive or unpleasant by any means - just *odd*."

"I thought she smelt lovely," Brinda said. "A bit like cake mixture." She was holding Gin's leg aloft, squeezing the arch of her foot with a pressure that was enough to stroke away the tensions but not enough to make Gin jump through the roof. They often pampered each other - and tonight it was Gin's turn to be indulged.

"Well I've never smelled that smell on anybody before," Lilea said, now patting her fingertips across Gin's forehead in an attempt to emulate the feel of raindrops.

"Apart from someone who's been eating cakes!" Mord said, flashing Brinda a wink.

Gin's eyes flicked open and she looked thoughtful for a moment. "I thought the man was stranger than the girl," she said. "Rembrae said he was nothing. And she's absolutely right - I couldn't smell or sense anything from him. He makes me more uncomfortable than the girl."

"I agree," Van remarked. "As much as the girl tried to hide it, I could sense her fear. But with the man, I couldn't pick anything up from him - not even the faintest waft of unease. It was as though he wasn't even there."

"Do you think he's some kind of dark sorcerer or magician?" Brinda asked.

"It's always possible," Mord replied. "Though highly unlikely."

"And why is that?" Gin challenged.

"Well, how many dark sorcerers or magicians have you ever known?"

"None, which is precisely the point. He could very well be one which would explain why he's not familiar to us. And there's another thing that bugs me. They weren't heading west away from Sunray Bay - they were walking east. What if there's somewhere else on the island that we don't know about?" She jumped up into a sitting position, her eyes wide and her body tense with excitement. As she swung her legs around she kicked one of the incense burners over with her left foot.

Mord stooped to retrieve it from the floor and scoffed, "Impossible, Rembrae would know about it if that were the case."

"Would she?" Gin surprised herself with her remark, but since she'd had the heated conversation with Reeve she'd been doing a lot of internal questioning and thinking. As much as she'd like to believe that he was nothing more than a pessimistic paranoid fool, she had given his comments some thought. He believed Rembrae was leading them all a merry dance, and even though it pained her to think ill of the Queen, she'd opened her mind to the possibility.

"There's only one way to find out," Mord said.

Each of the five roommates looked hesitant.

"You mean speak to Rembrae about it?" Lilea asked.

"No," Gin said, springing to her feet. "That's not what she means."

"Oh? Well what does she mean? Where are you going?"

With a devilish grin, Gin tugged at her bunched up hair so that it sat more comfortably on her head, and said, "I'm going back down into the dungeon to see if he can pull a rabbit from behind my ear."

"You're going to talk to the prisoners?"

"Yes." She had her hand on the door already. "Who's coming with me?"

Back through the darkened maze of corridors all five of them headed to the dungeon. When they reached the staircase, Gin held a finger up to her lips and hushed them all. Tilting her head and cupping her right ear with her hand, she said, "Shhh, we might hear them talking."

"I can't hear a thing," Lilea announced after a few moments had passed.

"Me neither," Mord agreed.

"They're probably sleeping," Gin said. "Come on."

In a commotion of white limbs and floating fabric, they all made their way down the steps, their bare feet slapping on the smooth stone, echoing loudly.

"They'll be awake now," Van laughed. "The noise we're making is enough to raise the dead."

But when they reached the bottom they were greeted by nothing but mangled iron bars lying on the floor. The torch on the wall burned low, showing the empty cell beyond the heap of heavy metal on the floor.

"How's that even possible?" Brinda asked, her voice high with astonishment. "I mean, seriously…?"

"Shitting hell," Gin gasped. "I'm buggered if I know. And worse still - one of us is going to have to tell Rembrae."

Chapter 29

Friday, 8:43pm: The Dungeons, Sun Castle, The Grey Dust Bowl

He'd lost count (and hope) after his sixth attempt but after what seemed like a hundred more, the bars moved in their stone foundations. Breathless whilst holding his right shoulder, he stood still for a moment because the searing pain from the jolted joint sent shocks of hurt right down to his fingertips. His face contorted as he waited for the intensity to subside, yet amidst the feeling of physical exertion and blinding agony he felt hope returning. The cell bars were finally starting to give. Bending over double he put his hands on his thighs and tried to regulate his breathing.

Having psyched himself up for another go he let out a vein-popping roar and lunged forward, hammering the framework of iron again with his immense bodyweight. As with all previous attempts his shoulder bore the brunt of the collision and he might well have cried out in pained defeat had the rectangular panel of metal bars not toppled forward and hit the stone floor with a resounding *clang*. Instead he wheezed, "Fuck yeah."

For a moment he panted and clutched his upper arm, pressing his fingertips deep into his deltoid and massaging around his collarbone too - it felt like every bone in his body was jarred, but the pain was worst there. Without delaying too long he knocked his sunglasses back into place and stepped from the cell; negotiating his feet through the bars he made his way to the steps.

Firstly he was determined to find Libby, and if Prince of Spandex had done anything untoward to her he made a resolve that he would kick seven kinds of shit out of him. In fact, the mere thought of the vampire made his top lip curl upwards. His snarl was just about audible.

Then secondly, he was going to see if…

To make sure that Della and Daisy weren't there at the castle. His aching body tensed at the thought, it was not something he looked forward to.

Making his way up the staircase he clung to the wall, his left shoulder grazing the stonework where he used it to guide himself in the dark. He trod with purpose but all the while he was alert, listening for hints that anybody might be close by. But he heard nothing except the mournful singing of the wind that haunted the castle's corridors and passageways, leaking in through window gaps, door chinks and wall cracks. It was a lonely, sorrowful sound which, in turn, made him think of his own body - an empty shell just like the castle. He wondered if the hollows where his soul had once lived echoed just as sombrely; void cavities that denied him all-ending peace singing a curse of forever-ness.

At the top of the stairs he took a moment to decide which way to go. Looking right and then left, and right again, he expected he'd end up getting lost anyway so he headed left. The passageway stretched forth into a blackened vacuum of uncertainty. As he passed empty chambers along the way he wondered how many of the castle's rooms were unused - and how many Blōd Vampyres actually lived there. He realised they could be watching him right now, hanging over him in shrouds of fog maybe. He remembered Thad Daniels of The Ordinaries telling him how they could change into fog and bats and wolves - but he wasn't sure what else. Whatever their morphing capabilities, it was sneaky-arsed trickery that he could do without.

His pace quickened when he felt a rush of warm air on his bare skin. Turning a corner, he saw an arched doorway straight ahead of him. The door lay open and beyond it he could see a courtyard that was lit by the moon's grainy silver light. *About frigging time*, he thought. Another light breeze rushed in to greet him, but instead of bringing a refreshing waft of the outdoors it brought with it a fetid stench of decay and body odour. The smell was so bad it hit him as solidly as a slap in the face. It made his eyes water and he could almost taste its tang. As he resisted the urge to retch, the source of the stink stepped into the doorway, blocking the view to the courtyard and bringing with it an even more powerful, concentrated stench. It was a person whose combined smell was of bad breath, dirty hair, dried-up piss, human excrement and rotted meat. Gagging, Grim coughed and moved backwards.

The new arrival stood still, unflinching. If he had to hazard a guess Grim would say the person before him was a man. His hair, what little there was on his shiny scab-encrusted scalp, stuck to his scrawny neck like tendrils of dead seaweed. It didn't appear as though he could close his mouth because the flesh and muscles of his lower face had wasted away, leaving grey jawbone exposed. His entire body was emaciated and sinewy. Skinny arms with clunky elbow joints hung by his sides and folds of hoary skin hung loose from his upper arms, a tell-tale sign that he must have had a healthier body at some point in his existence. Now his body was covered in purple welts and black scabs, open sores and yellow pus. His nose looked like an open wound with no nasal structure and no top lip. Yet however horrific all of this was, none of it was the worst aspect. Grim was far more unsettled by the man's eyes - seeing, but unseeing in their total whiteness. They looked exactly like his own.

The man was a zombie and Grim knew this was what he should look like, yet through some twist of fate he didn't. Silently he prayed to whatever god might be listening that Della and Daisy didn't share the same fate as this man. It was too awful a thought.

The zombie edged forward and expelled a low groaning noise from the depths of his stomach, which brought with it a new nauseating stink like stagnant water. Grim choked back a cough and pitched forward to grab the man around the neck. The cold, moist skin of the fevered dead man slipped in his hands as he yanked the man's head down sharp. The sound of snapping bones was no more significant than brittle twigs breaking underfoot. Grim released his grip, wiped his hands down the fronts of his trousers and let the limp body slump to the ground. Stepping over it and heading outside, he hoped the poor bastard had at last found peace.

Striding out into the cobbled courtyard he breathed in great gulps of fresh air, trying to rid his lungs of the contaminated stench of the zombie lest it taint him and trigger the benign virus within himself to become a malignant wasting disease. Movement in the far right side of the courtyard immediately caught his attention, but the slow cumbersome gait of the silhouetted figure suggested it was another zombie rather than a Blōd Vampyre. Leaning against the outer wall of the main building, he kept to the shadows and looked up to the sky, thinking. As he did so he saw two figures sitting up on the battlement wall, and even though they were silhouettes under the luminous spell of moonshine he could tell without doubt that it was Libby and the vampire. Relief gushed over him in a welcome torrent. He'd found her so easily, and she looked safe and well.

Scanning the courtyard he saw that the north tower stood nearest to the section of the battlement where she was. Creeping stealthily towards it, he intended to reach her that way, sticking close to the walls and using the shadows as he went. Every now and then low groans of the undying dead scuttled across the courtyard to chew at his nerves, eerie and disturbing calls from their paper-dry throats. *It's not them, it can't be,* he told himself, *Della and Daisy can't be here!*

Although the entrance to the tower was a gaping black hole, unsheathed and door-less and leading to more uncertainty, he stepped over the threshold with a sense of relief that he was leaving the noises and the things in the courtyard behind. Running his fingers along worn stone and allowing his eyes to adjust, he saw light filtering through a slit window above which highlighted a spiral staircase that followed the circular contour of the tower. He took steady strides, sticking to the outer wall where the steps were wider and more accommodating for his size twelve feet. He knew he must be nearing the battlement when he could see ghostly shafts of moonlight filtering more strongly into the stair passage. The stairs continued up and onwards into whatever chamber lay above but Grim halted when he reached an arched opening that led out into the night. Taking a deep breath he laid his back flat to the wall; craning his neck he peered out of the opening to gauge the situation outside. And nothing could have prepared him for what he saw…

Libby and the vampire were sitting close together on the battlement wall. They had their backs turned to him yet despite his limited vantage point it was plain to see that they were kissing. And what made it inherently worse was that Libby wasn't struggling or resisting. She was actually *sharing* the kiss.

He stumbled backwards as though he'd taken a punch to the stomach. *You fucking idiot*, he growled to himself. *Why did you let her in?*

Chapter 30

Libby's entire body jolted.

"*What?*" she gasped excitedly. "You're going back to Earth? You mean…you mean there's a way to get back?"

Reeve studied her reaction for a moment, his blue eyes more sincere than she could ever have imagined considering he was a vampire. Light amusement dimpled his cheeks, as he said, "Yes there's a way back.

"But how?"

He looked thoughtful for a moment, as though deciding whether or not he should tell her. Eventually, having decided that he would, he said, "Have you heard of Sunray Bay's weighing scales?"

She nodded, having a vague recollection of the conversation she'd had in the kitchen of Knickerbocker Gloria's just days ago. Gloria had told her about the scales then, about how they were used for weighing souls so those suitably redeemed could pass on to whatever lay beyond Sunray Bay. In the same conversation her own soul issue had been highlighted - not that she had that issue now. When Rufus had died he'd taken it with him. Now she was completely soulless and the weighing scales were of no use to her at all.

"We'll be using them to get back home," he said.

"So you have an appointment with the courthouse?"

He laughed. "No. Gin and I stole them from the courthouse last night." His grin was a shade off being smug.

"But how will you make them work? If you're not dead, how can you redeem yourself? Is it possible?"

"We have the blueprints. Thackery, one of my fledgling brothers, has been studying them. If anybody can get them to work, he can."

She looked dubious.

"Without meaning to sound condescending at all," he said, raising his hands, "The scales probably aren't what you imagine they are. Their intricate design is not solely intended to usher people off to heaven once they've proved they can be star pupils in the lessons of life, morality and etiquette. Granted, that was what Godfrey Manning was keen on using them for - but, no, they're much more elaborate than that. They're a portal between life and death itself, between planets and universes and space and time and…you get the gist. A piece of apparatus that could give us a greater awareness of other civilisations, they have *so* much potential, can you imagine?"

"And you have the scales and the blueprints to do all of this?" she asked incredulously.

His eyes glinted and he flashed a mischievous grin.

"That's madness," she said. "So…what do they look like, these scales?"

He shrugged his shoulders. "Just like your average set of weighing scales, I guess."

"So, basically, you propose to get back to Earth on a set of bathroom scales?" She couldn't stifle a snigger. "Now that I would love to see."

Reeve laughed.

"Anyway…" she eyed him with suspicion. "If you and Gin acquired the weighing scales last night and Thackery has already been studying the blueprints, then how come you haven't gone already?"

He groaned. "We have my mother to thank for the hold up," he said. "She has it in her head that we must navigate Blain's sons back to shore. In fact, she means for me to go back into Sunray Bay this evening to source a bulb for the bloody lighthouse lantern. When my search proves fruitless, which it will because I have no intention of going, she had better just forget about that part of her plan because sooner or later we're going to have Civilian Court Guardians launching an attack. They're doubtless searching high and low for the weighing scales and it's just a matter of time until the finger of blame lands upon Sun Castle."

"What about Casiphia?" she said. "Won't she be seriously pissed off when she finds out you've gone back to Earth without her consent?"

He wafted his hand dismissively. "We haven't heard from her since the turn of the last millennia. For all we know she's forgotten about us."

"So tell me," she said. "If you can't even remember Earth, what's your reason for wanting to go back there?"

He looked up at the sky, the stars a spray of white on barely-black. "Because I crave the freedom that Earth offers. As I understand it's richer in variety than it is here, in a whole array of contexts. I want to feel the unbound sense of exploration without being stifled by limitation. I want to enjoy the diversity that it has to offer, culturally and climatically. There're so many different reasons for me to want to go and just as many for me to want to leave here."

"Do the other Blōd Vampyres share your views?

"In what way do you mean?"

"Well from what you've just said, I think your reasons sound perfectly acceptable, but I can't help but wonder if a heartier food supply might be a big factor, you know?"

"You could well be right. I won't lie - we do need a healthier diet. The others follow my mother's lead, they do as she says, and what I do sense is that she wants to go back to Earth because she's…well, erm…because she's dying."

"Oh I'm sorry."

"Don't be," he said. "I'm not."

"But how will going back to Earth help her? Wouldn't she just end up back here again anyway?"

"My mother is cunning above all else," he said, shaking his head. "I've no doubt whatsoever that there will be method in her madness - but, alas, I don't know what it is. She hasn't exactly told me she's dying, I just know it. It would piss her off if she knew that I know, because it'd be the one thing she hasn't been able to hide from me." A devious grin crept to his lovely mouth. "And maybe I'll tell her that I know soon. I'll describe how I can see her fear, and not just the fleeting look that haunts her eyes lately but I'll tell her about the black mesh-like aura that hangs over her like Death's parasol. I'll ask her if she can feel it weighing down on her."

"She's still your mother though…"

"I don't need reminding," he said, his body becoming stiff. "When I return to Earth I never want to see her again. And I don't care how easy or difficult her demise might be - there'll be no words of comfort for her here. In fact, I never want to set eyes on another Blōd Vampyre for as long I live - however long that shall be. My mother is Queen of the Blōd Vampyres, but I'm no prince, Libby. I said it to impress you, I'm ashamed to say. I know it sounds foolish and childish perhaps, but it's true. I claim no title over a race that I've grown to hate."

She gasped. "But why do you feel that way?"

"I've experienced nothing but heartlessness and spite from my people." He lifted a strand of red hair that trailed over her shoulder. Running the length of it between his thumb and forefinger, his eyes widened and glittered as though he was sifting rubies through his fingers. Libby didn't move. She sensed an unequivocal change in his mood.

"Just so you know, this isn't a sob story. I don't mean for you to pity me," he said, his voice soft. "That's not what I want at all. What I want is a normal life. As normal a life as I'm capable of having, anyhow."

"And how do you define normal?" she asked. He let go of the strand of hair and looked at her curiously. "I'm just not sure it even exists."

"You're probably right, normal is a word that ignorant folk use, isn't it? I hope I didn't come across as being ignorant?"

"No," she said. "I wasn't implying that you might be ignorant, I just wanted to understand more what it is you want."

203

"What I want is to be more like you and your kind, Libby. That's what I would class as normal."

Christ, he doesn't know the half of it, she thought with a sense of irony.

"I want to experience the closeness that is so often shared by humans and their families, but most of all I'd like to find a companion. Someone who will let me see the sun through their own eyes. Someone who will love and care for me." He dipped his eyes and smiled sheepishly. "Does all of that sound sad?"

"No, not at all," she said.

His eyes fixed on hers and she could see absolute conviction there, the irises pale like the shallows of a tropical sea. Enticing, warm and beautiful, yet the longer she lingered the deeper and more dangerous they became - dragging her into some underlying emotional torrent. She imagined she could swim and then drown in them, and at that moment she was treading water because she just couldn't look away. She wondered if this was what Finnbane Krain had referred to when he'd said that vampires were masters of persuasion, because there was something irresistibly persuasive about Reeve's eyes right now. It felt as though something subliminal was happening to her senses, and yet she couldn't summon the power to look away in order to protect herself. She just couldn't break the spell he had over her.

"Why did you bring me here?" she asked, all too aware that his face was now closer.

"I just wanted to talk."

"What about?"

"I don't know. I just wanted you to listen."

"And I've listened. Did I make a good agony aunt?"

"An agony what?"

"Never mind."

"It's just that, well…it's like this, I…I think I've dreamt about you before."

"Really?" She blushed and fumbled with her fingers, sensing an awkward moment. "Was it a nightmare?"

"No. Far from it. You were the one to describe the sun to me."

"Oh. How did I do?"

"Not well, every time you started to speak I'd wake up."

"So how did you know that I could describe it?"

"I had faith in you. I *have* faith in you."

"You *have* faith in me? Oh no, you're very much mistaken." She shook her head profusely, her eyes still affixed to his. "It's very flattering, but she couldn't be me."

The light blue of his eyes dulled a shade or two. "Are you sure?"

"Yes, I'm sure," she said, her voice a trance-like monotone.

The blue-ness within his eyes moved; throbbing and spinning. And the darker rim pulsated, growing wider and then becoming thinner. She could do nothing but stare. Her mouth was agape and she edged forward to get even closer still. The detail was mesmeric, it was as though his eyes were literally pulling her in.

"Unless of course…" he said.

"Uh-huh?"

"Unless of course you'd like to think on it?"

"To think on what?"

"Whether or not you'd like to go back to Earth with me."

And with that she was swept away, her body serene as his lips closed over hers. Somewhere deep within she kicked and fought but her body paid no heed as she sank deeper. She felt fingers combing through her hair, gentle but fervent. Warm and *different*. Sharp teeth scraped the skin of her bottom lip, a strange and not unpleasant sensation. None of it was quite right - but at the same time, it was so right. Her mind was swimming and she was blinded by a vortex of muddied perception and bright colours, and suddenly she couldn't remember where she was exactly. The only thing that made sense was that something wasn't right. Something was too different.

Warm probing lips carried on tasting her, yet she couldn't fathom why that should arouse a sense of wrongness. It felt so nice, but then the lips weren't - *cold*. And for some reason they should be. They should be cold and refreshing like raspberry ripple ice-cream.

She reached out to stay the hands that were stroking her hair and found that they weren't right either. They weren't cold enough.

They weren't cold and they didn't belong to...

It was coming back to her. She could almost remember. This person who was embracing her right now wasn't...

What?

Wasn't *Grim!*

Pushing herself backwards, she broke the spell and gasped, "*No!*"

Chapter 31

Friday, 8:59pm: North Tower, Sun Castle, The Grey Dust Bowl

He couldn't think straight. Couldn't see past the maelstrom of rage and confusion that pounded and throbbed red behind his eyes. Libby kissing the vampire, he just couldn't comprehend it. There was no denying what he'd seen either; there could be no innocent misunderstanding.

And what perhaps riled him the most was that upon seeing her with the vampire like that he'd felt - *jealous*. Jealousy was nothing but a sneering emotion that betrayed his wits and completely fucked with his head. Jealousy was out of his control.

He *hated* that he felt jealous.

She'd spent days chasing after him and leading him on, yet now it appeared she was throwing it all back in his face in favour of a vampire who wore skinnier jeans than she did. And although it was entirely plausible, somehow he couldn't accept the thrill of the chase had worn off so soon. He'd seen the look on her face when they were together - the look he'd tried to ignore. But after much persistence, in the end she'd worn his defences down.

It was true - he'd met his match in her.

He liked how she wasn't overwhelmed by him. She wasn't fazed by his potentially-intimidating stature, his bad-temperedness, his mood swings…or even his past. She'd stuck around, actively making it difficult for him to resist her.

Okay, so it wasn't as though they were in a relationship. Neither of them had to answer to the other. She wasn't his any more than he was hers. But still, there were boundaries. Lines that shouldn't be crossed once an interest had been mutually sparked - which is what he thought had happened.

Not trusting himself to confront her, he edged back down the stairs of the north tower. As much as he wanted to beat the living hell out of the vampire and then throttle him with his own hairband, he just couldn't bear to see *her* or hear any excuses. Feeling hurt and betrayed, he also didn't want her to see what she'd done to him. The whole episode and subsequent pangs of jealousy had left him feeling inadequate somehow, and this made his anger reach a new peak. As he replayed the scene in his head once more he decided that the short-lived bout of emotional weakness he'd indulged himself in over the past few days was now over. From now on he was going it alone again.

Emerging from the north tower into the courtyard he crossed over towards the stables on the opposite side. The cobblestones on the ground were raised and aligned so that they ran in a circular design. They reminded him of a great big tortoise shell and at that moment, as he walked across its back, they were tinged a reddish hue. Looking up, he was surprised to see that the moon was dusky pink and the black sky was tinged deepest carmine at the edges. There was an overall bloodiness to The Grey Dust Bowl that matched the colour of his anger.

Red sky at night, I hear their plight, he said to himself with a newfound determination. Clenching his fists and tightening his jaw, he was set to kill every single zombie that lived within the castle's grounds. Then he was going to leave Sun Castle and head west.

Alone.

Chapter 32

She could sense Gin's dread as soon as the young vampire stepped into The Great Hall. Although she was treading softly across the stone floor in a controlled and sneaking manner, Rembrae could hear her approaching. *Silly girl, have you learnt nothing about me. Nobody creeps up on me unheard.*

"What is it, Ginnifer?" she called out, her voice hoarse and dry. The size of the hall and heat within it seemed to absorb the words, making her sound old and feeble. *I am old and feeble,* she thought, irritably.

She heard the thump of Gin's heart quicken, trebling in pace, and she knew something was wrong.

"Your Highness," the young vampire said when she reached the foot of the throne. Rembrae didn't open her eyes but she could imagine Gin bowing her head. "As you requested, I locked the prisoners in the dungeon…"

"But? I sense a but…"

Gin's nervous gulp of disquiet sounded as loud to Rembrae as it would have had she been standing right next to her.

"But…they're not there now."

The wolf's eyes opened and she saw a wide-eyed, worried expression on the pretty fledgling's face. "And were you worried about telling me that?"

Gin's face flushed pink and she nodded her head. With a small cough she said, "Yes, Your Highness."

"My sweet girl," Rembrae said. "There's no need to worry. You did as I asked, what more could you do?"

The young vampire shrugged her shoulders, her expression somewhat unsure.

209

"Remember, there are lots of us and only two of them. Do you really think it's worth getting your smallclothes in a twist over?"

"But the weighing scales, Your Highness, what if…"

"Don't worry about them, they're quite safe," Rembrae said. She stood up, attempting to neutralise the expression of pain on her face as her hind quarters sagged with sharp, pinching jolts that froze her arthritic hips. "Lilea is fond of hide and seek, is she not?"

Gin nodded, and if she'd noted the Queen's discomfort she didn't let on.

"Good, that means she must be good at it. There'll be no hiding tonight though, you're all seeking. And make sure you do it before sunrise."

"Very well, Your Highness." Gin bowed her head low and turned to leave.

Rembrae waited until the young vampire was facing away before she slid herself from the throne. Using front paws that were sturdier than the back ones, she pulled herself forward so that her hind legs dragged from the cushioned seat. She winced as they landed on the floor. "Oh, and Ginnifer?"

"Yes, Your Highness?" The young vampire turned around. The glow from the fire outlined her supple figure and basked her in a warm honey-coloured light. With her skin so smooth and tight, she reminded Rembrae of herself when she was younger.

"If you should discover that Reeve has anything to do with this…this tomfoolery…" Rembrae snarled. "Then tell him I want to see him. *Immediately*."

"Of course, Your Highness." Gin bowed once again.

Rembrae could never be too angry with Gin, she almost loved the girl. Her blackened heart wasn't capable of truly loving, so she was merely fond of her as much as was feasibly possible. She saw a lot of herself in the youngster; a headstrong streak of independence, with a healthy mix of rebellion and toughness. She'd raised her well.

Rembrae wondered what she herself might look like in human form now. She hardly dared to imagine whether her face would still be smooth, or if it would be lined like a crone's beneath the wolf's façade. She'd never been strikingly beautiful, she accepted that, but she'd had a face that was noble and attractive nonetheless - and she couldn't imagine it being old and withered. In the same vein, she wondered whether her body would be tall or stooped and whether her fingers would be straight or gnarled. It was Casiphia who had denied her womanhood for all these years; she was cursed to live the remainder of her life as a wolf.

It was a punishment dealt by the moon goddess, spanning back to the Reposition era. None of her Blōd Vampyre fledglings knew it, not even her own son Reeve. The younger vampires could only remember as far back as the mid-Biding era (she believed boredom and lack of stimulation in the dustbowl had somehow stunted their brain development, because she could remember right back to her own youth with crystal clarity), so they had no recollection of Casiphia themselves. They had no idea how vengeful their goddess could be because Casiphia had been silent since the early-Biding era. As far as they were concerned, it was Rembrae's own will to maintain the image of a wolf - and she gave them no reason to think otherwise. She wouldn't be seen as weak.

And now, more than ever, she *was* weak. She was dying. Time was running out and she needed to get back to Earth. She needed to search for the moonstone of Death Valley because then, and only then, would she have retribution. She'd be more than a self-made queen, more than a Blōd Vampyre and more than a worn-out old wolf - she'd be an immortal goddess.

Chapter 33

That woman was back. The peculiar one she'd first seen at the poolside in North Point cave system. Somehow she had replaced Reeve and was now sitting next to her behind a hazy mesh of grey that swirled, moved and changed like smoke. Soon the miasma vaporised, clearing until everything was well defined.

The older woman's eyes were squeezed tight shut in concentration. A purple nylon blouse fastened tight to her thick jowly neck with little black buttons that gleamed like garden beetles. She wore face powder that was a shade darker than the skin on her neck, it sat on her dry skin in matte particles and rested heavy in the deep grooves of her old-lady wrinkles. Lilac eye-shadow was intended to match purple lipstick that sat bitty on her thin lips and bled into the vertical creases of her top lip. Continuing the purple theme, she smelt of lavender; a powerful sickly smell that made Libby nauseous because of its closeness.

The woman's lips twitched, revealing teeth that were yellow and crooked with brown stains creeping from the crevices of eggshell-white gums. Libby flinched and moved backwards when the smell of halitosis mingled with lavender intoxicated her nostrils.

"Who are you?" she demanded.

The older woman's eyes popped open, as did her mouth, and as she fixed her eyes on Libby she looked both surprised and excited.

"I've got her again," she cried in a cigarette-hardened voice. "I've got her!"

"What are you talking about?" Libby asked, bewildered. "Who the hell are you?"

"Don't be afraid," the woman said.

"I'm not," she snapped. "I just want to know who you are and why you keep pestering me!"

The woman nodded her head and, although she was seated right next to Libby, she squinted as though she were far away. "My name is Peggy Spirittalker. I'm a clairvoyant, so please don't be scared. I'm an expert in these matters - I can help you."

"Are you taking the piss?" Libby said. "You don't look or sound very professional. I mean, how do you suppose you could possibly help me?"

"I'm here to listen. You can talk to me and tell me what happened. I can counsel you through your grief and shortcomings."

"You can counsel me? What, so you're a clairvoyant-come-psychiatrist now?"

"Well no, no I'm not," the woman answered, looking flustered. "But I speak with dead people regularly. I've got experience in these matters."

Libby was growing angry and impatient. How dare this interfering old cow keep inflicting her bloody awful presence upon her? Uninvited too.

"Look missus, I don't want or need your help - I've got much more important things to be doing than sitting around nattering with some batty old woman who thinks that just because she can communicate with dead people she has a right to counsel them. Now sorry if I'm being a bit off and all, but sod off and stop hounding me please. Go and find a dead person who actually wants to listen to your patronising nonsense. Or better still hurry up and die, then you'll have as many dead people as you like to chat with."

"Well, I never," Peggy Spirittalker gasped, her purple lips straight like two lines of merlot-stained skin. "There's no need to be like that. Sometimes people appreciate my guidance, I'll have you know."

"Your guidance? What the hell could you possibly know about what I'm dealing with right now? What could you know about Sunray Bay?"

213

"Sunray Bay? What's that?" The woman's drawn on eyebrows puckered, making them look even more wonky.

"Exactly," Libby said. "You've just proved my point."

"Look dear, I understand, really I do. Death can be a very traumatic experience…"

"A very traumatic experience? *You're* telling *me* that death is a very traumatic experience?" She laughed in outrage. "I bloody well know it is - *I'm* the one who's dead here!"

"And it's easy for a person to deny the fact that they're dead," the woman continued, ignoring, or failing to notice, the scorn in Libby's response. "It's easy for some to become depressed, anxious and frightened - or even lost."

"Well I could definitely become depressed listening to the sound of your voice if you keep just popping up whenever you feel like it. And anxious? Of course I'm bloody anxious," she said, "But I'm *not* denying anything - I know that I'm dead. How can you make that better? *Do* you think you can just come along and make everything alright?"

"I can certainly try my best to give you the best support and guidance, if you're willing to cooperate. But I can't promise that it'll make everything better, as you might hope."

Libby rolled her eyes. "What exactly would you hope to guide me on, Mrs Spirittalker?"

"I can talk with you about your death. I'll tell you what happened with the accident, if you'd like, and I can help you come to terms with it."

"I don't need help coming to terms with it. I'm over that part already."

"Denial. That's what you would have yourself believe."

"I'm sorry, but as much as it may come as a surprise to you, I seriously couldn't give a flying fuck about the car accident. Why aren't you listening to me? What good would it do for me to know who was sitting behind the driver's wheel? Whether it was a drunk or someone rushing to work or even a bloody joyrider, it's all irrelevant now. It won't change this and I have more important things to be concerning myself with right now."

"It'll help you find peace."

"Help me find *peace*? There is no peace in Sunray Bay!"

"Ah but I think it *would* help you find peace. You need to release yourself and be free, don't you understand? There is no such place as Sunray Bay, your mind has created some sort of coping mechanism."

Libby was furious; her nostrils flared to show as much. "How dare you, you patronising old cow. You think I've made Sunray Bay up as a coping mechanism? *A coping mechanism, for Christ's sake?* That would be the shittiest coping strategy ever! I suppose you'd also say that it's my mind's way of dealing with things if I told you that I'm surrounded by vampires and werewolves and castles and cave trolls? Oh and get this, the best coping mechanism I've come up with so far is to have sex with a zombie. Really. Hot. Sex. So put all of that in your counselling pipe and smoke it, you interfering old twat! How dare you tell me how to *cope*!"

"Well I never," Peggy Spirittalker shrieked, her face contorted. "How very rude and ungrateful, young lady. Actually no. You're no lady, not using vulgar language like that."

"Whatever you say," Libby snapped. "Just piss off, otherwise I might get some of Sunray Bay's finest to haunt you - and believe me they're a bunch of crazy bastards at best."

The old clairvoyant gasped and patted her chest with the palm of her hand as though she was going to suffer a heart attack.

"*Libby!*" A different voice rang out, distant and fuzzy as though it was on the other end of a bad line. "Did I not teach you better manners than that? I know you must be upset, darling, but since when did you *swear* so much? You've got a mouth like a potty!"

"*Mother?*" Libby gasped, reeling back in shock.

215

"Yes, darling, it's me. It's so lovely to speak to you," Merilyn Hood said, an emotional quiver making her voice break. "But I hope that bit about the zombie isn't true, young lady, else you're in big trouble."

Libby groaned inwardly and Peggy Spirittalker gave her a haughty look.

"She's all yours, Mrs Hood, I've got nothing else to say to her," the old woman muttered. "Young people of today, tsk."

Peggy Spirittalker faded, and then in waves of bright colours she was replaced by Libby's mother. Merilyn Hood's red hair was scraped back, unkempt and shining white at the roots. She didn't have a scrap of make-up on, not even mascara or pencil to define her fair eyelashes and eyebrows, which was very unlike her. Quite frankly, she looked dreadful. Just as bad as she'd looked in the dreams Libby had been having of late. Libby reached forward to hug her, but her arms met with nothing and the image of her mother rippled and faded away. She pulled her hands back quickly, scared she'd lose the vision completely. Merilyn looked alarmed and sat forward.

"Libby? Are you still there?"

"Yes, I'm still here," she said, relieved that once her arms were back by her sides the image of her mother was crisp and clear again.

"Oh thank goodness, I thought I'd lost you again. I've been trying to reach you since - well, since - you know…"

"No, I'm still here," Libby said. "How are you?"

"How am I? Oh, I've certainly been better," Merilyn answered, shaking her head. The rims of her eyes looked red raw and she started to nibble at her fingertips - which was a nervous habit of hers. "What can I say? We're all missing you like crazy. It's so hard. The funeral's tomorrow, you know. It's just awful, truly awful. But we've ordered a wreath of your favourite…" She started sobbing hard, her shoulders hunching over. "Of your favourite orange roses."

"It's okay, it's okay, I'm sorry I asked. It was a stupid question." Libby said, overwhelmed by her mother's

hysterics. "But I'm okay. Seriously, I'm doing alright here."
She hated to lie, but she also hated to see her mother in such
a state. She'd never seen her like this before.

"Are you?" Merilyn looked up, desperation etched into
her eyes. "Are you *really*?"

"Yes. Although…there's some stuff I need to talk to you
about."

"Oh?" Her mother's puffy eyes developed an element of
sheepishness, as though she knew what was to follow.

"Yes. I met somebody here. A man who said he knew
you."

"Go on…"

"His name was Finnbane Krain."

Her mother let out a long sigh and put her head in her
hands. Dragging her palms over her face she eventually
looked back up and her expression was pretty much all the
confirmation Libby needed. What Finnbane Krain had said
was true.

"I'm so sorry, darling.," she said. "I'm sorry you had to
find out that way. I'm sorry you had to find out at all. That
is…he did tell you everything didn't he?"

"Yes, he told me everything," Libby said, sighing. "So
it's true then?"

Merilyn looked away, unable to meet her daughter's
gaze. "Look, darling, I thought it best you didn't know. It
was a silly mistake. He was much too old for me anyway, it
would never have worked out. But when he…after he died, I
met your dad - I met Dennis - and he loved you like his own.
He'd never have had it said that you weren't his daughter."

"So he knew as well?"

"Of course he did." Merilyn put her hand next to Libby's
on the stone merlon. "You don't hate me for it, do you?"

"No, of course not. But - it's just…"

"Just what?"

"Well, about this whole vampire and faery business."

"Oh. That."

"Yes that."

"I'll be honest, you never showed any vampiric traits. In fact, the older you got the more I convinced myself that you *were* Dennis's. You were much more like him than you ever were Finn."

Libby cringed when her mother referred to Finnbane Krain as Finn.

"But what about the faery aspect?"

"Look, darling, we need to talk about that over time. It's too much for you to take in." She broke a sad smile. "I'm so sorry you had to learn this way, but we can't talk for very much longer - Peg is exhausted. Can we talk again soon? Will you let Peg in again?"

"Well she usually just barges into my thoughts unannounced anyway, so I don't see that that'll be a problem. Why break a habit?"

"Watch that smart mouth, don't be so cheeky," Merilyn chastised. "We can go over everything that happened, but it'll take time. We could grab sessions here and there - so long as Peg will oblige. You did say some pretty mean things to the poor woman. I'd be surprised if she's not offended."

"Yes, I know. I'm sorry, Peggy," she said, reluctantly. "But before you go, can you tell me anything about what being a faery entails?"

"Well, you're only *part* faery, and even though that'll still have its implications, don't go reaching for your spandex leotard and star-ended wand just yet, Twinkle Toes - there's too much to learn."

"And you wonder where I get my smart mouth from?" Libby said. "You could at least give me something to go on."

Her mother rolled her eyes. "Okay I'll give you a quick example, but that's it for today. At a very basic level, sometimes we can look to our dreams to find the truth."

"Can we? I mean, can *you*?"

"I used to be able to, before I started taking medication to stop the dreams. Sometimes it's best *not* to know the truth."

Libby thought of her younger sister for some reason. "Have you told Izzy the truth? Does she know that she's half-faery?"

"We all miss you very much, darling," her mother said, blatantly ignoring the question. "We all love you. Me, your dad and Izzy."

Her mother's image beside her on the merlon began to fade.

"Wait, don't go yet," she said, when something else dawned on her. "Is Alex a *werewolf*?"

But her question was met with nothingness. Her mother was already gone and everything went black.

Chapter 34

He withdrew from her, confused. She had initiated the kiss and he had gladly reciprocated - but when she pulled away he didn't understand.

"What…what did I do?" he asked, his hands held out defensively.

She wore a vacant expression on her face as she talked, making no sense whatsoever. It was as though she was looking straight at him, but straight through him at the same time.

"Libby, are you okay?" he asked. "I thought that's what you wanted - *you* kissed *me*. I would never have… I wouldn't have kissed you back if it wasn't what you wanted."

"Who are you?" she barked.

Reeve shook his head, beyond confused.

"I'm *Reeve*. You know who I am. What's the matter Libby? What's wrong with you?"

She didn't seem to hear him, not responding to his voice at all. Instead she muttered more nonsensical words and became visibly agitated and distressed.

He edged away from her, fearing their kiss might have sent her doolally. He'd wanted to kiss her so much, but he never would have forced himself on her. *Ever*. He wanted to placate her, but he didn't know how. He didn't dare touch her in case it upset her further and made her go even more crazy.

"I'm not," she said. "I just want to know who you are and why you keep pestering me!"

"Libby please, what are you talking about?" he pleaded. "I'm *Reeve*, you know, Prince of the Blōd Vampyres…"

220

"Are you taking the piss? You don't look or sound very professional," she said. "I mean, how do you suppose you could possibly help me?"

"*Professional?* You're not making any sense," he shook his head, flummoxed.

"You can counsel me? What so you're a clairvoyant-come-psychiatrist now?"

"I didn't suggest I *would* counsel you. And *clairvoyant*…what's that about?"

Her red hair beat the air, framing her troubled face. Reeve watched her for a while and stopped trying to interact with her senseless ramblings. So far as he could gather she believed she was talking to some old woman about dead people and vampires, but that then changed and he thought she believed she was talking to her mother instead, purporting to be half vampire and half faery. It was madness. He snapped his thumb and forefinger in front of her face, to see if it might break her trance.

"Libby, it's okay," he said firmly. "I won't touch you again and I won't force you to go back to Earth with me if you don't want to. I'll go on my own."

"Wait, don't go yet," she gasped, lurching towards him. "Is Alex a *werewolf?*"

"I'm…I'm not going anywhere just yet. And who the heck is Alex?"

She looked at him for a split second, actually seeing him this time. He could tell by the glimmer of recognition reflected in her eyes, but then her body slumped forward and she fell over the side of the battlement wall and tumbled down to the ashy floor fifty feet below.

Chapter 35

Gin couldn't quite believe how well Rembrae had taken the news about the prisoners. Not that it was her fault they'd escaped, but still, the wolf had been very calm about it. In fact, the more she thought about it, the more it became apparent that the Queen was somehow different. Changing. When they'd spoken just now Gin saw how very worn Rembrae looked, and despite the Queen putting on a brave face she'd seen the effort it had taken for the once-thought-invincible wolf to stand. *When did this happen?* she thought, *Why haven't I noticed before?*

Having left The Great Hall, she flitted across the cobblestones of the main bailey, making her way to collect the other girls from their dormitory. When she heard curious *shwack-crick-thud* noises coming from inside the lower bailey she came to a halt. The lower bailey was mostly used by the servants, where they congregated near the stable area and drew water from the well. They seldom made much noise, apart from the odd long-drawn-out groans, so the commotion of what sounded like a fast-paced kerfuffle was not a familiar one and it surprised her somewhat.

Turning on her heels she ran to the archway that connected the main bailey to the lower bailey, intrigued by what she might find. By the time she got there the noises had ceased, but as she looked towards the stables she inhaled in disbelief.

"What the pissing hell?"

Bodies lay strewn all over the floor. Unmoving heaps of twisted limbs and already decayed flesh. Without emotion she could tell that all the servants were dead. *Lilea will be happy,* she thought. Slight movement caught her eye,

222

diverting her attention. One of the prisoners, the man, was sitting on the edge of the well with his head cradled in his hands.

Uncertain as to whether he knew she was there or not she didn't bother creeping. She strode boldly towards him, but not once did he look up. His solid physique was like that of a professional wrestler, she thought, and the height to go with it made him a dangerous opponent, she was sure. *He's a bloody big bugger for certain,* she summarised, by the time she reached him.

Only when she was standing at an arm's swiping distance away did he look up. He showed no element of surprise and there was a look of melancholy to his face that turned his lips down at the sides in a frown. There was little sign of physical exertion about him considering he'd just killed over a dozen servants, and Gin knew that Rembrae had been correct - this one was dangerous. Placing her hands on her hips in a manner of dominance, she asked, "Who are you?"

At first she thought he was going to ignore her, but after a lengthy silence he sighed and said, "Nobody."

"What's your name?" she demanded, growing tired of his downbeat charade.

This time he answered straight away, his voice husky and low. "Grim."

She reached out intrepid fingers and plucked the sunglasses from his face. He fixed her with his white eyes and grabbed her wrist tight in his right hand, squeezing hard to let her know he could easily shatter the bones. She gasped with shock, but his grip slackened and he released her. Hooking one of the sunglasses' arms down the front of her bikini top, to free up both hands, she asked, "What the hell are you? You're not a zombie…"

"I don't know," he said, the answer honest and dejected.

She grew more and more suspicious of him. "Where's the girl?" she said, sweeping the courtyard with her eyes, wondering if they'd laid some sort of trap.

"I don't know," he said. His tone was uncaring but there was something in his expression that betrayed his intended manner of indifference.

"You're lying," she snapped. "Where is she?"

His face hardened and he growled, "With one of your lot."

"*Reeve,*" she assumed. She could almost imagine the poet reciting poetry to the pretty red-head or some such nonsense. Rembrae was likely to go ape shit when she found out.

"Yeah." Grim confirmed her notion.

She laughed spitefully and said, "I take it you saw something you didn't like?"

"I don't know what you mean," he said, his eyes unwavering on hers, unsettling and dangerous.

"Reeve can be quite the charmer," she said. "He can talk the talk, you know? But not to worry, he's a pussy cat really. I guarantee you, he won't harm her."

"He can do what he likes with her," he said, reaching out and pulling his sunglasses free from her top. "She's not my responsibility."

Once he'd put the sunglasses back in place, she pointed to the display of bodies near the stables and said, "What is the meaning of all that?"

"I was looking for someone."

"I take it you didn't find them?" she said, her tone sarcastic.

He shook his head.

Tilting her head to the side, taking a keener interest in him, she said, "And did you *expect* to find this person in a stable full of zombies?"

He surprised her when he answered. "I came to find my wife and little girl."

"Your wife and little girl?" she repeated, her thin eyebrows scrunching in the middle. "But why would you think they'd be here?"

"I didn't know. I just needed to see."

"So your wife and daughter are they…zombies?"

He tipped his head once. "Maybe."

"How long since they passed over?"

"Two years, three months and four days."

Her eyes opened wide in astonishment. "Well if you'd just asked in the first place I could have saved you going to the trouble of killing all of our servants. They're not here."

"How do you know that?"

"The last batch of servants we lured here was well over five years ago. It's not often we take on new recruits - every ten years or so. Their only intended purpose is to make the place uninviting to any unwelcome visitors that should happen to pass by during daytime hours. They're slow and hopeless most times, but you should see the suckers move when they smell human flesh and blood. They're like greased lightning." Glancing back at the lifeless bodies near the stables, she cocked an eyebrow and said, "*Were* like greased lightning." Narrowing her eyes, she looked him up and down. "I noticed that you didn't have that effect on them…"

But he didn't appear to be listening to her anymore. "Are you sure?" he said, his face distracted. "About the zombies. You're sure there haven't been any more in the last couple of years?"

"Of course I am," she said, placing her hands on her hips. "I'm telling you, we don't have your wife here and we most definitely don't have your daughter. We've never taken children."

He leaned backwards, gripping the edge of the well, and made a long sigh that sounded like relief, or perhaps grief. Gin was pleasantly surprised to see a tear roll from beneath his sunglasses, tracing the line of his cheek, down the side of his nose and coming to rest in the groove between his lips.

Maybe he wasn't so dangerous after all, she thought.

Chapter 36

Friday, 9:09pm: The Lower Bailey, Sun Castle, The Grey Dust Bowl

Standing up from his seat on the edge of the well he towered above Gin, even though she was pretty tall herself. He displayed a non-threatening demeanour, feeling little more than deflated and emotionally burnt out.

"I'm off," he said, seeking neither permission nor advice from the vampire.

"Where to?" she asked. If she meant to block his way, she made no attempt of showing it.

"West." His voice was growling and matter-of-fact. He rubbed his chin where two-day-old stubble itched. "Toward Spewing Mouth and beyond."

"But why? The conditions nearer Spewing Mouth are extremely hostile, you'll never make it."

"Yes I will. And if not, so what?"

She looked at him with blue eyes that were deeply scrutinising. After a few moments she shrugged, seemingly content with his intended plan. She stepped to the side, a gesture that said she would let him pass. Tipping her head in the direction of the drawbridge's archway but never taking her eyes off him, she said, "Come. If that's what you wish then let me escort you outside."

They walked together in silence. All around them in the walls of Sun Castle black window slits and door holes lurked, and he wondered how many of them concealed voyeurs at that very moment. A distinct and uncomfortable feeling of vulnerability gnawed at his wits because he knew he was at a definite disadvantage, he was a walking target. He'd be only too relieved when he was back out in the open space of The Grey Dust Bowl, on neutral turf.

As they neared the drawbridge, he wondered whether his journey would be resumed without interference or whether he'd be required to kick some Blōd Vampyre arse. It seemed strange that they would let him go so readily. There was a thick stillness hanging in the air - a peculiar feeling that indicated to him that something was about to happen. Something bad. Casting a quick glance up to the battlement wall, he saw neither Libby nor Reeve there. He wondered how she would react when she found out he'd left. The vampire would help her get over it, he was sure.

When they passed beneath the portcullis, Gin halted and thrust her arm across his chest. Expecting a struggle to ensue, he was confused when she merely signalled with her eyes for him to look left whilst holding an index finger up to her lips to hush him. Humouring her instruction, he glanced across to the left and saw two figures sitting on the ground. They were close enough to see that it was Libby and the male vampire. She sat cross-legged, filtering ash through her hands at either side of her. And Reeve was leaning backwards, stark bollock naked. He looked like a plastic figurine, shining a surreal white under the moon. His perfectly formed body was smooth and pretty much hairless, apart from a neat patch of pubic hair that was on display for all to see.

Libby was concentrating on black flakes lying in her upturned palm, and Grim heard Reeve say, "I have to ask you again, just to be certain. Will you go back to Earth with me? Won't you consider staying with me?"

He was shocked by the question, and curious about her reply.

"I'm sorry," she said. "But I'm not the one to give you the sun. I'm sure you're a really nice person, even if you can hypnotise people and make them do stuff they don't want to do..." She laughed in her usual playful way. "Unintentionally or not. But I can't do what you're asking of me."

"We could take it slow. You could get to know me better."

227

Grim hated that he was more or less spying on this interaction between the two of them; it made him feel creepy and weird. It wasn't his style - and yet, somehow he was fascinated all the same. Had it all been a big misunderstanding after all? Had he really almost left Sun Castle, leaving Libby behind to the mercy of the Blōd Vampyres, simply because he couldn't handle his own feelings of insecurity?

"It's not that," she said. "I just don't...you know...I just don't feel that way about you. And besides, I'm sort of involved with someone else. It's complicated, but that's how it is."

"Oh." Grim noted that Reeve's face was laden with disheartenment. "Grim?"

He watched as Libby nodded.

"So do you love him?" Reeve asked.

Grim felt his pulse quicken and he found himself holding his breath. Suddenly he didn't want to be there, he didn't want to know what the answer to that question was.

"No," she said, laughing in a way that suggested the question was an absurd one. "I only met him a few days ago. Love comes with time...but I *am* in lust." A dreamy grin spread across her lips. "It's strange, but I miss him when he's not with me. I *want* him with me. So, I think in time I could love him."

And Grim remembered to breathe.

Chapter 37

"What happened?" Reeve asked.

"I could ask you the same…" Libby murmured, pushing herself away from him. She was lying in his arms and he was sitting on the ground. No longer on top of the battlement, they were now at the foot of the curtain wall amongst the ashes. *"And why the hell aren't you wearing any clothes?"*

He groaned. "Ugh, it's probably not what you think. You fainted. You fell. I jumped after you."

She looked up to the battlement, suspicion sullying any gratitude she might feel.

"And you thought to take your clothes off first?" she asked.

"You don't understand. I had to transition in order to be able to catch you. I can't adapt my clothes to suit!" His voice now sounded peeved.

She moved from his lap, careful not to touch anything about his person that she really shouldn't. Smiling modestly, her cheeks now pink, she said, "Thanks."

"So what happened up there?" he asked, leaning back and resting on his arms, evidently blasé about his lack of clothes. "Who did you think you were talking to? Because it certainly wasn't me."

"My mother." She almost couldn't believe her own words. But it was true. She'd been talking with her as though she'd been sitting right next to her. "She used a clairvoyant to contact me from beyond the grave. Well, actually that's not technically true, is it? It's me who's beyond the grave…anyway, you know what I mean." Her voice was excitable and she fidgeted with her hands, combing ashes through her fingers at either side of her.

"So that's good news then?" he asked.

"Of course it is," she laughed. Then remembering Reeve's relationship with his own mother, she added, "We get on well, you know?"

He smiled and shook his head. "Not really. But I understand."

They sat for a while in silence and she played the whole conversation with her mother back in her head and wondered when she'd make her next appearance.

Reeve sat up straight. "All that talk about vampires and faeries...it's true?"

For a moment she was apprehensive, unsure whether to tell him or not. But considering he'd obviously heard the extent of the conversation anyway, she saw no reason to lie. Lowering her head sheepishly, she said, "Yeah, I guess so."

His kohl-lined eyes widened. "So that's what the old bitch couldn't fathom, isn't it? You're a faery!" He chuckled.

"What's so funny about being a faery?"

"Oh nothing, I'm just delighting in the fact that someone fooled my mother."

"Anyway, you!" she said, her eyes narrowing as she jutted her finger accusingly in his direction. "Never mind all of this. What the hell happened up there? What did you do to me?"

He shook his head, bewildered, hugging his knees up to his chest as though to protect himself from her sudden accusations. "I don't know what you're talking about. What do you mean?"

"Don't pretend that it didn't happen," she scolded. "You kissed me. Why? What did you do to me?"

Looking dazed and innocent, he said, "But *you* kissed *me*."

"I most certainly did not."

"You most certainly did. You started it."

"But that's a lie. I wouldn't have done that..." She studied him for a moment to see if his resolve would break so that he would stop telling bare-faced lies, but then it dawned on her. "It's your eyes! You…you hypnotised me or something with your eyes."

"That's ludicrous, I wouldn't hypnotise you into doing something you didn't want to do…" He dropped his legs back flat to the ground, his expression troubled. "I mean, if I did…I, I didn't mean to."

And the funny thing was she actually believed him.

"Well make sure it doesn't happen again," she scolded, throwing a handful of ashes onto his legs. He nodded his head and smiled at her, his teeth flashing dazzling-white. Satisfied that the misunderstanding had been cleared up, he took on a more serious tone and said, "I have to ask you again, just to be certain. Will you go back to Earth with me? Won't you consider staying with me?"

"I'm sorry," she said, feeding soft ashes through her fingers. "But I'm not the one to give you the sun. I'm sure you're a really nice person, even if you can hypnotise people and make them do stuff they don't want to do…" He sat forward, about to object, but she laughed and quickly added, "Unintentionally or not. But I can't do what you're asking of me."

"We could take it slow. You could get to know me better," he tried one more time.

"It's not that. I just don't…you know…" She felt really awkward, suddenly wishing she was back in the dungeon cell with Grim. "I just don't feel that way about you. And besides, I'm sort of involved with someone else. It's complicated, but that's how it is."

"Oh." Libby could tell how genuinely disappointed he was. "Grim?"

When she nodded her head, he asked, "So do you love him?"

"No." She was quick to reply, giving a little snort of laughter at the thought. It was ridiculous, she'd never throw her heart around as easily as that - would she? "I only met him a few days ago. Love comes with time…" Imagining Grim and all they'd been through in the past couple of days, she added, "but I *am* in lust. It's strange, but I miss him

231

when he's not with me. I *want* him with me. So, I think in time I could love him."

"Okay," he said, rising so that he kneeled before her. "I completely understand. I'm saddened, but I understand. Come on, I'll take you back to him." He held out his hand to her, but as she moved to take it his eyes sparkled with mischief and he said, "Actually, since you're a faery does that mean you can grant wishes?"

She rolled her eyes and heaved a sigh of humoured despair. "That depends on what you'd wish for."

"Ha." He slapped his thigh. "Damn, you saw right through me, but you can't blame me for trying. So what would you wish for if you could wish for anything at all?"

"Me? That's not how it works. I'm the faery and faeries grant *other people's* wishes."

"Says who?"

"That's how it happens in the fairy tales."

"A wish is a wish no matter who it's for. And since we're only talking metaphorically, tell me, what would you wish for?"

"Hmmm." There were so many things she could wish for. She could wish she wasn't dead for a start - but then she wouldn't have met Grim and she would probably be going through the untidy business of breaking up with Alex right now. A smile spread across her face as something trivial but important, nonetheless, came to mind. "I wish I had some clean clothes for a start," she said, tugging at the legs of her dirty, worn jeans.

He laughed. "Well I didn't like to say, but you are a bit...*scruffy*."

She narrowed her eyes and gave him a threatening glare, but she couldn't keep a straight face for long and she was soon laughing herself. After a few moments she became serious, her tone saddened. "Actually, I wish that Rufus, my dog, was still with me too."

"Hey, that's two wishes," he protested. "Isn't that greedy?"

She crossed her arms defiantly and said, "It's well known that faeries grant three wishes in total."

"Begging your pardon," he said mimicking her and crossing his arms over his own chest, "but that's genies."

She laughed and moved up onto her knees, eager to see Grim again. "Oh okay, smart arse, you might be right. But I wasn't going to use my third wish anyway." She stuck out her tongue.

"Why not?"

"I was going to save it for a rainy day."

He stood up and offered his hand to her once again, pulling her to her feet.

"That's a shame," he said. "It hardly ever rains here."

"Well it doesn't matter anyway since we were only being metaphorical," she answered. "Go on, your turn, what would you wish for?"

His blue eyes glittered with mischief and a wicked smile played about his lips.

"You know what? I wish that the lighthouse lantern was alight so that I wouldn't have to listen to my old snark of a mother mithering on at me because I didn't go back into Sunray Bay to look for a bulb." He winked at her. "Come on, I'll get you back to Grim before I face the music."

Lifting her hands she blew the remnants of ash from her fingers and then wiped her sooty palms down her thighs, leaving black marks on the blue denim of her jeans. The particles of ash flittered into the air and began dancing like a swarm of midges. She jumped back in surprise and Reeve looked in awe. There was no breeze at that moment and yet the ash swirled mid-air right before them. Growing in size, the pieces fluttered like a rabble of black butterflies. Colour began to form on their backs, liquid gold. They beat their wings in a more and more frenzied rhythm until they generated a buzzing noise. A crackling clap of lightning that sounded as though the very air around them had split rang out and then the whole vortex of lively black and gold merged together and shot upwards. It streaked through the now-burgundy sky, a sparkler leaving a trail of shimmering bronze behind.

Reeve drew in a deep breath as they watched it explode like a massive firework somewhere off in the distance above Sunray Bay.

"Oh my goodness," he murmured, his mouth agape. Instead of dissipating, the firework now hung suspended in the air, a big shining orb. "Is it the sun?"

She was lost for words for a few moments, but then shook her head, "No, I don't think so."

And then Reeve started jumping up and down clapping his hands together. "You did, Libby. You actually did it!" he cried.

"I did what?" she asked. Her brow was furrowed, yet all the while she couldn't help but smile. His exhilaration was most contagious.

"That's Prospect Point Lighthouse over there!" he laughed. "I wished for it to be lit, and you've…somehow you've done it."

Her own mouth fell open in wonder as she stared at the orb in utter disbelief. Could what he was saying be true?

She smiled when a familiar icy hand grasped her own.

Without taking her eyes off the miniature sun that shone above Prospect Point Lighthouse, she said, "It would appear that I can make wishes comes true."

Grim wrapped his arm around her waist and pulled her close. "I could well believe it."

Epilogue

As all attention was diverted to the skies of Sunray Bay and to the glowing light above Prospect Point Lighthouse, a freak breeze whipped up a maelstrom of ash in the corner of Sun Castle's lower bailey like a miniature tornado. Small black-grey particles danced and moved mindfully, like a cluster of corn flies. At first they swarmed together in gentle circular motions, but then they became a frantic mass of energy, swapping places, curling and then rearranging.

Finally a small head with two pointed ears took shape, followed by a small, squat body and a stumpy tail. No legs came to fruition, the figure simply hovered above the ground with no clear connection between its body and the floor. The small ghostly dog made of ash shook its head, sending black particles flying into the air like jumping fleas. As its blinky black eyes took in its surroundings, its nose sniffed the air loudly.

"Ah, flipping heck," it groaned. "Not this place again!"

About the Author

Rachael H Dixon lives in the cold and windy northeast of England. She craves sunlight and warmth, and as such her skin is so white it's almost translucent. She's been writing ever since she could hold, albeit strangely, a pen. Her love for the macabre stems from reading James Herbert novels and watching Vincent Price films when she was small.

As well as writing, Rachael loves reading, walking her two dogs, drinking red wine and admiring Gil Elvgren art work. And she often wonders whether she's the only writer in the whole world who doesn't like coffee.

Her debut novel, Slippery Souls, was short-listed for the Writing Magazine's Self-publishing Award 2011 and is the first book in the Sunray Bay Series.

To see what Rachael is up to, or to contact her, go to:

Official website: **www.slipperysouls.co.uk**
Blog: **www.rhdixon.blogspot.com**
Facebook page: **Rachael H Dixon**
Twitter: **@RachaelHD**
Email: **rachaelhdixon@gmail.com**

Lightning Source UK Ltd.
Milton Keynes UK
UKOW041826260413

209847UK00001B/2/P